For Simon Jones

The Bridge

MATT BROLLY

THOMAS & MERCER

Text copyright © 2023 by Matt Brolly
All rights reserved.

Published by Thomas & Mercer, Seattle

www.apub.com

Amazon, the Amazon logo, and Thomas & Mercer are trademarks of Amazon.com, Inc., or its affiliates.

ISBN-13: 9781542031455

eISBN: 9781542031448

Cover design by Tom Sanderson

Cover image ©Pictorial Press Ltd / Alamy Stock Photo; Joe Dunckley / Shutterstock; JoseDG / Shutterstock

Printed in the United States of America

The
Bridge

Prologue

How he hated the antiseptic corridors of the hospital. Each step through the echoing hallways brought with it the haunted memories of his childhood, and the more recent horrors of watching Mother go through her agonising descent.

Absently he rubbed the scar on his back, a legacy of his formative years, as he helped Mother through the hospital doors towards the car park. The oncologist had given them the prognosis they'd expected. This time the chemo had failed to take and although the hospital had offered to try again, they'd decided enough was enough.

Opening the passenger side door for Mother and helping her inside, it pained him to feel how little she weighed. The cancer had eaten away at her flesh, at the strength that in the past had seen her take on things that would have destroyed most people. It was a warm, sunny day, but she shivered as he placed the seatbelt across her. 'Come on, Mother, let's get you home,' he said.

She was clearly suffering but managed to summon the strength to match his smile before replying. 'OK, Father, that would be nice.'

It was a quick journey to the detached farmhouse he'd inherited, the only good thing his parents had ever done for him. Easing Mother from the car, he grimaced at the feeling of her trembling bones. He glanced around to check all the security cameras were working. 'Let's get you inside, Mother,' he said, punching the six-digit code for the front door.

Watching Mother shuffle through the entrance was like viewing another person. Age and illness had crept up on her, and he knew it wouldn't be long. He needed to start making plans for life without her – something he'd never known.

But first there were things to finish. He needed to make her remaining time memorable, and had already set things in motion to achieve that.

He made her hot cocoa and together they sat on the ancient, flower-patterned sofa where he'd occasionally been allowed to sit as a child, smells of nicotine and old food reaching his nose every time he moved. Those were the good memories. The rare moments of freedom, where he'd been allowed space. If his parents had been feeling charitable, they would even allow him to watch the family's black and white television. Moving pictures had enthralled him and, during those precious times, he would imagine the outside world as one gigantic television programme – an image that was shattered when he was finally allowed to start school.

Foam from the cocoa formed on Mother's lips, and as he leaned over to wipe it, he caught a whiff of decay from her breath and skin. Her cheekbones were prominent, poking through her flesh as if they were trying to escape, the rest of her little more than skin-covered bones.

Only her eyes retained their steeliness. And as she smiled and thanked him, he could tell there was still a little life left in her.

'What would you like to do now, Mother?' he said. 'Perhaps you should go to bed. Rest up.'

'Not yet, Father. I'd like to watch a little before we go to sleep.'

He chuckled at her response, unable to hide his joy. Watching gave them both peace, tethered them to the past.

'I have the beginning of something special for you,' he said, hearing the excitement in his voice. 'Let's see how he's faring, shall we?'

Mother held her hand out and he lifted her insubstantial body through the narrow corridors, out towards the garden. A light breeze was up and Mother shivered as they crossed the overgrown lawn, where he punched in a second digital code on the keypad to their special room. The door slowly eased open, and they moved into a second space – a room within a room – where they hunched together on a love seat.

In front of them, close enough to touch, were a bank of black and white TV monitors. Most were switched off or contained images of empty spaces, but on the three central screens there was movement within. Three captive people staring back at them, as if they knew they were being watched.

Chapter One

With a groan of effort, Louise Blackwell bent down and cleaned the toilet bowl. She'd spent the last thirty minutes on the bathroom floor, waiting for the walls to stop spinning. Showering and changing in a rush, she opened the private entrance to her parents' half of the house and went downstairs.

Her nausea was clearing but the last thing she wanted was for the family's dog, Molly – a two-year-old Labrador – to be jumping up at her. 'Get down, Molly,' she mouthed, her voice a dry rasp.

Despite being in her early forties, and having a separate floor of the house, sharing a building with her parents often made her feel like a teenager. In the kitchen, her parents were eating breakfast with her eight-year-old niece, Emily.

'Good night?' asked her father, pushing a plate of freshly made pancakes towards her.

It was such a familiar refrain, but Louise fell for it every time. She sat down without answering, offering her father nothing but a wilful look as she poured herself a glass of orange juice. It had been nearly three months since she'd fallen pregnant, but she had yet to tell her parents. The only person who knew was the baby's father – her boyfriend, and ex-colleague, Thomas Ireland. Louise had told herself it was too early to go public, but in reality she was scared about what would happen next. And most of that fear centred around the girl sitting opposite her, her niece's beaming smile evident through a mouthful of uneaten pancake.

Louise's parents had become Emily's guardians following the death of Louise's brother, Paul. Initially, they'd lived in Bristol but her parents had struggled with Emily and they'd decided to move in with Louise in the house on the outskirts of Weston-super-Mare. She'd talked with Thomas about moving in together, but the logistics of any move felt so complicated at that moment. She could never leave Emily behind, but was also worried about what would happen to her parents if she moved away. Couple that with the responsibility of her work as a detective inspector in Major Crimes, and the fact that Thomas had a son of his own, Noah, from a previous marriage, and the situation became a mess that she feared would never unravel.

She watched her father as she ate her pancakes. The lines around his mouth and eyes seemed more pronounced than ever, and there was a slight tremor in his hand as he held his coffee cup to his lips. The last few years had been testing for both her parents, although looking after Emily had given them a fresh lease of life. But such an arrangement couldn't last forever. The pregnancy was forcing her to consider things she'd rather not dwell on. The more she watched her father, the more she realised that soon her parents would struggle to look after Emily. If there was ever a time for her to consider adopting Emily it was now.

'We're ready to go when you are,' said her mother, who'd been suspiciously quiet ever since Louise had arrived.

It was the last day of Emily's school holidays, and they had a full day ahead of them. 'I'm sorry. Have you been waiting for me?' said Louise, wincing as she took a bite of her pancake.

'Yes,' said her mother, shooting her a withering look. 'The day is getting away from us.'

'Understood,' said Louise, getting to her feet, fighting the momentary dizziness. 'Let me get my walking shoes and we can be off.'

Emily clapped her hands as she jumped down from the table and, thirty minutes later, they were walking through Worlebury Woods – Molly and Emily running ahead, delighting in one another's company. Louise's morning sickness had faded. As she walked arm in arm with her father, she noticed how slowly he was moving through the dry undergrowth of the woodland. They'd both met Thomas on a number of occasions, and knew Louise was dating him. There would never be a better opportunity to tell them. She'd spent enough time at his place that it wouldn't come as a shock, but again she found herself regressing to her teenage self. She tried to formulate the news in her head, but couldn't quite find the words. She had no doubt that her parents would be delighted for her, but still she was reluctant to tell them. Maybe she was thinking too much into it, but it was so early in the pregnancy and she worried how they would react if something went wrong. They'd already endured so much loss in their lives, and she didn't want to risk putting them through more anguish.

And there was Emily. Although they would welcome the freedom Louise adopting her niece would bring, wouldn't that also be a loss of sorts?

Her phone rang, rescuing her from the immediate dilemma. She apologised to her father as she broke away from him. 'Blackwell,' she said.

'Louise, it's Greg. Sorry to bother you on a Sunday.'

Louise's stomach lurched at the words. She whispered to her parents to carry on, and that she would catch them up, before replying. 'This better be important,' she said to the caller, Detective Sergeant Greg Farrell, one of her team in Portishead.

'We have a body,' said Greg, as if that was all the explanation needed for him to be calling on her day off.

'Why are you bothering me with that?'

'You're the only DI on call, I'm afraid.'

Louise lowered her eyes, her hand instinctively going to her belly, which at that moment felt hollow, not filled with life. *You have a lot to answer for,* she thought to the thing she hoped would one day be a bump. 'I take it this is a suspicious death?' she said to Greg.

'I'm at the crime scene now. Avonmouth Docks. A routine search of the shipping containers uncovered the body. I'd handle it myself, but the assistant chief has got involved and requested someone over my pay grade.'

'People smuggling?' asked Louise, under her breath.

'Possibly. We've yet to identify the body. The SOCOs are working through it now. The victim appears to be twenty-five to thirty, no ID. A secret compartment was uncovered in the container. A few airholes drilled into the outside. Just her and empty food tins, water bottles, bucket for a toilet. Not a pretty sight.'

'How long has she been dead?' said Louise, glancing around to make sure she wasn't being overheard.

'Not long. Possibly the last twenty-four hours,' said Greg.

'You really need me to come in for this?'

'You know I wouldn't ask if I didn't need to. I've had to close down operations for the time being, and it's getting very heated. The assistant chief requested you personally.'

'Did he now? It's going to be an hour before I get there. Are you able to hold the fort until then?'

'I'll do my best.'

8

Louise had been in this position too many times before: down on her haunches, face to face with her niece, about to impart some bad news. The hardest thing was seeing the weary acceptance in Emily's eyes as she apologised for cutting the day short. She gave Emily one more hug goodbye before leaving, noticing how fiercely her niece hugged her, giving her parents a quick shrug of apology as she headed back towards the car park.

Traffic on the M5 was light and she was at the Avonmouth Docks within thirty minutes. Her journey into the secure area was stopped twice – first by the gates at the railway crossing as a local train went by, and then by the transport police officer guarding the area. Louise waited for the barrier to rise before following the flashing lights of the abundant emergency vehicles to the correct spot in the vast area. She passed what appeared to be a gigantic rubbish tip to reach a cordoned-off section where hundreds of shipping containers were piled high. To one side of her she could see the Avonmouth Bridge she'd just driven over, and, on the other, the longer shimmering white of the Prince of Wales Bridge.

After displaying her warrant card to the uniformed officer guarding the barrier tape, Louise caught sight of DS Greg Farrell, who was in a heated exchange with a man in a three-piece suit. A look of relief washed over Greg's face as Louise approached.

'DI Louise Blackwell, this is Raymond Atkinson, operations manager for the dock company.'

Atkinson, a rotund man in his fifties, looked her up and down before speaking as if deciding on her seniority. Although he was wearing a suit, he appeared dishevelled, his chequered tie hanging loosely from his neck, sweat dotted on his forehead and cheeks. 'DI Blackwell, glad you could make it,' he said, unable to hide his disdain.

'Did you find the body, sir?'

'No, it was one of your lot,' said Atkinson, wiping the sweat from his brow.

Louise looked at Greg.

'Customs and Excise,' said Greg.

'You're responsible for these containers?' asked Louise.

'For the whole area, yes. I've been called in, the same way I imagine you were. Not the best way to spend a Sunday. I was half-way through a roast lunch.'

Death can be so inconvenient sometimes, thought Louise, remaining silent.

'Could you kindly tell me when I'll be able to get things moving again around here? We were already delayed by this bloody search,' said Atkinson.

In the distance, Louise heard the gentle hum of traffic on the bridge. Although there were three ships in the man-made harbour, there appeared to be little activity. The giant red cranes were unmanned; the only motion she could see was the whirl of the numerous wind turbines dotted around the surrounding area, which added to the already alien landscape. 'What was the search in aid of?'

'Random check,' said Greg.

Louise nodded, turning her attention to the operations manager. 'We'll get things moving as soon as we can, but we have a suspicious death on our hands so I can't offer any firm timescales.'

'That's not good enough,' said Atkinson, throwing his arms in the air like a pudgy toddler having a tantrum; something even Emily had long since grown out of.

Louise turned her back on the man. 'Show me,' she said to Greg, ignoring the operations manager's protestations as she moved off towards the crime scene.

◆ ◆ ◆

More barrier tape had been placed around a set of shipping containers a further three hundred yards inland. The area was busy with SOCOs – Scenes of Crime Officers – their white protective suits glittering in the sun.

'The second one up,' said Greg. 'C&E already had this in place,' he added, pointing to the metallic stairs that led to the open container.

Louise changed into a protective uniform before making her way up the portable staircase, her shoes clanging on the metal steps.

'I'd suck in some air before you go inside,' said Greg.

She took a deep breath before placing on her face mask, but even still, as she moved inside, she was immediately overwhelmed by the putrid smell of decay. The acrid taste of that morning's sickness reached her throat, and it took all her strength not to head back outside. The pathway through the container was narrow and dark, and every step sent waves of nausea through her body. Reaching the second section of the container, she was stopped by one of the SOCOs – an old colleague, Janice Sutton.

'I just love these Sundays, don't you?' said Janice, who appeared impervious to the smell of excrement, body odour and something indefinable lingering in the air that Louise always associated with death. Just behind Janice was the body of the victim, who was still being processed by two other SOCOs.

'No ID. We estimate her to be twenty-five to thirty years old. It's hard to say for sure,' said Janice, repeating the information given to Louise by Greg.

'The cause of death?' asked Louise.

'If I was to hazard a guess, I would say dehydration.'

Louise shook her head, breathing through her mouth as she looked at the corpse lying in a pool of excrement and urine.

'Greg says you place the time of death in the last twenty-four hours?'

'Looks that way,' said Janice. 'We've been here before,' she added.

Louise nodded, recalling the case from five years ago where nineteen asylum seekers had been discovered in shipping containers in the same port. None had survived the ordeal, and to this day no one had been prosecuted.

Louise glanced around at the discarded tins of food and water bottles. 'She'd made provisions to stay?' she said, shuddering at the idea of submitting to such confinement. The very thought made her feel claustrophobic, and she looked back at the exit route, fighting the sense of being trapped in the container. 'Where did the boat come in from?' she asked.

'That's the thing,' said Janice. 'This container hasn't come from anywhere. It was due to be shipped out tomorrow.'

Chapter Two

Louise couldn't get out of the container quick enough. She tried not to run as she left the crime scene, ripping her mask from her face as she reached the exit and sucking in lungfuls of the salty air. Still the smell of death remained, and she drew further shallow breaths as she took slow steps down the metal staircase and over to the forecourt area where the operations manager, Raymond Atkinson, was gesticulating to anyone he could find.

'Mr Atkinson, a word,' said Louise, looking beyond the manager to the sight of the Avonmouth Bridge, looming over the dirty river. 'The container where we found the body. I understand it was due to be shipped tomorrow?' she asked.

'Is that so?' said Atkinson, his wide eyes suggesting the question had no merit.

Louise looked towards the vast ship already piled high with multicoloured containers that made it look like an oversized children's toy. 'Where is that ship headed?'

'India.'

'How long have these containers been waiting to be loaded?'

Atkinson shrugged his shoulders, sweat dripping off his forehead on to his pudgy cheeks. 'I will need to double-check the exact time. We've had some delays of late. My guess is those containers have been there for three to four weeks. Non-perishable goods.'

Louise closed her eyes, the piercing rays of the early September sunshine making her dizzy. 'The victim could have been in that container for a month?'

'It's feasible, I suppose. Listen, I haven't even seen the body. I don't really know what the hell is going on, and no one is telling me much,' said Atkinson.

'Who has access to these containers?' said Louise, ignoring the man's protests.

'Forklift drivers, site managers, security personnel, you name it. Not that anyone could drag the body into one of those things once it's stored here.'

'Why is that?'

'Look around you,' said Atkinson, pointing up at the numerous cameras. 'We have hundreds of CCTV cameras in this area. Every square inch is monitored twenty-four-seven.'

'It happened before though, didn't it?' said Louise.

The operations manager closed his eyes, his head hanging between his shoulder blades as if the memory was too much to bear. 'That's why they're there. We never want that to happen again.'

Louise wasn't prepared to let up. 'What about before the containers arrive? I presume they arrive prepacked?'

Atkinson's face brightened, the smallest hint of a smile creeping on to his lips. 'Yes, they do,' he said, as if the riddle had been solved. 'I can give you a list of our contractor firms and find out exactly where that container came from, and when it was packed.'

Louise nodded. 'When is that ship due to leave?' she said, nodding her head towards the vast container ship in the harbour.

'Tomorrow, if we can resume loading shortly.'

Louise shook her head. 'That's not going to happen any time soon, I'm afraid. We're going to need to search every single container, including the ones you've already packed on board.'

14

'Have you lost your mind?' said Atkinson, glaring at her as if she was stupid.

Louise fought her anger. She'd long lost any sense of surprise at the reactions of people like Atkinson but his lack of empathy still grated. 'A woman has died, Mr Atkinson.'

The previous hint of a smile on the man's face had been swallowed by rage. 'That could take days,' he said. 'You can't even imagine the cost.'

'I'm sure you have insurance for such eventualities,' said Louise. 'You wouldn't want to take the risk of another body lying undiscovered?'

'I don't think you quite appreciate the consequences of what you're suggesting. The knock-on effects would be unmanageable. The fines for the delay in shipping, the overtime backlogs, not to mention we have two more container ships coming in next week. Sorry, it just can't be done.'

Louise took a step closer to the operations manager, forcing him to move back. 'That's not your decision to make, Mr Atkinson. Furthermore, we will need to complete a mass DNA screening of all your workers over the next couple of days,' she said, daring him to argue.

Atkinson took another two steps backwards, as if fearing he was about to be struck. 'I know the chief constable,' he said, under his breath.

This time it was Louise's turn to smile. 'So do I. Lovely guy, isn't he?'

Louise walked away from the operations manager, not willing to talk financials when less than a hundred yards away lay the dead body of an unknown woman. She caught up with Greg, who was chatting to one of the SOCOs near the crime scene. 'The first thing we need to do is find out who that poor woman is. If Atkinson is correct, she could have been in there for at least a month, if not longer,' she said.

'Could she survive that long?' asked Greg.

'She had food and water, at least to begin with. It wouldn't have been pleasant, but it would be feasible. We'll know better when we've had the pathologist's report.'

'When was she placed there? I understand people wanting to get smuggled into the country, but smuggled out?'

'I don't think that was ever the plan,' said Louise. 'It just wouldn't make sense. Even if she'd been placed in that container recently, it wasn't set up for surviving a long journey. Maybe she was hiding there and found herself trapped. No point hypothesising on it now. We need to find out details of the container firm that shipped that here. When it left, when it arrived. We need to find out exactly who had access to the container and, despite what Atkinson says, I need all the CCTV video for the last month. I need you to go through it all.'

They both knew it wasn't an easy job, but Greg didn't raise any objections.

'Just one more thing,' said Louise.

Greg raised his eyebrows, acknowledging her Columbo reference. 'I hate it when you say that.'

'We need to check inside every single one of these containers and those aboard that ship.'

Greg winced. 'That is going to take a long time,' he said, echoing Atkinson's sentiments, if not quite in the same cynical way.

'Better get going then,' said Louise. 'No other container leaves this site until they've been checked.'

It was another ninety minutes before the SOCOs were finished. Louise spent the time with her phone glued to her ear, arranging for extra workers to be called in from the various local police stations in the surrounding area. Already the job of searching all the containers looked unfathomable but there was no other option. As she worked, Louise tried not to think about what the victim had been going through during their last days, the idea of being trapped in such a small, confined space triggering her own mild claustrophobia.

By late afternoon, a crowd had gathered outside the barrier tape, the press having been alerted to the suspicious death. A hush descended over the group as the victim's body was moved out of the shipping container on a gurney, and down the metallic staircase into a waiting ambulance.

As the SOCOs began wrapping up, Louise donned protective overalls once more, and took a final look at the crime scene. Despite the container being open for the last few hours, the influx of fresh air had made no difference to the smell. How the SOCOs were dealing with it was a mystery to her as she stepped through the narrow corridor of boxes towards the area where the body had lain.

Despite her fears, and her own claustrophobia, Louise closed her eyes and tried to imagine what the victim had endured. With the container sealed, the victim would have been left in almost complete darkness. From what Janice Sutton had said, death had been prolonged. There didn't appear to be any signs of struggle on the victim's body and Louise wanted to believe that she hadn't suffered even though the evidence suggested otherwise.

She opened her eyes and took one final look around her at the filth-ridden floor and walls of the metal container before heading back out, where Janice was waiting for her.

'You still think dehydration or starvation?' asked Louise.

'I think so. We're going to get the container moved, see what's inside those surrounding boxes. I think she was trapped there. I'm no expert but by the emaciated nature of her body, I would say she hadn't had water for at least two or three days.'

Greg brought them water as the three of them watched the container craned from its spot and placed on to the ground. The side panels were opened and the SOCOs returned inside, slowly retrieving the contents from within.

'Better go back,' said Janice, donning her mask.

There was a sense of unreality to the scene, the bright red shipping container in the middle of the forecourt as, behind it, a never-ending container ship framed the curving structure of the Avonmouth Bridge.

As the SOCOs continued working, the ambulance carrying the unidentified body drove away. Seconded officers began to arrive and soon the time would come for Louise to organise them. She supervised as the first pallet came out of the container, one of the SOCOs undoing the lock with the key supplied by Atkinson. Louise half-feared they would uncover another body, but the pallet contained nothing more than electrical goods.

Another two hours went by before the victim's container was empty and still the search of the other containers hadn't begun. Atkinson had asked for other workers to be called in but was finding it difficult to get the staff on a Sunday.

'I think we've found something,' said Janice, summoning Louise and Greg over to one of the pallets. 'I don't know how we missed this,' she added apologetically, as she gestured towards the interior of the pallet, which was all but empty except for what appeared to be a solitary video camera. 'We found this in a secondary compartment. It looks like it was purpose-built, definitely not standard. There is a small gap in the pallet here,' she said, pointing to a circular hole. 'That would have been facing the victim.'

Louise glanced at Greg, seeking verification but the DS just shrugged.

'You're saying she was filmed?' said Louise.

'You'll have to get your tech team in to verify. All I can say is the lens was pointing in the direction of the body. It could be that her death was recorded.'

Chapter Three

Louise called her colleague from the IT department, Simon Coulson, and asked if he could join her. As expected, he dropped everything and was at the docklands within thirty minutes. He worked methodically, picking out the camera, the various wires and battery packs until he'd seemingly reached some sort of conclusion.

'Pretty ingenious, in its way,' he said to Louise, as they both stood gazing at the arrangement. 'It must have taken some organising. You see the multiple battery packs? One was automatically activated after the other had depleted.'

'Meaning?' said Louise.

'It's a remote-activated camera, and with the battery packs it could have worked for days – weeks even.'

'You're saying that camera has been recording our victim?'

'It certainly looks that way.'

'Where's the recording?' said Louise, refusing to get too excited by the news. 'I presume it's recorded on to the camera's hard drive?'

Coulson frowned. 'That's what would usually happen, yes,' he said. 'The camera has a built-in flash drive and room for memory cards. See,' he said, pointing to a number of slots that appeared to be empty. 'Unfortunately, whoever set this up had other plans in mind,' he said, reaching to a number of thin black strands protruding from the camera. 'I will have to double-check, but I believe these wires were attached to the shell of the container. If I'm not mistaken, they were used to facilitate access to Wi-Fi.'

'You think the camera was sending out signals?' said Louise.

'I believe so. I'll take the camera in and look at it, obviously, but I don't think anything's been recorded on it. I think all the footage was being sent to another device. I guess that means someone, somewhere, was watching the victim.'

'Jesus,' said Louise. 'What the hell is going on here? Would you be able to determine where the images were sent?'

'It's possible. Depends how switched on the perpetrators are,' said Coulson. 'Unfortunately, it's not that hard to use VPN or relay the signals. And if they've gone to all this trouble, I doubt they would overlook such things, but you never know. We'll do everything we can, Louise, you know that.'

It was midnight before she finally left the docks. The day had dragged, the searches of the containers painfully slow – the delay due to the lack of personnel and interference from Raymond Atkinson who was continually throwing different obstacles in their way. She sent a text message to Thomas before leaving. He called back five minutes later as she was approaching the M5.

'I thought you'd be asleep. Didn't want to bother you,' she said.

'I can't believe they called you in on your day off for that,' said Thomas.

'Tracey and half the team are away,' said Louise.

'What about Greg?'

'He was first on the scene, but the assistant chief requested me personally.'

'Teacher's pet,' said Thomas.

'Now, now. No need to be jealous,' she said, teasing him.

It was a shame that Thomas was no longer part of the team. She'd enjoyed being able to share everything with him, and his input as a detective had been invaluable. He didn't like to admit it, but she was sure he missed the work, especially after his disastrous foray into private contracting, which had almost seen him arrested.

'How about you? How did it go with Rebecca today?' she said, easing on to the motorway, which was all but deserted.

'Not great, I'm afraid. She started crying at one point. I think it was the idea of Noah having a half-brother or sister.'

Rebecca was Thomas's ex-wife. When Louise had first moved to Weston, Thomas had still been married to her and Louise had met her on a number of occasions. Rebecca had always seemed a lovely woman and it felt strange to be in this position. Like it or not, Rebecca was now going to be a big part of her life and she wanted to get along with her.

'It must be a bit of a shock,' she said to Thomas.

Though Rebecca had known that Louise and Thomas were dating, they'd only been together for a few months. The pregnancy had come as a surprise to Louise, and she could imagine how Rebecca must be feeling.

'Now it's your turn,' said Thomas.

'I told you, I'm not telling my parents until we've had the scan,' said Louise. Thomas had wanted to tell Rebecca early as he wouldn't be seeing her again face-to-face for another month, but Louise still wasn't ready to tell anyone else. Her concerns over Emily and her parents aside, she was in her forties and that brought with it extra complications in regards to being pregnant. Things could go wrong, and the less people knew beforehand the better. 'I still haven't worked out how to tell Emily, either,' she added.

'I know, let's not worry about that now,' said Thomas. 'Your family are going to be over the moon to know they have a little grandchild on the way. Emily's going to have a baby cousin – who wouldn't want that?'

'Hope so,' said Louise. 'You ready for your interview tomorrow?'

Ever since that last ill-fated job as head of security for a local firm, Thomas had been looking for a new role. She'd sensed his frustration over these last few weeks. He was used to working, and wasn't suited to having time on his hands. It had to be hard on him watching her go off every day to do something that he'd once excelled at, and she hoped he found something soon.

'Ready as I'll ever be. I can't wait to start work again, if I'm honest. Being a man of leisure is not all it's cracked up to be.'

'At least it gave you some time to practise doing the house-work,' said Louise.

'What does that mean?' said Thomas, with pretend out-rage. They'd yet to make a firm decision on moving in together, although it was an inevitability and something she was sure they both wanted. Thomas's two-bedroom house would be enough for them for the time being, though everything depended on what was going to happen with Emily.

'Nothing, just that I expect a certain amount of cleanliness,' said Louise, before saying goodnight.

The potential impact of the baby on Emily was still troubling her as she left the motorway and headed through the back roads of Worle towards her house near Kewstoke. She'd only touched on the situation with Thomas, but she'd been wondering more and more about Emily moving in with them. It was going to be hard enough being a new mother without the added complication of a second child. But she loved Emily like a daughter, and although she didn't see her as often as she would like, she couldn't bear the idea of living away from her.

Pulling up outside the house, Louise shut the car door and tiptoed across the pebbled driveway towards her separate entrance.

Again, she was struck by the absurdity of having to sneak into her own house late at night and wondered if that feeling would ever disappear, or if, to a certain extent, part of you always felt like a child. Making herself some Malai chai tea, she collapsed in front of the television. The day had exhausted her and she would have loved to have gone to sleep but was still too wired, with so many things playing around her mind.

Her relationship with Thomas was going well, but it had all happened so quickly. It was only in the last couple of weeks that they'd told one another they were in love, and here they were on the verge of moving in together, and raising at least one child.

Distracting herself from the complications of her private life, Louise turned her thoughts to the victim found in the shipping container. With the discovery of the video camera, and the potential extent of the commercial disruption, the investigation would now take precedence over her many other outstanding cases.

Hopefully things would be clearer in the morning, but as yet they still had no identification for the victim, no idea how she'd got placed in the container, and certainly no idea as to why.

Louise switched off the television and sat for a few minutes in silence. Allowing her eyelids to close, she pictured the victim in her confinement and tried to consider the mental strain she must have been under. With the low ceiling and the surrounding pallets, it must have been like being buried alive, and Louise thought her sanity would have snapped within hours if she'd been placed in that position. She had spent so many hours during her career wondering at the lengths people would go to inflict pain on others, but still things like this ate away at her. How anyone could do such a thing to a fellow human was beyond her. The camera had been there for a reason, and images formed in Louise's mind of the dead woman's last minutes. The pain she would have endured, the panic in her eyes as she drew her last breaths. While somewhere, someone watched for their own twisted pleasure.

Louise tried to shake the visions from her head. Knowing falling asleep on the sofa would play havoc with her in the morning, she managed to drag herself to the bedroom. She didn't even bother undressing, falling into a night of uneasy dreams the second her head hit the pillow.

Chapter Four

Julie Longstaff pulled up outside her detached house in Henleaze early Monday morning. It was the first time she'd been back to the property since Saturday, having spent the last two nights at her mother's house. It must have been all in her imagination, a fallout from Saturday's events, but the place felt different. There was a tinge to the air outside the house, a smell of ammonia in the drains she'd never noticed before.

The argument with Patrick on Saturday night had spiralled out of hand so quickly. Now, with some space, and a fresher head, she realised that maybe she'd gone too far.

She was looking forward to seeing him again to put things straight. Some of the truths she'd shared with him had been plainly hurtful. He was never one to hide his feelings and the heartbreak in his crumpled features as she told him she wanted a divorce had haunted her through yesterday's hangover.

Life together had grown stale and increasingly claustrophobic, but divorce wasn't the way forward. She'd been with Patrick forever, and she struggled to see a future without him. On Saturday she'd noted in her e-diary that it had been five years to the day that they'd given up their wild plans of IVF. Conscious or not, that had been the catalyst for the argument on Saturday, and she wished she could have the day back again.

Opening the front door, she pictured the last time she'd seen Patrick as he'd stormed out, no doubt on the way to the nearest bar. She hoped he'd got it out of his system, though from the increasingly incoherent messages she received late Saturday evening she doubted that was the case. He'd refused to answer his phone yesterday – he'd been punishing her, and she probably deserved it – and would be at work now, so she had time to prepare something for him on his return.

The air inside the house was musty, as if she'd been away for days. Photographs lined the stairway, smiling images of their wedding and holidays making her feel worse about the argument.

After Patrick had stormed out on Saturday, she'd left for her mother's and told her she'd asked Patrick for a divorce. Her mother had always loved Patrick, and after much dithering she'd asked Julie why she wanted to leave him. Even in her angry and drunken state, giving her an answer was harder than Julie had imagined and now she knew she'd made a mistake by acting so hastily.

She went upstairs and showered. As she changed, she was surprised to see that Patrick hadn't made the bed. That wasn't like him. He had a need for tidiness that bordered on the obsessive.

She made her way back downstairs and brewed a pot of coffee. Taking the drink through to the lounge, a nagging doubt entered her mind. She'd left for her mother's an hour or so after Patrick had stormed off. Glancing around the place it became apparent to her that Patrick probably hadn't returned. That would explain the unmade bed, the empty coffee cup on the sideboard, and Patrick's gym bag still being out in the hall; all things that would have been moved had he returned.

Julie sighed and tried his number, worried that his drinking had got out of hand on Saturday night and had continued into the Sunday. It wouldn't have been the first time, and with recent events, she was worried that he could have got himself into some trouble.

The phone went straight through to voicemail, which was unusual during a work day. There'd obviously be a simple explanation, but she still felt on edge. She thought back to that distraught look on Patrick's face when she'd told him she wanted a divorce. The furrow on his brow, the light wrinkles at the edge of his eyes that had deepened over the last year. She'd never met someone who wore their emotions so openly and he'd reacted as if he hadn't expected it at all.

As the minutes dripped by, she grew concerned that she'd been too harsh with him and he'd done something stupid. She called his best friend, Martin Peters, who claimed he hadn't seen him for a few weeks but would ring round his other friends. She wanted to call Patrick's work but was worried about how it would sound. Instead, she called her mother, who told her not to panic. 'He's probably sleeping off a hangover somewhere, or drowning his sorrows still,' she said.

'But you know Patrick. He's emotional.'

Her mother went silent. Five years ago, after the final round of IVF, Patrick had tried to take his life. He'd been discovered trying to climb the railings on the Clifton Suspension Bridge. He hadn't managed to follow through, and had received counselling ever since. Julie had begged him then to give up his drinking, but somehow he'd continued with the routine and she hadn't stopped him.

'I can come round if you want?' said her mother.

'No, that's fine, Mum. I'll try his friends again. I'm sure you're right, and there's nothing to worry about.'

But worry she did. She wasn't in the least bit superstitious, but something had been off from the first moment she'd arrived back at the house that morning. Maybe it was all the stress from Saturday but she couldn't shake the feeling that something was seriously wrong. She waited another thirty minutes before calling Patrick's work, speaking to Patrick's PA, Alistair.

'Oh, hi, Julie. How are you?' said Alistair, unable to hide the tone of surprise in his voice.

'Fine, thank you. I was wondering if Patrick was there. I can't seem to get through to him on his phone.'

The line went momentarily silent. She could almost hear Alistair working out how he was going to reply. 'I was actually going to call you, Julie. I'm afraid Patrick hasn't turned up this morning. There's a very important meeting at lunch over in Bath. I'm hoping he's on his way there now. I can't get through to him on his mobile phone either.'

Julie's heart was pounding against her chest. It felt like an extreme reaction, but her body was acting of its own volition. She pictured Patrick on the bridge, searching for a gap in the safety barriers to throw himself off. 'Where's the meeting, Alistair?' she said.

Alistair hesitated. 'I'm not sure we can tell you that,' he said, after a second's delay.

'I'm not a spy, Alistair. He works for a maritime insurance company. Tell me where the restaurant is.'

'The Bull and Boar on Bath Road. The meeting's supposed to be at one.'

Julie rubbed her chin, hoping to God this all meant nothing. 'OK, Alistair. Keep trying his phone. I'll let you know if he turns up at the meeting.'

Chapter Five

Louise awoke at 6 a.m. with a jolt. Although light streaked through her curtains, it took her a few seconds to adjust to her surroundings. Her dreams had been plagued with visions of being trapped underground. She spent so many nights at Thomas's nowadays that the place was almost like a second home to her. Stretching, she rolled on to the other side of her bed, saddened that Thomas wasn't there. Although her section of the house was separate from her parents, Thomas was yet to sleep over. It was laughable in so many ways. Thomas was now the father of her child, for heaven's sake. But he had his own place and it just felt easier being there, away from the glare of her family. She dressed in a hurry and rushed downstairs, keen to see Emily before her first day back at school.

The girl was already up, Louise's mother running around frantically despite them still having another hour before they had to leave.

'Look how grown up you look,' said Louise to her niece, whom she hadn't seen since yesterday morning when she'd been forced to leave for the docks. Emily wasn't one for holding grudges. She moved over and gave Louise a hug, before her grandmother began brushing her long hair.

'You'll be in secondary school before you know it,' said Louise's father, looking up from his newspaper on the kitchen table.

'I'm only going into year four, Granddad, don't be silly,' said Emily, trying to shrug off the hairbrush.

'Year four,' said Louise, sitting down next to her father. *How had she got so old?* It felt like yesterday that she'd visited her brother Paul and his wife in the maternity ward and held the girl for the first time in her arms. That Emily had endured so much tragedy since – her mother's losing battle with cancer, and Paul's slow-drawn alcoholism and eventual violent death – was something Louise would never fully be able to come to terms with. She felt responsible for her in so many ways that the idea of not living with her any more seemed inconceivable.

'Do you want to give me a lift to school, Aunty Louise?' said Emily.

Louise glanced at her mother, who shrugged. 'If that's OK with Grandma and Granddad.'

'We can come too,' said Louise's mother, her stern voice suggesting the change of events was down to Louise.

'That's fine, but we'll have to take two cars. I have to head straight off to work afterwards.'

'I'm not going to miss my granddaughter's first day back at school, am I?' said her mother, as if Louise was somehow trying to steal her thunder.

'That's settled then,' said Louise, glancing at her father, whose eyes remained firmly on his newspaper.

It was a glorious September day as Louise drove along the old toll road into Weston. The tide was in, lapping at the sea wall, a ray of light glancing off the water at Marine Lake as they drove along the seafront. Strange to think how much Weston had become part of her life these last few years. She'd come to the town under duress, forced out of her position in Major Crimes by a man who was now in prison, but had now fallen in love with the place.

'Are you looking forward to going back to school?' she asked Emily, who was lost in thought, staring across the water at the distant outline of Steep Holm.

'Sort of.'

'Sort of?'

'I hope I'm in the same class as my friends. Some of us will be in a different class, and I'm worried they'll all go without me.'

Louise parked up outside the school. Emily had gone through so much with the death of her parents that it pained her every time she saw her niece unhappy. 'I'm sure that wouldn't be the case, and even if you are in different classes, you'll still see your friends at breaktime and lunch.'

Emily frowned, and Louise feared she'd said the wrong thing. 'What say we go out this weekend. Just you and me?'

The frown disappeared from Emily's face, replaced first by a smile then a look of concentration. 'Thomas and Noah can come too, if you want?' she said.

Louise kissed her niece on the head. 'You are a very thoughtful girl,' she said. 'Now, let's get you to school before I get in trouble with your grandma,' she added, wondering if in the not-too-distant future she would be having the same conversation with the child growing within her.

◆ ◆ ◆

The journey from the school, up the bypass and along the M5, was a slow one. It was a toss of the coin when it came to the state of traffic along this stretch of motorway. Sometimes she sailed through to Portishead within the blink of an eye, but at times like this when she caught the rush-hour traffic, the vehicles moved snail-like towards Bristol and beyond. It started to clear out as she neared the

Avonmouth Bridge, her speed picking up so much that she barely had time to glance over at the area of yesterday's crime scene.

DCI Robertson summoned her into his office when she arrived at headquarters fifteen minutes later. They'd barely seen one another over the last couple of months following Louise's most recent case in Weston-super-Mare. That investigation had involved an explosives expert who had detonated a number of bombs in the seaside town. Louise and Robertson had tracked the culprit down to an allotment near the town centre, and for a brief period it had just been the three of them: Louise, Robertson and an elderly man who'd been responsible for a number of atrocities.

Louise had seen a different side to Robertson then, and he'd seen a different side to her. They'd both come close to stepping over a moral line no police officer should cross. That they'd felt justified in doing so wasn't the point. It was now a secret between them, and Louise still wasn't sure if it would eventually play on their relationship.

If it was bothering Robertson, he wasn't letting it show. He looked his usual dour self as she entered the office. 'Close the door, Louise,' he said, in his rough Scottish brogue.

'Iain,' said Louise, taking a seat.

'Still no ID for the victim at the docklands?'

'Unless you have any news to tell me, sir,' said Louise. 'We'll be working on it flat out. I've ordered a mass DNA screening.'

Robertson scratched his head, a tell-tale sign that he was delaying telling her some bad news. 'We're getting a lot of grief from the shipping company,' he said eventually.

'That's to be expected, isn't it?' said Louise.

'I guess so. I've just had the nod from the assistant chief that we're going to deploy some more bodies to help you with the search of the shipping containers and the DNA screening. If you think it's necessary.'

'Is that so?' said Louise, thinking how strange it was that sometimes resources were available, and sometimes they were not.

'I see from your report that we're ruling out people smuggling,' said Robertson.

'Not ruling it out completely. That container's been there for a month and it's possible the victim's been there for the same period. And as you know, people are normally smuggled into the country, not out of it.'

'This camera, what do you make of it?'

'It's such an elaborate set-up. Could be some sort of punishment. I've read about things like this before. Organised crime keeping people in detention, streaming the results. It wouldn't surprise me if someone connected to the victim has been forced to watch her demise as some sort of deterrent.'

'Deterrent?'

'Deterrent, show of power, you name it.'

'Why here? Why now?'

'I guess that's what we have to find out, sir.'

Louise took a deep breath as she stood by the door, the nauseous feeling moving up to her chest. She blinked her eyes, fighting a brief bout of dizziness.

'Everything OK?' said Robertson.

Louise tightened her grip on the door handle. 'Need something to eat,' she said, leaving before Robertson could question her further. She hadn't been sick that morning, but if she was to become nauseous now, then it would definitely be a case of the wrong place at the wrong time. She'd yet to tell anyone else about her pregnancy, but knew she would be obliged to tell Robertson once her three-month scan was complete. She'd been trying to put it off for as long as possible, knowing that as soon as it was official, things would change for her. She would still be allowed to do her job, but a pregnant woman was a health and safety issue in the police, and she wasn't yet ready for any special treatment, and definitely wasn't prepared to be away from the action, especially with the shipping container investigation being in its infancy.

She made herself a cup of tea, still fighting the wave of dizziness. Her eyes struggled to focus, her vision blurring as she carried the tea to her desk. She considered calling Thomas for some moral support, but didn't want to be overheard talking about the baby. Instead, she uploaded her itinerary on the screen, delegating all her other cases, giving the shipping container investigation priority. Already she'd had a knock-back. Simon Coulson had left her an email. He'd been working all night on the camera they'd found in the container, and, as he'd suspected, there was no way to trace the signals from the camera beyond a list of improbable relay destinations spanning the globe.

DS Greg Farrell arrived ten minutes later. As usual he was wearing a high-end suit, immaculate from head to toe. Only his deep-set eyes showed the signs of a late night. 'Coffee?' he said.

Louise had been off coffee ever since falling pregnant. The smell had made her nauseous even before the positive test. Now with the bouts of morning sickness, the very thought of drinking it made her want to go to the toilet. 'Rooibos tea,' she said, ignoring the rumbling noise in her belly. 'Are you going to tell me about your late night?' she said, when Greg returned with her tea.

'That obvious?' said Greg, rubbing his bloodshot eyes.

'I've seen you looking better,' said Louise.

'Been working all night on the missing person reports, got a bit carried away with it in the end and went national, going back months and months. I think I have an identification for our victim.'

Louise sat up straight at the news. She hadn't got on well with Greg during her first years in Weston-super-Mare – he'd had a youthful arrogance about him at the time, which he'd thankfully grown out of – but now he was one of the few people she fully trusted. 'You sure?' she said.

Greg loaded photographs on to his phone and handed it to her. 'Aisha Hashim,' he said, as Louise flicked through a number of images of a bright, smiling woman.

'Went missing six months ago,' said Thomas. 'Age twenty-three, originally from Huddersfield, moved down to London for work. Apparently found a flatshare in Sydenham, south-east London. Made a few calls to her parents but no one's heard from her since. She was reported missing in London. I spoke to the investigating officer this morning. There was a lot of family turmoil. The parents didn't agree with her life choices, which in part explained the move to London and possibly why she hasn't been back in contact.'

Louise loaded the crime scene photographs from yesterday on to her computer screen and gazed from the screen to Greg's phone, trying to equate the two women: the smiling face of Aisha Hashim in the days before she went missing with the sunken eyes of the victim they'd found in the shipping container. The similarities in eye colour and facial structure were obvious, but the body in the container had lost a considerable amount of weight, the face gaunt, her bones angular in comparison with the more rounded features of Aisha Hashim.

'I just got off the phone with Dempsey,' said Greg, as if reading her mind.

Dempsey was the county pathologist. 'And?' said Louise, wondering why Greg was keeping her in suspense.

The DS took his phone back and loaded some more images. 'The parents supplied this image when she went missing,' he said. 'A birthmark on her right thigh.' Louise scrolled to the counter-image on her screen of the unidentified victim. There it was, in plain sight, the crescent-shaped blemish on the woman's thigh.

'Dempsey's confirmed the mark is the same?' she said.

Greg nodded.

'We have to get the parents to identify the body,' said Louise, moving her hand to her belly. Some things never got easier, but the thought of giving a death notice to a parent now felt harder than ever. She hadn't even given birth, yet she felt the sense of protectiveness of her unborn baby envelop her in a way she'd never experienced before. It was overwhelming, and it was impossible to conceive of the pain Aisha Hashim's parents would endure when they found out what had happened to their daughter.

'Already on to it,' said Greg. 'I called the team in Huddersfield CID. Going to do the death notice this morning and they'll get someone to drive the parents down later today.'

Chapter Six

As soon as she ended the call with Alistair, Julie rushed outside to the car. It was possible she was overreacting, but she couldn't resist the sense that something was very wrong. Not only had Patrick not returned home yesterday, he hadn't called into work. If Patrick was anything, he was dependable. Maybe a little too much so. She'd never known him to miss work because of a hangover, and there was no way he would miss an important meeting without letting anyone know.

After briefly considering driving to the Clifton Suspension Bridge, she swerved through the Bristol traffic out towards Bath. She blamed herself. Patrick had looked genuinely shocked when she'd told him about the divorce idea. It had been such a stupid error of judgement. Of course it had crossed her mind over the years, but all couples went through that. She'd been hurting and had spoken through anger. She understood that now, but at the time had been blinded with her rage. She would have liked to think that Patrick would have understood too, but he didn't do well with confrontation. She should have stopped before he'd left. When she saw him next, she would tell him that.

Meandering through the traffic, she thought about all their happy times together as she tried to fight images of him freefalling from a bridge. She smiled as she recalled when they'd got together.

A group of them from school had gone for the day to the river, and she'd fallen for his cheeky confidence, the way he'd been mature for his years without being boring. They'd been together ever since and she didn't regret a single day, despite what she'd said on Saturday.

He didn't deserve any of this. He'd wanted them to have children because she'd wanted them to have children. And when they'd been unable to do so, he'd blamed himself. It had taken him a long time to get over it, and there were things she'd kept from him, but she still loved him the same way she had that day by the river, despite the staleness that had slowly crept into their marriage.

She honked her horn, swearing as a car pulled in front of her from a side street. Her behaviour wasn't rational but she didn't care. She had an unwavering need to see Patrick again, just to make sure everything was OK.

She arrived at the gastro pub five minutes after the meeting was due to take place. She left the car, her body drenched in sweat and shaking as she peered through the windows of the building. She'd met some of Patrick's clients in the past, but couldn't recognise anyone in the bar area. One thing was for sure, however: her husband wasn't there.

She called Alistair again. 'Any news?' she said, before he'd even had the chance to say hello.

'No, I keep getting a dead signal.'

'I'm at the restaurant,' said Julie. 'He's not here.'

Alistair mumbled something down the line, clearly uneasy about the situation.

'Do you want me to go in? Speak to the client?'

'Not sure how that's going to look,' said Alistair. 'Maybe Patrick's spoken to the client to explain why he's late. Give me five, I'll call the client, see if he's heard from Patrick.'

Julie hung up and pretended to scan the menu on the outside window as she waited. From her vantage point she could only see four occupied tables. When a smartly dressed man in a three-piece suit lifted his phone, she knew he had to be Patrick's client. The man looked around, nodding a few times, before placing the phone on his table.

In seconds, Alistair called her back. 'This is a shitshow,' he said, seemingly more concerned about the business than Patrick's safety. 'The client hasn't heard from him.'

'What's his name, Alistair?' said Julie.

'What do you mean?' said Alistair, playing dumb.

'The client's name, of course.'

'Tristen Ainsley,' said Alistair. 'Though I don't think it would be a good idea to go and speak to him,' he added, but Julie cut him off before he had a chance to protest any more.

Julie knew how inappropriate her behaviour was. It was so out of character for her as well. She could feel the sweat dropping off her body and imagined her hair was a frantic mess, as she walked straight over to the table where Patrick's client was sitting. 'Mr Ainsley?' she said.

The man glanced up at her, his eyes full of surprise. Julie wondered if he thought he was looking at a madwoman.

'Julie Longstaff, Patrick's wife.'

Ainsley's mouth hung open as if he couldn't quite process what he was being told. 'Oh, Mrs Longstaff, please take a seat,' he said, after a few painful seconds of silence. 'Have you heard from your husband?'

Julie sat down. 'No, that's why I'm here. I'm really sorry to trouble you. I know the office has just spoken to you as well. I haven't seen Patrick since Saturday night and I'm growing increasingly concerned that something might have happened to him. I wanted to know when you last spoke to him.'

Ainsley's face mellowed. 'I haven't spoken to him since early last week. We exchanged a brief email on Friday. Let me check,' he said, scrolling through his phone. 'Yes, here we are. *Look forward to seeing you on Monday, hope you have a good weekend. All the best, Patrick.* Confirming our meeting, obviously,' said Ainsley, his brow furrowed in concern.

'Nothing since? Nothing over the weekend?'

'Afraid not. Listen, is he *missing* missing? When did you last hear from him?'

'We had an argument on Saturday night, I stayed at my mother's house and Patrick hasn't been home. This is so out of character, that's why I wanted to speak to you,' said Julie, worrying she was oversharing.

'Oh, I understand. I know this is a horrible question, but have you checked the hospitals?'

All Julie's energy drained from her. 'No,' she whispered. 'I guess that would be the most logical thing to do. OK, Mr Ainsley, thanks for the suggestion. I'll get on to it now,' she said, standing, using the back of the chair to maintain her balance, the restaurant momentarily swirling out of focus.

'Here, let me help,' said Ainsley.

'No, it's fine,' said Julie. 'Obviously you'll let the office know if you hear from him?'

'Of course.'

'Thank you, Mr Ainsley, and I'm sorry for your inconvenience.'

Ainsley shook his head as if it was of no importance. Julie heard him say, 'Good luck,' as she left the restaurant, and rushed back to the car, where she broke down in tears.

Chapter Seven

Having a name for their victim changed everything. Louise began the process of setting up her incident room, officially elevating the investigation from a suspicious death to murder. She made calls to the investigating officers both in Huddersfield and Sydenham while waiting for the Hashims to arrive, and familiarised herself with the files.

Aisha had left school aged sixteen with a handful of GCSEs, a bright girl by all accounts who was easily distracted. She'd found a job at a local café waiting tables, but started working in local pubs when she turned eighteen. As Greg had stated earlier, she moved to London six months ago and had been registered missing two months later.

It was hard to decipher how thorough the investigation into her disappearance had been. The sad fact was thousands of people went missing every year. In a place like London people often disappeared on purpose, not wanting to be found. The investigating officers in Huddersfield and London had done their due diligence, but beyond interviewing friends, family and former employers, the search for Aisha had been a dead end from the beginning.

Aisha's body had been taken to the county mortuary in Nailsea. Louise arrived thirty minutes early, scanning through her files while she waited for the Hashims to arrive. She'd been here so many times before that it was second nature to her. For the Hashims it would be a life-changing experience. Death notices were never easy at the best of times, but having to identify the body of your child was always particularly cruel.

Louise noticed her hand resting on her belly. Though her earlier nausea had faded, she'd still had nothing to eat and her appetite was close to zero. She stood as two uniformed officers from Huddersfield entered the building and introduced her to the grieving parents. Louise ran through all the necessary preliminaries before guiding them both to the mortuary.

'We only need one of you to identify the body,' said Louise, as they stood on the threshold behind which the body of the Hashims' daughter lay.

'We'll both see her,' said Mr Hashim, holding her gaze.

Louise opened the door and motioned for the parents to step through. The smell of antiseptic, formaldehyde and another rich, coppery smell she always associated with the place hung in the air. Louise acknowledged the technician standing by the body. She wanted to warn the parents about what they would have to see. Though Aisha didn't have any noticeable physical injuries, her features were gaunt and shallow and such a stark comparison to how her parents would remember her, but there were no real words she could offer that would sufficiently prepare them. Instead, she looked both parents in the eyes and said softly, 'Ready?'

Both parents nodded and Louise removed the sheet covering the corpse, studying the parents as they looked down on Aisha. The father remained stoic, nodding to affirm it was his daughter. The mother had to look away, letting out a sharp noise as if a scream had been caught in her throat.

The sound hung in the air. Louise had to take a few seconds to compose herself. Despite her usual detachment, Mrs Hashim's despair resonated with her in a way she couldn't fight.

'Thank you,' Louise said, her voice unsteady. 'You can spend some time with her alone if you wish?'

'It's fine,' said Mr Hashim. 'Please.'

The technician covered the body and Louise led the parents away.

◆ ◆ ◆

Louise asked the two uniformed officers to drive the Hashims to headquarters. She didn't want to put the parents through any more trauma, but they needed to be questioned. Until proven otherwise, everyone had to be considered a suspect in Aisha's death. From the reports it seemed they'd had, at best, a difficult relationship with their daughter, and as always in these types of investigations, family members had to be considered credible suspects.

Louise had noted the differing reactions from both parents to seeing their dead daughter, but nothing was a given. Mr Hashim's stoicism didn't mean he wasn't in pain, and Mrs Hashim's scream of despair didn't mean she wasn't hiding something.

Her appetite returning in a surprising rush, Louise stopped at a service station on the way back to Portishead to eat a cheese sandwich washed down with a herbal tea. Setting off again, she called Greg and checked how things were progressing at the docks.

'As well as can be expected,' said Greg. 'We've had to send a number of workers home. There's a general sense of unease, but I guess that's what we expected.'

'How far are you through the searches?'

'I'd be surprised if we've gone through half of the containers yet,' said Greg.

'Keep going. I'll join you when I've finished with the Hashims,' said Louise, hanging up before driving up the hill to headquarters.

The Hashims had been placed in an interview room, and both were nursing cups of tea as Louise entered. After once again offering her condolences, she told the parents she would be recording the conversation before asking the pair about their daughter. Louise went through her notes, going over everything that had been given to her from Huddersfield and Sydenham.

'I understand the last time you spoke to Aisha was four months ago. Is that correct?' she asked the parents.

Mr Hashim nodded. 'Aisha called my wife,' he said.

Louise found his face unreadable, which wasn't something she was used to. 'How did she sound?' she asked, turning her attention to Mrs Hashim, who'd barely spoken since they'd met.

'She sounded fine – said she was enjoying living in London and the freedoms it offered.'

'That sounds about right,' said Mr Hashim.

'What do you mean?' said Louise.

'I'm afraid Aisha was big on her freedoms,' said the man, as if that was something to apologise for. 'We're partly to blame. We lost control of her at a young age – fourteen, fifteen. She started hanging around with the wrong crowds, you know how it goes. Smoking at school, drinking in the park. She was a bright girl, my Aisha. We had big plans for her. She was due to study biology for A levels. We hoped she'd go to medical school.'

Mr Hashim talked about Aisha as if she was his property, as if she was a thing to be moulded into the shape he wanted. He didn't seem to be displaying any signs of mourning, aside from regret at her past behaviour. That in itself wasn't so strange, people handled grief in many different ways, but she wondered if something was being left unsaid.

She'd seen her own father's despair after the death of her brother, and it was nothing she wanted to ever experience again. But she would have liked to see a flicker of despair in Mr Hashim.

Maybe he was putting on a brave face to protect himself, fearing an unstoppable onslaught of emotion should he let his guard down. Or maybe his relationship with his daughter hadn't been that strong. It happened more than people thought. The unbreakable bond between parent and child wasn't always as robust as society dictated it should be, though the way Louise already thought about her own growing baby made her find that difficult to believe.

'She left school at sixteen?' she asked.

Mr Hashim nodded. 'She could have stayed on to do her A levels. Her grades weren't as good as they should have been, but we talked to the school and they knew her potential. She wasn't interested – wanted to go out drinking, seeing boys. We had to sever ties.'

'Sever ties?' asked Louise.

Mrs Hashim let out a strangled cry at the question, similar to the noise she'd made at the mortuary.

Louise looked at Mr Hashim, hoping he would do something to comfort his wife, but he didn't reach out to her.

'We told her to leave,' he said, as if warming to his subject. 'I'm not ashamed of it. She needed to learn the realities of life. I hoped to shock her back into the real world,' he continued, seemingly speaking for the pair of them.

'Where did she live?' asked Louise.

'She was a fortunate girl – she moved in with some friends. I think she did some sofa surfing. I think that's what they call it.'

'How long did that last?' asked Louise, trying to hide her surprise at Mr Hashim's dispassionate way of speaking about his daughter.

Mr Hashim stared at her as if she'd just issued a challenge but didn't answer.

Louise matched the gaze before turning her attention to Mrs Hashim. 'She didn't move to London until she was twenty-three, did she?' asked Louise, wondering what it was the pair were hiding from her. She glanced down at her notes. A man called Malcolm Knotsford had been questioned when Aisha first disappeared. Knotsford had a couple of prior convictions for possession, and had been arrested but not charged on a set of up-skirting videos that had appeared online.

'Do you think this might have anything to do with Malcolm Knotsford? He was Aisha's boyfriend, wasn't he?' asked Louise.

'Don't say that name to us,' said Mr Hashim, patting his wife's arm.

'Mr Hashim, I'm afraid we need to go through these questions. I'm sure you want to find out why this happened to your daughter.'

'She moved in with him,' said Mrs Hashim, shrugging off her husband's hand. 'She was seventeen. They lived together for three years. He wouldn't let her see us,' she added.

Louise wondered if that decision had been solely down to the boyfriend, considering the parents had banished their daughter when she was still so young.

'And what happened between Aisha and Malcolm?'

'They split up around her twenty-first birthday. Came home to us then, crying, bags on her shoulder like we were a launderette,' said Mr Hashim.

Louise couldn't tell if the mother was fully subjugated in the marriage or was just allowing her husband to blow off steam for appearances. This time, it was Mrs Hashim who laid a hand on her husband's arm, a way of telling him to be quiet.

'She was heartbroken,' said Mrs Hashim. 'Malcolm had been seeing a number of women behind her back. It was all she'd ever known since she'd left home, and she was too young to know how to deal with it.'

'How long did she live with you after that?' asked Louise.

'She lived with us until she moved to London,' said Mr Hashim, as if the very idea was still traumatising him.

'She took a bookkeeping course and was going to do her accountancy exams,' said Mrs Hashim, smiling for the first time, her face alight with pride.

'That's why she went to London?' said Louise.

'We thought so. She got a temp job with a charity in east London. She said things were going fine. She used to call us every couple of weeks and then one day she just stopped.'

'How did she sound on that last call?' said Louise.

Out of nowhere, Mr Hashim slammed his fist against the table. 'We've answered all these questions before,' he screamed, the vein on his neck throbbing as he tried to contain his anger.

Louise was surprised by Mr Hashim's outburst, the show of emotion a stark contrast to the composed way he'd previously been behaving. 'I understand how difficult this must be for you,' said Louise. 'Every piece of information you give us could be influential, however irrelevant it might seem at the moment.'

'She sounded OK, but I knew she was hiding something,' said Mrs Hashim, ignoring her husband's outburst. 'She sounded discontented, as if London hadn't proven the dream she'd hoped it would be. That was to be expected and I tried to encourage her to keep going with things. If I'd known then that it would be the last time I spoke to her I would have said more, would have pushed her to find out what was happening in her life.'

Louise lowered her eyes. She had no words of condolence that would make the parents feel any better. 'Did she mention anyone else? Or even if this Malcolm had turned up?'

'No, Malcolm was long gone by this point. We didn't really have that sort of relationship, you understand. Talking about boys and things like that,' said Mrs Hashim, as her husband rolled his eyes at the mere suggestion.

Louise ignored the husband's gesture. 'Had she forgiven you?' she asked, noting the tension in both the parents at the question.

'Forgiven us for what?' said Mr Hashim.

'Kicking her out, Arjun. What else do you think?'

Mr Hashim tensed again, his mouth tight, as though he was grinding his teeth. Louise couldn't tell if it was because of what Mrs Hashim had said, or the manner in which she'd said it. 'What you both don't understand is that this was always bound to happen the day she quit school,' he said.

'Don't be so ridiculous,' said Mrs Hashim.

'It's true. We did our best for her and how does she repay us? Going off to live in sin with some druggy layabout. And then when we let her return to our house? She ups and leaves for London, as if we didn't even exist.'

'And this?' said Mrs Hashim, getting to her feet. 'Getting murdered? I suppose this is all her own fault as well,' she said, screaming at her husband.

'Maybe if you'd been a proper mother to her this would never have happened.'

Louise saw that the words had hurt Mrs Hashim as hard as if her husband had used his fists. Her face crumpled, and she turned towards the door.

'Please, take a seat,' said Louise. 'You're both upset and saying things you don't mean.'

'He means it all right,' said Mrs Hashim. 'I'm not going to say another word while he's still in the room.'

Chapter Eight

Julie returned to the house. It may have been in her imagination, but already she sensed Patrick's absence everywhere she looked. She wanted to believe that any second now he would open the front door and walk in, head hung low, but somehow she knew that wouldn't be the case. She wasn't spiritual, didn't believe in anything such as fate, but she couldn't shake the feeling that something was wrong.

She spent the next hour calling local hospitals and police stations, phoning friends and family, but still there was no news of Patrick. Whilst boiling the kettle, she opened the fridge for some milk, and noticed the half empty bottle of Sauvignon Blanc which, despite the early hour, looked particularly enticing. Upon taking the bottle from the fridge, she held it in her hands, feeling its weight. She winced as she pulled the cork, the acrid smell of the wine telling her that it was no longer fit for drinking. Throwing the contents down the sink, she decided to retrace Patrick's movements from Saturday evening, which had started in the kitchen.

Despite his anger, Julie recalled the sadness in his hound-dog eyes as she'd mentioned divorce. There had followed a few minutes of heated recriminations before he'd left, slamming the door behind him. No doubt, his first stop had been the Dog and Duck, the local pub only a few hundred yards from their house – the place he visited every time they had an argument.

With no better options available, Julie locked up and made the short walk to the bar. Her dismay must have been visible as she walked into the pub. The bar manager, a strange little man she knew only as 'Rich', stopped her, a genuine look of concern on his face.

'Is everything OK, Julie?' he asked, placing his pudgy hand on her shoulder.

Julie found herself clenching her fists, nails digging into her palms as she tried to control the overwhelming urge to break down in tears. 'Hi, Rich,' she said. 'I was wondering if you'd seen Patrick recently?'

Rich's eyes were downcast. She couldn't be the first woman to come looking for her husband at the pub, and although she was sure there was some sort of unwritten rule for such occasions, she wasn't going to be leaving without an answer. 'Come and sit down. Let me get you a coffee or something,' said the manager, as he hobbled towards the bar.

Julie felt the eyes of the staff on her as she took a seat on a tall stool, as if they were party to a secret. 'Have you seen him, Rich?' she said, as the manager placed a coffee in front of her.

'Not today, love. He was here Saturday night, though. We almost called you.'

'We had an argument,' said Julie.

Rich lifted his hand as if no explanation was needed. 'That much I gathered. He was knocking them back at a hell of a rate.'

'What time did he leave?' asked Julie.

'We were quite busy. I think it must have been sometime between nine and ten. I saw him stumble out of the door. I presumed he'd gone back to your place. Did he?' asked Rich, his eyes wide in anticipation.

'That's the thing, I don't know. I stayed the night at my mum's and didn't come back until this morning. There's no sign of him at the house and he hasn't turned up for work today.'

'Dianne,' said Rich, looking over at a pretty, young barmaid who walked over, a smile lighting up her face. 'This is Julie, Patrick's wife. You know Patrick, don't you?'

It was only for a second but Julie saw something in the barmaid's eyes, a flicker of recognition tinged with a hint of disdain. 'Yes, of course,' said Dianne, the smile not fading.

'Did he say anything on Saturday about where he might be going? I thought he was going home,' said Rich, repeating himself.

The smile faded from the barmaid's face. 'I don't know,' she said. 'He mentioned something about going into town. He was trying to get a few of the regulars to go with him but you know this lot, they only ever leave this place when it's closing time.'

Julie closed her eyes. Of course he hadn't gone home. When Patrick started drinking, especially when he was worried about something, he didn't like to stop. 'If you hear anything, will you let me know?' she said, standing.

'Of course,' said Rich, walking her to the door of the pub. 'I'm sure he'll turn up, love,' he said, following her outside. 'Listen, it's none of my business, but he told me what your argument was about. I'm sure he's just drinking it off somewhere. He'll turn up, mark my words,' he added, as if that was all the explanation she needed at that point.

She called Alistair again as she walked back towards the house, and an hour later she was meeting him outside the local police station in Henleaze. Ashen-faced, Alistair seemed unsure of the etiquette of the situation.

'Thank you for coming, Alistair.'

Nothing about Patrick's PA's body language was reassuring. His shoulders were slumped, his eyes downcast. If anything, he looked more worried than Julie felt. 'I have called everyone I could think of,' he said.

'Thanks, Alistair. I know you would have done your best. Let's go in.'

After explaining their reason for being there, they were buzzed through to the foyer and told to wait for the next available police officer. Julie noticed Alistair's legs twitching as they sat down together, his immaculate Italian leather shoes bouncing along to some unheard rhythm.

After twenty minutes, the door buzzed open again. A young, uniformed officer introduced himself. 'Mrs Longstaff? I'm PC David Jackson,' he said.

Julie stood, acknowledging the man who barely looked old enough to be out of school.

'This is my husband's PA, Alistair Whitehall,' said Julie.

The police officer nodded and led them through to a small interview room in the heart of the building. 'Please, sit,' said PC Jackson, taking a notepad and pen. 'This is about your husband?'

'That is correct,' said Julie, telling the officer about everything that had happened in the last couple of days.

'Just to confirm, the last time you saw him was approximately three p.m. on Saturday afternoon, and you first became worried about him being missing this morning, is that correct?' said PC Jackson.

'As I said, after our argument I went to visit my mother.'

'And you're sure he hasn't been back in the meantime?'

'I've asked our neighbours and called all our friends. Everything in the house seems untouched to me, but the most worrying thing is he didn't turn up for work. There is no other explanation.'

The officer pursed his lips. It was the third or fourth time he'd repeated the gesture since they'd arrived. To Julie, it seemed a self-satisfied mannerism he used when he doubted what he was being told. 'And you've called all his friends and family?' he asked.

'We've tried everywhere,' said Julie. 'What I don't think you're understanding is how unlike Patrick this behaviour is. He wouldn't just go missing. He certainly wouldn't miss a client meeting, that's for sure. Something has happened, I'm sure of it,' said Julie.

The officer pursed his lips again, and Julie found herself clenching her fists once more. All she wanted to do was to reach out and slap the gesture off the young man's face.

'Has anything in Patrick's life changed recently? You mentioned you had an argument?' said PC Jackson.

Julie looked to Alistair, and back to the officer. She didn't really want to share the details with Patrick's PA but there were more important things to worry about at the moment. 'The argument came about because I asked Patrick for a divorce,' she said, noting how alien the words sounded when said out loud.

PC Jackson offered her a half smile, and she could tell he had come to some sort of conclusion in his head.

'It was stupid of me, just a heat of the moment thing. It doesn't explain this behaviour, if that's what you're thinking,' she said, pre-empting him.

'No, of course not,' said Jackson, scribbling away on his notepad. 'I think I have enough information now,' he added. 'We'll begin making enquiries immediately. I realise how worrying this must be for you, but these things do tend to happen when people are faced with life-changing moments. They escape for a few days, but nine times out of ten they come back.'

Julie's nails broke the skin of her hand. She couldn't believe the audacity of the man. He looked barely old enough to have completed his A levels, and here he was giving her life lessons, telling her that Patrick would probably turn up in a few days' time as if he were a lost dog.

'This isn't good enough,' she said, Alistair placing his hand on her shoulder as he got to his feet. Julie shrugged the PA's hand away. 'Something has happened to him, I can tell,' she said.

PC Jackson nodded, also standing. 'I'll pass the information on to everyone in the department. We'll do our utmost to find your husband for you. In the meantime, if you can think of anything else that could help, you can call me here,' said the officer, handing her a business card with the police station's phone number on it.

Julie grabbed the card from his hand. 'You don't understand. Alistair, can you leave us for a second?'

Alistair smiled uncomfortably. 'Of course,' he said, looking baffled as he left the room.

'Patrick has a history of mental illness. His work don't know. We decided to keep it from them. Five years ago, he tried to take his own life.'

'I see,' said PC Jackson, nodding. 'You're concerned he might do the same again?'

'Of course I'm concerned about that.'

'I do understand. I will adjust my risk assessment and pass the details on to a senior member of my team. There are certain things we can do, such as checking bank card use. I assume you're sure he's not at your home?'

'Of course.'

'Do you have a car?'

'We do, but it is still at home.'

'Any sign that Patrick has packed anything?'

Julie shook her head.

'All this information will be passed to the team. We will keep checking the hospitals for you. You have done the right thing coming here,' said Jackson, getting to his feet.

Julie felt the anger wash over her body. She was being dismissed, Patrick's disappearance seemingly an irrelevance. Before she knew it, she was back outside, the heat of the sun stinging the back of her neck. 'That was a bust.'

'It'll be OK,' said Alistair.

'I wish people would stop telling me that *it'll be OK*,' said Julie, mimicking the tone of Alistair's voice. 'He's missing, and something is wrong. I know it in my blood.'

'We'll find him, I promise,' said Alistair, trying to hold her gaze.

Enraged by Alistair's pointless platitudes, she mumbled a goodbye and walked away. As she turned the corner, she caught site of a man in a beige-coloured saloon who appeared to be staring straight at her from the driver's seat. As she returned the look, the man started the car and drove away.

The driver's face had been blurred by the sun, but she was sure she recognised his narrow blue eyes from somewhere; the memory of where and when was tantalisingly out of reach. It remained out of reach an hour later as she stepped into the wine cellar, retrieved two bottles of white wine and placed them in the fridge.

Chapter Nine

Louise was still reeling from her conversation with the Hashims as she pulled into the car park at the Avonmouth Docks. She'd seen a coldness in Aisha's father for much of the conversation that she hadn't much cared for, and explaining it away as grief was proving to be more and more difficult, especially considering his outburst of anger towards the end. Aisha's mother was a different story. She was clearly grieving for her daughter, and the differing emotions of the two parents had come to a troubled end, Mr Hashim having to be escorted from the station before Mrs Hashim would leave.

On the way over, Louise called the missing persons team who had been allocated Aisha's case in London. She'd spent forty minutes trying to get through to the right person, and it had been arranged for her to visit the area tomorrow where she intended to question as many of Aisha's former work colleagues and flatmates as she could find. She'd also called Huddersfield CID and asked them to locate Malcolm Knotsford. She wanted to talk to Aisha's ex-boyfriend as soon as possible. She'd asked further questions about the arrest relating to up-skirting, but so far no one had been able to give her the information she needed.

The docks were a different proposition from yesterday. The cleared containers had started to be lifted on to the waiting cargo ship and the area was alive with activity. Greg met her at the entrance of the office buildings.

'Anything to tell me?' she asked.

'We've been getting through the backlog, and doing the DNA testing,' said Greg. 'Mr Atkinson is as pissy as ever, though I think it's finally dawning on them that this needs to be done,' he added, as they took the steps to the elevated office overlooking the docks.

Atkinson didn't get out of his seat as they arrived in his office. He was better dressed than the day before, as if he'd gone to a great effort to put on his best suit. 'Good of you to join us, DI Blackwell,' he said.

'I understand the searches are going well?' said Louise, ignoring the man's sarcasm.

'We're a day behind,' said Atkinson. 'Going to be a few thousand in late penalty fees, unless we make up the time on the journey, but I suppose you don't care about that.'

'Sorry for any inconvenience that you're experiencing,' said Louise, 'but may I remind you that a dead body was found on your premises.'

Atkinson's jaw muscles tensed. Louise was surprised at how quickly he was prone to anger, his face reddening as if she'd said something purposely to provoke him. 'I agree, it's a tragic business. These things do happen. We get stowaways all the time. It's just unfortunate that this one managed to lock herself in.'

This was the first Louise had heard about stowaways. 'How many stowaways do you get?' she asked.

'Not as many as we used to. Our security is state of the art nowadays. Occasionally they find their way on to the ships.'

'What's the process when you find them?' asked Greg.

'It depends where and when we find them. If we're close enough to land, we can get them shipped off. Sometimes they have to stay on the ship until the next port of call.'

'Do they usually use the containers for this?' asked Louise.

Atkinson shook his head. 'No, that would be suicidal,' he said, having the good grace to look shamefaced as he realised the inappropriateness of his comment. 'Let me introduce you to Bradley Davis, our head of security,' he added, getting out of his seat and walking her to a second set of doors, where a lone man sat in front of a bank of television screens.

'Bradley, this is DI Blackwell,' said Atkinson, making the necessary introductions.

Davis turned on his swivel chair and jumped on to his feet. He was a tall, gangly man, in his late fifties, a cascade of wrinkles breaking out on his features as he smiled and offered Louise his hand to shake. 'Hi,' he said. 'I'm responsible for all security in the docks.' His manner was bright and cheery, so much so that Louise wondered if he knew why she was here.

'Terrible business, naturally,' he said, as if reading her thoughts. 'I've been studying the camera footage from the last seven days.' He returned to his seat, fetching up footage of where Aisha's body had been found. 'Gone through it in triple speed. Naturally, I'll forward it to your department. The camera system is state of the art – each one has motion sensors built in as standard to catch every movement, however slight. I've gone through every occurrence over the last week. As you would expect, it was all triggered by wildlife or changes in the weather. Nothing to report but maybe your team can go through it more methodically.'

The man talked about the cameras with the enthusiasm of a child. 'And the days before that?' asked Louise.

'Again, I've sent that footage to your team. I haven't had the opportunity to go through it myself.'

'Is there any way of bypassing these cameras?'

Davis shook his head, smiling as if the very thought was absurd. 'No, any discrepancy would be recorded. For instance, we would get alerted if the cameras were disabled for any period, however small.'

Louise glanced at the screen, which was showing images of Aisha's container in triple speed. It was currently set to four days before her body was found, in the middle of the day. Louise wondered if Aisha had still been alive during the period, if she'd cried out for help only for her pleas to go unheard.

'In your professional opinion, is there any way the victim could have got into the container in the last four weeks?'

'I don't think even Houdini could pull off such a trick,' said Davis. 'Even if they'd been able to bypass the cameras, which is an impossibility, they would never have been able to force their way inside. Have you seen the containers? The way they're secured? You may have yourself a locked-room mystery here, Detective.' The head of security glanced around the room with a smile, as if he'd come up with something profound.

At times, you need the patience of a saint to do this job, thought Louise. A woman had been killed, and in such a profoundly horrible way, and here was the head of security treating everything like it was some sort of game. 'If not here, how would you suggest she got inside?'

'I've been thinking about this. I think you have two options. The logistics for the movement of the container are as follows,' said Davis, loading a new screen on his laptop. 'The empty container came from a depot in Sunderland. We have already been on to them, and they confirmed that the container was empty when it left their place five weeks ago. It was then transported by lorry to a packing depot in Chipping Sodbury. I've already been on to them for you as well.'

'You have been thorough, Mr Davis. And what did they have to say?'

'Naturally, they check each of the containers. Pack them by hand. Well, I say *hand*, they load them with forklifts. I don't think they're going to load a container with a woman inside now, are they?' he said, snorting.

'No, I guess you're right,' said Louise. 'Can you print those addresses out for me?'

'Already done,' said Davis, handing her a piece of paper.

Louise thanked both men and walked outside with Greg. 'The IT guy is a blast,' she said.

'Like chalk and cheese. You want me to chase on the packing depot?'

'No, you continue the work here. Give the container firm a call when you have a second. I'll make my way over to Chipping Sodbury,' said Louise, the sound of cranes lifting the shipping containers on to the waiting ship accompanying her back to her car.

Louise's mother's number appeared on the screen as she reached the outskirts of Chipping Sodbury, a small market town in south Gloucestershire where the packing depot was located. She came close to ignoring it, but her mother rarely called during the day so it could be important. 'Hello?' she said, answering.

'Hello? Aunty Louise?' came the reply.

Louise checked the clock, wondering how the day had gone so fast. 'Hey, Emily, how are you?' she asked her niece, as she was ushered through the main car park to a spot by the office buildings.

'I'm good,' said Emily. 'It was my first day back at school today.'

'Yes, I know,' said Louise. 'Was it fun?'

'They put me in Mrs Randall's class,' said Emily.

Louise wracked her brains, searching for the image of the young primary school teacher who, despite what Emily had called her, she didn't believe was married.

'Oh, Miss Randall.'

'Yes, yes, Miss Randall. Millie Waters got told off for calling her Mrs.'

'Are you happy to be in her class?' asked Louise, buoyed by the joyfulness in her niece's voice but mindful of what Emily had told her that morning about being split up from her friends.

'Yes, some of my friends were put with Mr Martinez, but I didn't want to be in his class because he is extremely strict,' said Emily.

'Well, that's good then. But some of your friends are in your class though?'

'Yes, Millie, Abigail, Sophie and Vickie are all in my class. It's a shame Izzy and Maisie are with Mr Martinez, but we still see them every breaktime.'

'Well, that is fantastic to hear,' said Louise, her niece's enthusiasm so heart-warming that a bit of Louise wanted her to remain that way forever.

'What are you doing, Aunty Louise?'

'Oh, you know.'

'Catching the bad guys?'

'That's right. I'm always catching the bad guys,' said Louise.

After saying goodbye, Louise felt overcome with guilt for not being there for Emily as she returned from school. More and more of Emily's life seemed to be passing her by. She felt the absence deep within her chest, and somehow found herself crying – something she couldn't recall doing on duty for years. 'This is what baby hormones do to you,' she said to herself, checking her face in the rear-view mirror. Wiping away her tears, she walked over to the offices. A few minutes later, she was wearing a bright yellow hard hat, and was being led around the loading area by the factory foreman, Nathan Hoskin.

'The containers come to us empty, as you can see,' he said, pointing to a forklift truck that was loading pallets on to an empty container. 'We fill them, seal them, ship them out, usually to Avonmouth.'

'Whilst you are doing that, would anyone be able to sneak inside?' asked Louise, showing the foreman images of the tight space where Aisha Hashim's body was found.

'Now why the hell would they want to do that? Even if these containers were shipped immediately, which they rarely are unless they contain perishable goods, it would be suicide entering one of these things. There's no air in them for one thing, or very little. I don't like being inside them even when the doors are open.'

'But theoretically, someone could get inside?' asked Louise.

'I guess so. But the containers are sealed shut out of hours. As you can see it's a busy place; you wouldn't be able to just walk off the street and set up camp.'

'Do you have cameras?' asked Louise.

'The footage is already with your team. I'm sorry I can't help any more,' said Hoskin.

Louise looked around at the busy cargo floor, agreeing it would be difficult for someone to smuggle themselves in unnoticed. One thing was for sure: Aisha hadn't been a stowaway. The placement of the camera and the wires was proof enough of that.

Someone had wanted Aisha to be in such a vulnerable position. The camera hadn't been placed there for posterity. It had been there because someone had wanted to watch Aisha's final moments. And to achieve that, someone must have coerced Aisha into the container.

Some sick individual had deliberately placed Aisha in her tomb, and Louise wouldn't rest until she'd found out who that person was.

Chapter Ten

Julie had spent the last thirty minutes pacing the house. Her mother had called five times in the last couple of hours trying to force her to spend the night with her or, worse still, suggesting she come over to help. Aside from desperately needing to see Patrick again, Julie wanted nothing more at that moment than to be alone. She didn't want anyone else to see the guilt she was carrying. The last thing she needed was her mother fussing over her, looking to glean every bit of information that would explain Patrick's disappearance.

Julie opened the fridge and stared at the two unopened bottles of chilled wine. She wanted to keep her wits about her, but could almost taste the alcohol on her tongue. As she pulled the first bottle from its confinement, she thought about the car outside the police station. The nondescript saloon, and the driver with his narrow eyes. Had she been mistaken, or had he offered her a smile as he drove away? She was convinced she knew him, but try as she might, she couldn't remember where she'd seen him before.

It seemed that every other weekend she was attending one of Patrick's corporate events. She would always drink too much to alleviate the boredom. She was sure she'd seen the man during one of those events but, for the life of her, the time and place – and definitely the man's name – eluded her.

The wine tasted like nectar, easing down her throat and sending a cool shiver through her body. She slumped on the sofa, first glass almost gone. How had it come to this? Only three days ago, she'd been a normal, married woman. Maybe not a super-contented one, but one without a missing husband. If she could have that time back now, she would never have said the things she'd said to Patrick on Saturday.

She drank some more wine, her head already fuzzy. She tried to pretend that she didn't know why she'd said those things but who was she kidding? The anniversary of the IVF treatment may have been a catalyst but that hadn't made her suggest a divorce. It was her guilt.

She drained the remainder of the glass in one gulp, a hollow feeling remaining in the pit of her stomach. She wanted another drink but was glued to the chair by exhaustion. Absently, she found herself scrolling the names on her phone, stopping on the entry recorded as 'DW'. Derek Watson. Her one-time lover.

Even now, she laughed at the idea of sleeping with someone called Derek. It had started six months ago. She'd met Derek at one of Patrick's endless work events. She'd seen him around before – he was a client of a client of Patrick's – but had never thought much about him until that evening when he started paying her some attention. They chatted the night away, Patrick too busy with his clients to give a damn about what she was up to.

Two weeks later, he had called her out of the blue. It had been fun while it lasted, ticking all the clichés – it was illicit, dangerous and exciting all at once. Still, she'd had that nagging feeling deep within her bones every time she met up with Derek. Things may have not been going well for her and Patrick, but he hadn't deserved this type of betrayal. Eventually, she'd called it off. Derek had taken it with good grace. He was married as well and by the way he handled things, she could tell it wasn't his first affair.

Maybe she should have told Patrick, instead of making stupid demands, but it would have broken his heart. The guilt she felt for the affair was for her to suffer alone, and if anything had happened to Patrick because of her selfishness she would never forgive herself.

Opening the second bottle of wine, she wondered what type of person she'd become. Not only betraying her husband but lying about it, before allowing him to disappear off the planet. He was such a sensitive soul. She should have spoken to him about her concerns long ago, and once he was back, she would make sure they did everything they could to remain together.

She picked up her phone again, and, as she had done at least once every hour over the last day, she tried Patrick's phone, screaming at her screen as it went straight through to answerphone. She wanted to call Alistair, and that all but useless policeman, but it was too late; not that either of them would have anything but meaningless platitudes to offer. Instead, she found her finger hovering over Derek's name.

Now that would be a betrayal, she thought to herself, spluttering on her drink that dripped down her chin and on to her chest. She threw the phone across the room, lest she succumb to temptation, and tried to think about all the good times with Patrick. They'd been so happy at the beginning. Was it so impossible to believe that they could be that way again?

Her helplessness was becoming unbearable, and she drank the rest of the bottle in a few gulps. She couldn't quite believe how quickly her life could unravel, and the fact that hardly anyone was taking her seriously made things so much worse.

'I will find you,' she said, slurring to herself. 'I will find you. I didn't mean what I said,' she cried, her head hitting the cushion on the sofa and sending her straight to sleep.

Chapter Eleven

Thomas's house in Worle was empty when Louise arrived later that evening. She let herself in, and cooked some pasta as she waited for him to return home. As she ate, her hand went to her belly, which felt no different on the outside but fluttered within. She wondered if this was something she would have to get used to, a lone mother sitting at home, waiting dutifully for her partner to arrive. It was a situation she'd never been in before and she had to concede it was this potential change in her lifestyle, not the pregnancy, that scared her the most.

Ever since she'd left university, all she'd known was work. More specifically, police work. She'd had lovers, but never really anyone serious enough she would consider settling down with. She'd made her share of mistakes as well. Her ex-colleague and lover, Tim Finch, who was currently behind bars, was testimony enough to that. The idea of domesticity in any form still didn't sit well with her. She could picture a future with a child, but not without being in the police.

She'd seen the subtle change in Thomas since leaving the police, and it had cemented her feeling that she couldn't leave. He was rudderless at the moment, and though that would hopefully change when he found a new job, Louise couldn't imagine not having the hectic challenge of her profession. Where that would leave them when the baby arrived, she didn't know.

Finishing her pasta, and needing to think about anything else, Louise uploaded her old case files from a people-trafficking investigation five years ago. Nineteen bodies had been found in a shipping container at the Avonmouth Docks. The container had been placed on the ship in Belgium, and those inside had spent just over a week onboard. Unlike the container Aisha's body was found in, the large container they had stowed away in had been purposely fitted with air holes and had previously been used to transport livestock. A computer malfunction had led to the container being incorrectly stored upon the ship, surrounded on all sides by other containers, which had given the poor, unfortunate souls within no chance of surviving.

Louise didn't consider herself very claustrophobic, but the idea of being trapped in a container sent shivers down her spine. What must they have thought as they heard the sound of the other containers being placed around them, the light fading, the breathable air being sucked away? It didn't bear thinking about, but the idea had crept into her head and refused to budge.

Uploading her case notes from the current investigation, she glanced again at the withered body of Aisha's corpse, wondering what combination of events had led to her demise. Maybe it had all been a tragic accident, though the addition of the camera suggested otherwise.

Thomas arrived an hour later, comically stumbling through the door, the smell of beer surrounding him like a shoal.

'Good night?' said Louise, an ironic smile playing on her lips as she shut the laptop.

Thomas held his arms out, his wide eyes giving him a youthful look. 'How's my baby?' he said.

'Are you talking about me, or the thing growing inside of me that is making me sick every morning?'

'Don't speak about my baby girl like that,' said Thomas, with a pretend frown as he walked over and placed his hand on her belly.

Louise slapped his hand away playfully. 'Stop calling it a girl – we don't know what sex it is yet,' she said. Everything felt so far removed at that moment that she couldn't imagine the baby as a boy or a girl; she couldn't think any further than the connection she felt growing within her.

'I know,' said Thomas. 'It's my baby girl, you'll see.'

'Let's get the scan done first, shall we, before we start choosing any names? Why are you so late?' she asked.

'I got the job. Sorry, I should have sent you a text. I went out celebrating with my new boss. Not sure it was the best idea, but he seemed happy when I put him in a taxi home.'

'I see. Get me pregnant, and next thing I know you're out every evening gallivanting with your pals?'

Thomas knew her well enough to know she was joking. 'Well, I've got you where I want you now, haven't I?' he said, leaning in to kiss her.

Louise kissed him back, feeling the slight irritation of his stubble on her cheek. 'You can brush your teeth before there is any more of that,' she said, pulling away.

'Harsh,' said Thomas. 'I'll make myself a tea.'

'That's such great news, Tom.'

'The tea or the job?'

'Both. Are you pleased?'

'As long as it doesn't turn out like the last one, I will be.'

Louise could already see the energy returning to him. He didn't suit being idle, and having led such an active life in the police, he needed to be out there using his experience.

'I'll have one too,' said Louise, as Thomas poured his tea. 'I'm off to London in the morning.'

'That shipping container girl?' asked Thomas, filling the kettle.

'Yes, I need to have a chat with some of her old flatmates. There may be an old boyfriend involved. I was going to ask, you were working on that people-smuggling investigation a few years back, weren't you?'

'I was working in Weston that night and they called me in. I've seen some things but that tops the lot. The way they were all arranged, Louise, lying there on the floor . . . tragic. And the smell.'

'I can only imagine.' So often it was the smell that remained with you. Every time she was near an open fire, she was reminded of a case where she had saved someone from a burning pier on Birnbeck Island, and she could still smell the decay and waste from the container where they'd found Aisha.

'Do you think they're linked?' said Thomas, placing her tea down.

'Not really, but I don't want to rule out any potential link.' The truth was, any link would make her job that much easier. At present, all they had was a victim with no known ties to the area. Without something to connect Aisha to the West Country, they could end up at a loss. Louise sipped her tea. They both understood the stark reality of the situation.

Sometimes people disappeared for no reason. Sometimes they turned up again. Sometimes they were never found. And too often, there was no explaining why.

Chapter Twelve

The day started as it usually did: Louise on all fours by the toilet bowl. She hadn't fully known what to expect during her pregnancy, but this seemingly daily routine was draining her energy. And it wasn't going unnoticed. Her mother commented on her dour appearance as she arrived back at her house to collect a notebook she'd left behind.

'You look like you're coming down with something,' said her mother, fixing Louise with a stare. 'Your skin is very pale. Are you sure you're feeling OK?'

'I'm fine, Mum,' said Louise, giving a concerned-looking Emily a quick smile before nibbling the end of some dry toast.

Her mother watched her eat, as if she could stare the truth from her. Eventually she looked away and poured herself a tea, but every now and then Louise caught her looking over and grew increasingly certain that her mother could tell she was pregnant.

Louise finished her makeshift breakfast, gave Emily a quick kiss goodbye, and headed upstairs to get her notebook. Ten minutes later, she was on the road, trying to beat the early morning traffic as she headed to Sydenham in south-east London where she'd arranged to meet a local detective at 11 a.m.

She craned her neck as she crossed the Avonmouth Bridge, trying to catch sight of the container ship, but the traffic was moving fast and all she caught were the lines of storage units waiting to be shipped.

Her left hand reached for her belly, a gesture she'd been trying to avoid in case it drew attention to her pregnancy. There was something comforting about resting her hand there, as if it was protecting the growing life within. It still felt unreal at the moment, and despite the morning sickness and feelings of lethargy, she refused to get carried away before her three-month scan. But the reality was that in six months' time she could be giving birth, and she'd never felt so unprepared in her life.

She arrived in Sydenham an hour early and managed to force down a cup of tea and a ham sandwich from a local café. She was supposedly eating for two now but her appetite was non-existent and she had to force the last half of the sandwich down.

Still, some of her energy was returning, and by the time she reached the block of flats on Belmont Road at 11 a.m. she felt almost back to normal. She didn't have to look hard for the police officer she'd arranged to meet. In plain clothes, the slender man sitting on the brick wall outside the ex-council apartment looked conspicuous and uncomfortable. 'You must be Louise Blackwell,' he said, as she approached. 'DC Stephen Brown,' said the officer, getting to his feet and shaking her hand.

'Good to meet you, Stephen. Thanks for taking the time to see me.'

Stephen shrugged his shoulders. Well over six feet tall, he was dressed in a light cotton suit that was way past its best. The detective had been responsible for the initial investigation into Aisha's disappearance, and Louise had studied his reports from that time.

'I was still on the beat when she went missing. Used to deal with a lot of missing people. I spoke to one of her former flatmates yesterday after your call,' he said, as they made their way into the building. 'Meryl Gatwood. In fact, she's the only one left in the flatshare who was there when Aisha disappeared.'

'Did you think there was anything suspicious about her disappearance at the time?'

Stephen shrugged again, already his signature gesture. 'The division was dealing with up to fifty missing people at a time. They often fitted the same pattern. Aisha moved to London from a smaller provincial town, decided she couldn't hack it, and upped and left, owing some rent money. We did what we normally do. Called friends and family, work colleagues and kept a track on it, hoping she'd turn up. One thing that was slightly odd was the amount of stuff she left in the apartment – quite a lot of clothes, which is unusual for someone making a break for it. But aside from that, nothing stuck out. I rechecked my notes last night. From the testimony of her friends, it appeared she didn't seem very happy here. London can do that to people. It's great when things are going well. When they're not, it can be the loneliest place on earth.'

The lift door pinged open. Louise retched at the smell of urine coming from inside.

'We can take the stairs if you want,' said Stephen. 'Though I doubt the smell will be any better.'

'It's fine,' said Louise, stepping inside the lift. 'I'll hold my breath.'

The journey to the eighth floor took such a long time that they may as well have taken the stairs. Sweat trickled down her brow as the lift made its laborious journey. She didn't know if the sensation was a continuation of her morning sickness, but she felt momentarily trapped within the metal box.

Despite knowing that the thin air would last, and the doors would soon open, she had to fight feelings of claustrophobia. She drummed her foot on the floor, willing the lift upwards, her thoughts turning to Aisha's last minutes in the shipping container.

She let out a breath as the lift arrived and the doors pinged, stepping into the corridor as soon as the opening allowed.

If Stephen had noticed, he chose not to say anything. 'Down here,' he said, walking along the threadbare carpet, past a corridor of identical doors until they reached 816.

A young blonde woman with braids in her hair, wearing a bright blue flowery summer dress, answered the door. 'Meryl Gatwood?' said Stephen, displaying his warrant card. 'I believe we met once before. This is my colleague, DI Blackwell.'

Meryl squinted her eyes, studying both warrant cards before allowing them inside. 'I can't believe this has happened to Aisha,' she said, taking them through a narrow corridor to a shared living area with a kitchen-diner. 'Please sit,' she said, pointing to a battered leather sofa.

They sat facing the largest flat-screen television Louise had ever seen. Louise tried not to fixate on the TV as her body sunk into the sofa, but it was such an anomaly to the meagre surroundings that she couldn't take her eyes from it. It must have been sixty inches wide, and in such a small room with low ceilings, it looked particularly out of place.

'Sebastian's,' said Meryl, noticing Louise staring. 'Quite the eyesore, isn't it?' she added, as she pulled a wooden chair from the kitchenette area. 'He's in Aisha's room, actually. I'll show you, if you like.'

'That would be great,' said Louise. 'First, a few questions about Aisha's time here?'

Meryl lowered her eyes. Louise noticed the woman's black Dr. Martens boots that seemed to be out of place with the pretty dress she was wearing. 'Well, this place holds six of us at any given time, people come and go every few months. I've been here for three years, and I've probably lived with at least twenty-five different people in that period. Obviously, I remember Aisha after everything that happened, but she was just one of so many, you know?'

'How long was Aisha here for?'

'I think it was about three months,' said Meryl, glancing over at Stephen.

'What was she like?'

'She was the salt of the earth, really. Very friendly, outgoing. I guess you would call her bubbly.' Meryl took in a large breath. 'I don't want to say anything bad about her, especially now, but sometimes I found her a little too much, do you know what I mean?'

'Not really,' said Louise.

Meryl frowned. 'I don't mean it in a bad way, honest. She was lovely, but sometimes she would just talk too much. I did wonder if she was masking something; you know, tears of the clown, that sort of thing. She'd talk lots and pretend to be happy when maybe she wasn't.'

'Did she say anything about that?'

'About what?' said Meryl.

'About her happiness. Did you talk about things? Perhaps her work, her love life?'

'She was working in telesales, there wasn't much to talk about. For most of us, it's work to live. As for love life . . . I think she had a couple of boys over here, I can't be sure. There was one guy who turned up a few times. I told you about him,' said Meryl, looking over at Stephen. Louise couldn't be sure, but the answers felt a little polished. As if Meryl was rehashing the same tale she'd told last time when Aisha had gone missing. It didn't necessarily mean anything. People were often nervous around the police, but she did wonder if the woman was hiding something.

'Please, if you could tell my colleague again,' said the DC.

'Fine. One guy by the name of Malcolm. I didn't care much for him. That's not unusual. Just came across as being a bit full on, do you know what I mean? Intense.'

'This him?' said Louise, showing her the picture of Malcolm Knotsford given to her by Aisha's parents.

'Yeah, that's him. Though he looks a bit better in that than he did in real life. He looked to me as if he was on something. His eyes struggled to focus, you know?'

'Aisha ever talk to you about him?'

'Not really. As I said, we weren't that close. Though she was always a lot quieter when he was around, that's one thing I can say. It felt to me that it was almost as if she was embarrassed by him. Either that or she was scared to be herself around him. Whatever the reason, I don't think he was good for her. But as I said, I didn't know her well enough to know more than that.'

Meryl showed them to the small bedroom where Aisha had lived. It was no wonder the owner of the giant TV had put the screen up in the living room going by the size of the bedrooms. Aisha's old room was little bigger than a store cupboard, the single bed taking up nearly half the floor space. With a narrow single wardrobe, and a small desk and chair, there was hardly any space to walk about.

'It's the smallest room,' said Meryl. 'I offered Aisha the choice of two rooms – the other one was bigger, but she said it was too noisy.'

'What did she leave behind?' said Louise.

'Well, she didn't really have that much to begin with from what I know. The few times I did come in here, the space looked quite clean, everything put away in that wardrobe. She'd keep a few books on the desk. The books were still here when she disappeared, and a few of her clothes, but there was no bag so I assumed she just packed in a hurry and left. She wasn't the first person to skip out of here with no notice.'

'Did you call the police?' asked Louise.

'No, that was the landlord. He was very pissed off when he found out she'd upped and gone two days before the next rent payment was due.'

'You haven't heard from her since? No phone calls, emails or anything?'

Meryl squinted, glancing up at Louise as if she'd been caught in a lie. 'There was something. No contact from her, nothing like that . . . but something I didn't tell you the first time around.'

Louise and Stephen exchanged looks. 'Go on,' said Louise, wondering if her earlier suspicions about Meryl withholding some information were about to be confirmed.

'I wasn't hiding anything from you, honestly. The only reason I thought of it was when I was told where her body had been found. I remembered she'd been pissed one night, just come back from a works party. We must have shared the better part of a bottle of vodka between us. She was telling me some pretty odd things.'

'Odd, in what way?' said Louise.

'Honestly, I can barely remember, I was that pissed. Just some weird sex stuff her and Malcolm used to get up to. They used to like doing it in small spaces or something. Each to their own, I guess. I remember her becoming quite animated about it, the excitement, the breathlessness, that sort of thing. I just found it funny, and we never talked about it again. She told me that there were groups that were into this stuff – she mentioned one of them was based out of the South West. As her body was found in Bristol, it must have jogged my memory. Sorry that I didn't mention it before.'

Louise had been right about Meryl holding something back, and though she pushed the woman for more information on Aisha's peculiar sexual peccadilloes, she didn't have anything else to share. It wasn't such an odd omission for Meryl to have made – it was an uneasy subject – but she made a note to check on Meryl when she got back to the station.

Later, Louise spent a couple of fruitless hours at Aisha's old workplace. A depressing, grey tower block with narrow corridors and small cubicles where hundreds of young people sat wearing earphones, repeating the same scripted sales pitch to unsuspecting citizens.

As at Aisha's old flat, the turnover in tenants was high and only a couple of people remembered her. Their feedback was generally the same as that given by Meryl: Aisha was bubbly, outgoing, but they didn't really know much about her. Neither had heard of Malcolm Knotsford.

By early afternoon, Stephen promised to have another trawl through his case notes and Louise thanked him before heading back home.

Later, as she drove along the M4, Louise was struck by the lack of remorse she'd heard from the people she'd spoken to about Aisha. For all the talk of the girl being outgoing, no one had seemed that bothered about her passing. Even Meryl had seemed more concerned to convey that she didn't know Aisha that well. No wonder Aisha had felt alone in London. All Louise had to determine now was if that loneliness had been the reason for her to leave, or if something more sinister had called her away.

She phoned Greg as she passed Reading and relayed details about her morning in London. Greg had travelled to Huddersfield police department that morning. Malcolm Knotsford was still AWOL. The last time anyone had seen him was three months ago at the Wetherspoons in the town centre. Huddersfield police had checked all his former addresses but there was no sign of him anywhere.

'I have some more information on the up-skirting arrest. Knotsford had been identified by one of the victims as being in the area on the day of the incident, but nothing beyond that. His place was searched, and he handed in his phone, but no incriminating evidence was found so no charges were forthcoming,' said Greg.

'His priors were only for possession with intent?'

'Some weed once, cocaine second time.'

'A clear escalating pattern. Hard not to think it could be the same with the up-skirting. We need to up our actions on that search,' said Louise. 'Knotsford has to be treated as prime suspect at the moment. I'd like a more thorough search on Aisha's online history as well,' she added, updating Greg on the information supplied by Meryl regarding Aisha's sexual preferences.

'I guess that would give her a reason for being in a container in the first place,' said Greg. 'Maybe she'd arranged it somehow with Knotsford, and things had got out of hand?'

'I'm thinking along those lines as well. But Meryl said Aisha had links to some sort of group in the South West. At least she knew people involved in the scene. There must have been some online correspondence.'

'I'll look into it,' said Greg.

'Get Huddersfield to send over everything they have. How are things going at the docklands?'

'Pretty good. I got a call through saying the last of the searches have been completed and the tanker is due to set sail tomorrow.'

'That will please Mr Atkinson and his chums,' said Louise. As she hung up, she thought about what Greg had said. Maybe this had all been a game that had got out of hand. A possibility that felt more likely now that the other containers had been found to be empty.

Taken in isolation, Aisha's death seemed strange, but Louise had come across enough weird practices in her time on the force that such a theory was easy to believe. People got up to all sorts, and were more than willing to put themselves in danger for a kick. If Knotsford had been involved in the up-skirting incident, then it wasn't a stretch to imagine him setting up a camera system so he could watch his girlfriend in the confined space.

Consensual or not, it didn't let Knotsford off the hook for murder. If he'd known Aisha was in that container then he'd been responsible for her, and should have alerted the authorities when things went wrong. Louise pictured Aisha cooped up in the container, wondering what had happened. Had the fact that she'd known Knotsford was watching made things worse during those last minutes? Knowing someone was out there, able to save her, but hadn't bothered?

Louise rolled down her window, recalling how she'd felt in the lift earlier that day. Her chest felt tight, and she couldn't shake images of Aisha from her head. The utter desolation she would have felt in those last seconds as she'd struggled for breath, knowing she'd been betrayed.

The thought was still troubling Louise ninety minutes later when she arrived back at headquarters. She knew she wouldn't be able to focus on anything else until they'd found Knotsford, but at that moment she was having trouble enough of her own. She was breathless just walking the short incline to the front doors of the station, the baby taking all her energy. She knew it was only a matter of time before someone would know the secret she was hiding.

She took the lift to CID, catching her breath, and checking her appearance on her camera phone. Glancing at her pale skin and sunken eyes she understood what her mother had said that morning about her looking tired. Though, as the lift doors pinged open, she thought ruefully that she was so often overworked – and because of that so tired-looking – that none of her colleagues would notice the difference.

◆ ◆ ◆

Louise was surprised to see her colleague and best friend in the force, DI Tracey Pugh, sitting in CID, a hand running through the big frizz of her black hair, her raucous laugh ringing out in the office as she kept a number of her colleagues entertained.

'What are you doing back?' said Louise, a surge of warmth running through her at the sight of her friend.

'We arrived this morning,' said Tracey. 'I think I wore Sam out. I left him at home to recuperate. I just missed this place too much,' she said, with a wink. 'The guys have been updating me on the shipping container girl. Sounds horrendous.'

'It was,' said Louise, recalling the stifling conditions inside the hot box, the image of Aisha's gaunt body on the metal floor.

'Buy me a coffee and you can tell me all about it,' said Tracey. 'Deal.'

It was comforting having Tracey back. Out of everyone at the station, she was the one person Louise would have considered telling about the baby. She felt at ease in her company, even welcomed the smell of her liberally applied perfume.

'Still not on the coffee?' said Tracey, as Louise ordered a cup of herbal tea.

'I don't want to get into the details but let's just say my insides no longer agree with it,' said Louise, smiling as Tracey feigned disgust. As they sat down by the window, Tracey opened her mouth to speak, and for a second Louise thought that she knew, that the detective in her had worked it all out. Maybe she had, but she'd decided to remain silent. Instead, she said, 'So, tell me about this container girl.'

As Louise began telling Tracey about the investigation, her colleague became animated, tapping away on her phone.

'I've heard about this before,' said Tracey. 'Remember there was that MI5 guy? They found his body in the suitcase.'

Louise frowned. She recalled the case, which had made national news, but she wasn't sure about its significance.

'Here, look,' said Tracey, handing her the phone. 'It's called claustrophilia.'

Louise took the phone from her. 'Should I ask you how you know about this?' she said.

'What can I say? I like to keep up with current trends,' said Tracey with a smirk.

The article made for interesting reading. Claustrophilia was defined as pleasure derived from being in a confined space, and, like most fetishes, there were extremes and different approaches, including being restrained within boxes and cages, as well as full latex body suits.

'That's quite a thing, isn't it?' said Louise. 'It would certainly support the theory that it was a sex game gone wrong between Aisha and Knotsford.'

'She may have just done it herself,' said Tracey. 'It could be it was the way she wanted to go out.'

'What about the video camera then?' said Louise.

Tracey shrugged. 'Posterity? Who knows?'

Louise thought about an investigation she'd conducted a couple of years earlier in Weston. A group of women had taken their own lives, though it was later discovered that each had been coerced by a charismatic man who'd been drugging them.

Louise would never reach any conclusion without supporting facts, especially so early in an investigation, but at that moment Tracey's suggestion didn't ring true to her. She could buy into the fact that perhaps Aisha had wanted to be in a confined space, but she didn't believe she had wanted to die. Though, at that moment, she couldn't give any evidence as to why.

'You know you're not supposed to be back in until tomorrow, but if you wanted to make yourself useful . . .' said Louise.

'You want me to do some research into claustrophilia groups in the South West?' said Tracey, raising her eyebrows.

'If you don't mind,' said Louise with a smile. 'Especially as it seems you already know so much about it.'

◆ ◆ ◆

It was dark by the time Louise left the station. All the talk of claustrophilia had left her with an uneasy feeling, and she was pleased to be out in the open, standing next to her car as she gazed at the clear night sky.

With her current workload, the investigation into Aisha's death was taking up more of her time than it should have, but she couldn't drag herself away. Again, she found her hand rubbing her belly as she thought about Aisha's last moments in the container. Forced or not, the thought of the young woman being trapped in the container was having an unusual effect on her and she felt breathless as she sat in the driver's seat. The interior of the car felt smaller than usual, and she had to take deep breaths and open the window before she was ready to set off.

More and more, she found herself reliving Aisha's last moments. Empathy for victims was something she never wanted to lose, but she'd learned early in her career that it could be counterproductive. The simple fact was that in her role she encountered things most people would never experience – some things most people could never even imagine – and getting too involved only got in the way of her job. It had been a struggle, especially early on in her career, but she'd learned to become more detached during her investigations. Sometimes it was the only way through the terrible ugliness she encountered, but she could never fully detach herself from the victims, and with Aisha that connection seemed deeper than usual. She couldn't shake the young woman's terrible death, and it was playing more on her mind than she would have liked.

The car still felt confined as she drove back to Weston, the cold wind from the open window stinging her face. Out of nowhere she felt hunger pains, a sudden desire for fish and chips. She drove into town, pulling up opposite the seafront, and ordered a haddock supper. Carrying the contents of the meal in grease-soaked paper, she sat on the sea wall, glancing along the mud-strewn beach towards the distant sight of the sea. To her left the lights of the Grand Pier flickered in the night sky.

Only three months ago, a middle-aged man had tried to detonate an IED inside the structure, which, if it hadn't been for Louise and DCI Robertson, would have taken the lives of hundreds of people. *It never stops,* she thought, finishing her meal and rubbing her belly. 'I hope you enjoyed that,' she said to the baby growing within her, hoping it was content in the comfort of her womb. 'You're not having that every night, do you hear me?'

Lights were still on in the family house by the time she reached home. She decided to pay her parents a quick visit, despite tiredness making her want to go straight to bed. Her mother was waiting for her in the living room and shot her the same glance she'd given her that morning – a mixture of concern and accusation that only she could muster. 'Everything OK?' she asked, her tone sounding accusatory to Louise, who collapsed on the sofa opposite.

'I've just had some fish and chips,' said Louise, regretting the words as soon as they left her mouth, as if she was giving away a secret.

'Stop, you'll make me hungry,' said her mother.

'Where's Dad?' said Louise.

'He wanted an early night. I was hoping I'd catch you before I went up.' The hint of accusation had disappeared from her mother's eyes, though her gaze was still searching.

'Everything OK with Emily?' said Louise, pulling herself up so she was sitting.

'It's not Emily I want to talk about, it's you.'

'You're not going to call me tired again, are you?' Louise tried to smile, but the exhaustion was eating away at her.

'You do look tired, dear. You know I don't mean that as an insult. I worry about you. I read about that girl they found near the bridge. Are you in charge of that investigation?'

Louise nodded.

'Remember you can delegate some responsibility,' said her mother.

'I hope you're not going to give me advice on running a police department now?' Louise didn't want to argue, but sometimes her mother tried to dictate her life.

'I know what you're like. You get obsessed with things. It was the same with all those bombings. You put yourself in so much danger. If I lost you . . .'

'It's part of the job, Mum, I don't have any option,' she said, though she understood now more than ever her mother's concern. It wasn't only herself she was putting in danger. She suddenly realised she could more easily understand all the years of anguish her parents would have gone through with her and Paul.

'You do, Louise, you know you do.' Her mother was sitting on the edge of the sofa now.

'You're not usually this forthcoming,' said Louise, wondering what had got her so agitated. She looked down to see both her hands were resting on her stomach, and moved them away quickly, but not before her mother had caught the gesture. They both stared at each other and Louise was baffled to find that she was crying. 'I'm pregnant,' she heard herself saying, her vision blurred by her tears.

It wasn't like her to show so much emotion, but her mother didn't care. She was sitting next to her in seconds, her arm around her shoulder, her hand lightly brushing away her tears – something Louise couldn't remember her doing since childhood.

Louise realised now how foolish she'd been not telling her parents. 'I know you are, silly girl,' said her mother, as Louise crumpled into her arms.

Chapter Thirteen

Julie woke with a paralysing hangover, the intensity of which she hadn't experienced since her early twenties. After waking last night, she'd spent an hour searching through old videos on Patrick's laptop, hoping for a glimpse of the man she'd seen outside the police station, before collapsing back to sleep.

She struggled from the bed and traipsed downstairs, pouring herself a morning coffee and collapsing on one of the dining room chairs. Glancing at the clock, she closed her eyes and tried to ease the tension from her head. Surely the police must start taking her seriously now?

She remained in that position for a few minutes before calling Alistair.

'Sorry, Julie, still no news,' said Alistair.

Did she hear a hint of impatience in his voice? *What is it with these people?* she thought as she hung up. Where was the panic, the desperation to find Patrick? Alistair had spoken to her as if Patrick's disappearance was a minor inconvenience. It was as if the world had already moved on and she was the only one keeping Patrick's memory alive. She kept picturing her husband's body, broken at the foot of a bridge. The police knew Patrick had issues in the past, yet they didn't seem to be treating his disappearance as a priority.

And she was to blame. If only she hadn't been so stupid. Her selfishness had resulted in Patrick disappearing, and she would do anything to take back those careless words; to take back everything, from her pointless affair onwards.

Finishing her coffee and immediately replacing it with a second cup, she moved to the lounge and opened the curtains, half expecting the man from outside the police station to be standing there. She understood it was all in her imagination; that she was fixating on the man as a way of dealing with Patrick's disappearance, but she couldn't shake that look from her memory. The smirk on the man's lips, the narrowing of his eyes, as if he knew something she didn't. The problem was she sounded hysterical whenever she mentioned Patrick. Maybe that was why Alistair was dismissing her concerns. The same could be said of the local policeman who, in her opinion, was treating Patrick's disappearance with the same reverence as a missing cat.

After making some breakfast, she glanced over at the wine rack. How easy it would be to fall back into oblivion? The irony wasn't lost on her. Part of their argument had been about the endless corporate shindigs Patrick attended where they would both drink too much and end up arguing. But it felt like the only way of dealing with things at the moment. She hesitated before deciding she needed to remain focused. Instead, she rang the local police station again – fifteen wasted minutes passing by as she waited for the young police constable to come to the phone.

'I can assure you we're doing everything possible, Mrs Longstaff,' he said, his tone similar to Alistair's.

'I don't believe that for one moment,' said Julie. 'Whatever has happened between me and Patrick, this isn't like him. He wouldn't just get up and disappear. Nothing we said was irreversible. He wouldn't just abandon his job and life. I think he may have harmed himself.'

'We've checked with all the local hospitals. No one with Mr Longstaff's name has been admitted.'

'That's not as comforting as you might think,' said Julie, trying to control her indignation.

'Sometimes no news is good news in these situations. Mr Longstaff could have gone away for a few days to get a break. I've seen it so many times myself.'

Julie doubted that as much as she doubted everything the young police officer was telling her. 'If you won't do anything about it, I will,' she said, catching a sigh from the officer before she ended the call.

She spent the next couple of hours orchestrating a social media campaign, posting pictures of Patrick on the various sites, asking people if they'd seen him. Responses started coming in immediately, though they were mainly from well-wishers.

Despite herself, her thoughts turned to Derek, which in itself felt like a double betrayal. She wanted to call him, to grab a crumb of comfort from his arms, but she couldn't do that to Patrick. Instead, she looked through his laptop again. If she'd cheated, maybe he had as well. It didn't seem like him, but people could keep secrets from one another – she was living testimony to that – and maybe some answers would be found that way.

But if he was cheating, he was hiding it well. He wasn't on social media and all his email communications were purely professional. *It's just you who's the liar and cheat*, she thought to herself, the lure of the wine rack stronger now than ever.

'Nope,' she said defiantly, as she grabbed her house keys and left the building.

The blast of heat came as a surprise, sweat prickling her brow. Her hangover still lingered in her bones, and rounding the corner on to the main road, she began to feel paranoid. It felt as if everyone was looking at her, passing judgement. *There goes the woman who cheated on her husband, and made him so upset that he disappeared from her life.* She turned around to see if anyone was following her, her paranoia telling her to turn home, but she fought the feeling and kept walking and soon found herself outside the police station once more, at the spot where she had seen the man staring at her. *Come on, you bastard, show yourself,* she mouthed, wondering if she was slowly losing her sanity.

She lingered for a few minutes before walking to the local bar, telling herself she would only order a coffee. She was halfway through the door when her phone pinged. It was a notification from Twitter, a direct message request. She accepted it and immediately checked the sender's profile which was just a combination of letters and numbers. They had no followers and were following no accounts. Julie was about to delete it as junk when she absently glanced at the message.

We're enjoying watching you, it said.

Chapter Fourteen

The container ship moved so slowly that at times Louise wondered if it was moving at all. She'd arrived at the docks at 6.30 a.m., and here she was two hours later, still watching the container ship – the AS *Matilda* – that would have taken Aisha's corpse, if it hadn't been discovered, across the sea.

She was here for more than just completion. She wasn't finished with the place. Despite what the operations manager, Raymond Atkinson, and his head of security had claimed, someone within the organisation could be responsible for placing Aisha in what would eventually become her tomb.

Atkinson was a much happier proposition than the last time she'd met him. He was resplendent in a tailored suit with matching waistcoat, an old school tie pulled snugly over the top button of his shirt. 'Thank goodness that's all over,' he said to her, as they stood together at the dockside, the container ship inching along towards the open sea.

'I'm afraid the interviews and DNA screening will continue,' said Louise. 'We need to speak to everyone who potentially had access to that container.'

'That's a lot of people,' said Atkinson, with a sly grin that suggested he thought this was all an irrelevance.

'Don't worry, we have the resources.'

'It's up to you, but in my opinion, you're wasting your time.'

'Opinion duly noted. We will be able to use your offices though,' she said, more statement than question.

'If you really must,' said Atkinson, the grin disappearing.

Louise's experience as a police officer meant it was rare for her to be overwhelmed by irritation when dealing with a member of the public, but Atkinson's lack of empathy for Aisha was riling her.

'We must,' she said, through gritted teeth.

Leaving others from the team to continue the questioning and screening, Louise left the docks and returned to headquarters. The talk with her mother the night before was still fresh in her mind. The relief of telling someone else had been liberating, and her mother's love and understanding had been everything she'd needed at that moment. They'd had their disagreements over the years but Louise was glad to have her on her side. She'd half expected her to raise concerns about Louise's age and how quickly she'd moved into the relationship with Thomas, but she'd been nothing but supportive – and had even offered to attend the scan that Friday.

With Greg in Huddersfield on the lookout for Malcolm Knotsford, and teams set up at the docks and the packing depot in Chipping Sodbury, the morning briefing ended up being just Louise and Tracey. Tracey had a number of investigations of her own pending – a week away having doubled her workload – but she still offered her full assistance.

'I had a rather intriguing evening,' she said, as they sat drinking tea in the incident room. Tracey was a trained CII – a covert internet investigator – and had worked undercover before online, using aliases to infiltrate different types of groups. 'Some of them are quite open, and were willing to chat to me at a low level. It never ceases to amaze me the stuff people get up to behind closed doors. Nothing I can think of that could be less arousing than being confined in a small space, but who am I to judge?' she said, running her hand through her tangle of hair.

'I take it there's nothing about potentially illegal extreme practices?' said Louise.

'Nothing about women being left to rot in a container, no. In some instances, it can be like a type of S&M. People can be left in confined spaces, or they stay together in them, but there's a big thing about safety words and that sort of thing,' said Tracey. 'People get off watching and being part of it. Frankly it scares the hell out of me. They're into coffins, going underground in potholes. If you can think of it, they've done it,' said Tracey, her thoughts trailing off. 'Anyway, I'll keep pushing.'

They both knew it would be some time before Tracey would be fully accepted into the community. Unfortunately, it was time they didn't really have. 'You should speak to Simon, see if he can help in any way. He might be able to track the location of some of these people. It would be handy speaking to someone face-to-face about all of this.'

'I'll speak to him,' said Tracey. 'You know what these things are like nowadays, shrouded in security.'

Louise left Tracey to it and made the short drive to Clifton to where Aisha's parents were staying. She found them in the reception of their hotel, sitting in silence on two armchairs. 'I'm sorry to bother you both, but could I ask a few more questions?' said Louise.

The last time she'd seen the pair, they hadn't been speaking to one another. The dynamic in the whole family was clearly off and Mr Hashim looked away as his wife answered for them both.

'Come up to the room,' she said.

Louise followed the pair to the lifts, the uncomfortable silence getting worse with each step. As they entered the lift, Louise was unable to banish thoughts of getting stuck and her being confined with Aisha's parents. The unusual circumstances of Aisha's death seemed to have made her more aware of her surroundings than usual, and she had to stifle a sigh of relief when eventually the doors pinged open.

The Hashims' hotel room was stiflingly hot. The air conditioning was switched off and the blinds were open, allowing a blast of sunshine through the large oval windows. Neither parent seemed to mind. Louise didn't object as she sat on the single armchair, with Mr and Mrs Hashim sitting on the edge of their bed.

'This is going to be very uncomfortable to hear,' Louise said, without preamble, telling the Hashims about her visit to London and the possibility that Aisha's death had been the result of a sex game gone wrong. Louise studied the parents as she spoke, surprised by their weary acceptance. She'd thought that Mr Hashim in particular would have been outraged by the suggestion, but both nodded along, Aisha's father refusing to meet her eye as she mentioned claustrophilia.

'I don't know what any of that is,' said Mrs Hashim, 'but there was an incident.'

Mr Hashim shook his head, stood up and walked to the bathroom.

'It was not long before Aisha left for London. We hadn't seen her for a couple of days. Late at night we heard a noise from upstairs. We have a small loft conversion where Aisha liked to be, particularly when she was younger. The noise was coming from there. Arjun went up to have a look. We have some storage space in the eaves up there. That's where we found her. Well,' said Mrs Hashim, turning from Louise's gaze, 'that's where we found them both. How they'd got there and how long they'd been there I don't know. They were naked when we found them.'

'Aisha and Malcolm?' said Louise.

Mrs Hashim nodded, glancing at the bathroom where Mr Hashim was still avoiding the conversation. 'Arjun went crazy,' she said, under her breath. 'He grabbed Malcolm by the ankle and tried to pull him out while Aisha was screaming. In a way it was almost funny. Malcolm's pale foot dangling through a hole in the wall. Arjun tried with all his might but he couldn't shift him. In the end we waited them out. Both came out naked. The embarrassment,' said Mrs Hashim, shaking her head. 'I threw them some dressing gowns and Arjun stormed off. Maybe I should have talked to her about it, but I just didn't know what was going on. I think they'd been there for a couple of days. The smell was horrendous.'

'Why didn't you tell us about this the other day?' said Louise. 'Surely you must see the parallels?'

'I just didn't think,' said Mrs Hashim, turning back to look at her, her eyes wide and lost. 'That's why Arjun hates Malcolm so much. He banned him from the house after that. Why would she want to do that to herself? Do you think she did it all on purpose? Do you think she took her own life?'

It was Louise's turn to look away. She wanted a few seconds to think of an answer that at the very least could offer Aisha's mother some hope.

It was now all too easy to put herself in the Hashims' position. The thought of ever losing her unborn child was too traumatising to even consider. But what sort of hope was there to give? The poor woman already knew her daughter was dead.

'I really don't know, Mrs Hashim. But I can promise you that we'll do our best to find out,' she said, understanding, as she spoke, how brittle her words must seem.

Chapter Fifteen

As Louise made the short journey back to headquarters, she kept thinking of Aisha and Malcolm Knotsford. The picture Mrs Hashim had painted – the pair of them naked in the eaves of the house – was vivid in Louise's mind. She could see Aisha cowering in the opening, as clear as if she'd been there herself.

Aisha had clearly had some obsession with confined spaces, and after what she'd read about claustrophilia yesterday, Louise was approaching the investigation with a different perspective. Mrs Hashim had asked if Louise thought Aisha had taken her own life, and although Louise couldn't rule it out as a possibility, she didn't believe that was what had happened.

Given this new information about Aisha and Malcolm, it could be that Aisha's death had been nothing but a tragic accident: a game that had got out of hand. However, from what Louise could tell, Aisha had spent those lost days in the eaves voluntarily with her boyfriend. Therefore, it followed that she had – on some level – enjoyed being in the confined space with him, or at least had trusted him enough to be there. The set-up in the container seemed to be at odds with this. Nothing about the camera, or the meagre provisions, and most importantly the fact that she'd been alone, suggested that Aisha's pleasure had ever been a consideration;

which in turn suggested that Aisha's final confinement hadn't been consensual.

CID was all but empty when she returned. Greg was still in Huddersfield and Tracey was working with Simon Coulson, trying to gain further insight into the claustrophilia groups.

As Louise made herself a tea she glanced over at Robertson's office. This time next week she would probably be forced to tell him about her pregnancy. It wasn't a conversation she was looking forward to. It could potentially lead to her being taken off the investigation and would mean she'd be all but desk-bound up until the time she took maternity leave.

But it wasn't just that troubling her. Things still felt off with her boss, and try as she might, Louise couldn't live with such uneasiness. She'd experienced so many poor relationships in her career before – a former colleague, DCI Finch, who was currently holed up in prison for the next ten years plus, being a prime example – that she couldn't let this one positive relationship sour. And although things with Robertson would never reach anywhere near those levels of antagonism, she knew if she let things fester, their relationship may never be the same again.

If Robertson was having the same thoughts, they didn't register on his face as she entered his office. 'Louise,' he said, rubbing his eyes as he glanced up from his laptop. 'How are things progressing with the shipping girl?'

Louise studied her boss as she sat down. The fine lines around his eyes and a slight swelling to his face suggested he'd put on a bit of weight these last couple of months. She updated him on the situation, informing him about her trip to London and her recent meeting with the Hashims.

Robertson sat back in his chair, considering what he'd been told about Aisha and Knotsford in the eaves of the house. 'Suicide? Accidental death?'

He listened intently as Louise worked through her thoughts. He'd been the one person in authority to have backed her one hundred per cent since her enforced move to Weston, and he would no doubt trust her on this investigation, but still she sensed the disquiet between them.

She was taken back to that day when they'd found the identity of the bomber who had been terrorising Weston-super-Mare and the surrounding area. The search had taken them to a small allotment site in Weston, where their suspect, Bryce Milner, had pulled a gun on them. The next few moments were still a blur in Louise's memory. At one point, Milner had been disarmed and then she had been holding the gun, pointing it squarely at the suspect. She recalled a buzz of noise as she demanded answers from Milner, only for Robertson to ease the gun from her hand.

Later, with time running out and the threat of hundreds of innocent lives being lost, the roles had been reversed. It had been Robertson who'd attacked the suspect and Louise who'd been the one stopping him straying too far beyond boundaries they'd both breached.

Robertson caught her looking at him, a flicker of indecision crossing his eyes. 'Something you want to say to me, Louise?' he said, a softness to his usual thick Glaswegian accent.

'Is everything OK between us, Iain?'

It only lasted a split second, but the hesitancy in his voice was unmistakeable. 'Of course it is.'

Maybe she was reading too much into it. It felt possible that they'd both crossed a line that day. But to what end? They'd saved a town from a tragedy it would have taken years to have recovered from, at the same time protecting themselves from the killer.

Yet, the silence between them was painful. It felt to Louise like it had changed their dynamic. That they shared a secret they were a little ashamed of, and there was now a growing distance between them that was preventing her from telling him about her pregnancy.

Instead, she took a deep breath and said, 'That's good,' before leaving the office.

Chapter Sixteen

Julie stared at the message for the hundredth time that day. It was so innocuous but she'd thought of little else since it had arrived. What little detection work she could do on it had proved fruitless. The message came from a Twitter account with no followers, the handle a combination of random letters and numbers: @17ahfret6

Her first thought had been to call the young policeman from the local station, but she'd soon dismissed the idea. Even if he was prepared to listen, he would have no better luck finding out its source than she could.

Next, she considered Alistair but dismissed that as well. She already suspected that he thought she was losing her mind. And part of her wondered if he blamed her for Patrick's disappearance, that she'd somehow driven him away.

What options did that leave her with? She couldn't call her mother, who would only make matters worse. That left Derek. It had taken Patrick's disappearance for her to realise how small her life was. With Patrick gone, life had become empty. Her demands for a divorce hadn't come from a desire to embark on a new life with Derek, or any other suitor for that matter. If it had been anything beyond a silly mistake, it had been a cry for help. A declaration about the way she felt her life was going. And now, the freedom she'd requested threatened to smother her. A cruel part of her wondered if it was all Patrick's doing. That, somehow, he'd staged his disappearance to punish her. But he didn't have the wherewithal to pull something like that off so quickly, and the truth was that he would never be so hurtful.

Trying to distract herself, she defrosted some lasagne. As she waited for the microwave to finish its cycle, she was drawn once more to her phone. Hundreds more messages had appeared since that morning. Patrick's disappearance was being taken seriously by social media, if not in the real world. People were retweeting her requests and sharing her posts on Facebook. Potential sightings were being sent to her, and it felt as if this other, virtual, world was on her side. Yet, all she could think about was that message.

We're enjoying watching you.

It was the *we* that freaked her out the most. She'd had an iron-clad certainty that the man she'd seen outside the police station was responsible but that *we* had thrown her, and at present it was something she couldn't get past. Dealing with one crazed stranger was difficult enough, but if there was more than one of them?

And what did it all mean? She had no idea who would want to hurt Patrick and her in such a way. It was probably all a cruel prank. But it if wasn't, what if someone had hurt Patrick and was now coming for her?

She jumped as the microwave pinged, putting her hand over her mouth to stifle a scream. The lasagne was still a frozen mess. She broke it down further with a fork, and placed it back inside. As she shut the microwave door, she heard a clattering of metal from the rear of the garden – possibly foxes rooting through the bins. She glanced down to see her hands were shaking. Usually, she would have ignored such sounds but now her mind wouldn't settle. Her heartbeat intensified as she moved towards the rear of the house. Resting her hand on the kitchen worktop, she closed her eyes to steady herself. In her mind's eye, she imagined opening the door, only to be greeted by the man she'd seen watching her outside the station.

'Pull yourself together,' she muttered under her breath, but her limbs didn't want to move any further. From the side, she withdrew the sharpest knife she could find from the wooden block. Holding it aloft, she stared at it as if she'd never seen it before.

'This is absurd,' she said, the bread knife shaking in her hand as she edged slowly towards the back door, which was ajar. For a brief second, she couldn't remember having opened it and convinced herself she must have done so in a haze that morning.

It was still warm outside, and a gentle breeze blew through the door as she stepped over the threshold. She could only imagine what her neighbours would think if they happened to peer over the fence and caught her moving down the garden, knife in shaking hand.

'You'll get yourself committed,' she said to herself, taking a deep breath as she walked across the patio, noticing immediately the source of the sound she'd heard. The lid of the compost container at the back of the garden had come loose and was rattling against the fence. In all the years they'd had it, at least ten by a quick estimation, she'd never known that happen before. The lid was heavy, and screwed down on to the container. Even the fiercest of storms hadn't dislodged it, so how could it have happened now?

Julie hesitated on the patio. Her eyes darted around the scene, and her body tensed as she half expected the stranger to pop up behind one of her neighbours' fences like a jack-in-a-box. She lowered the knife so it dangled by her thighs and moved towards the rear of the garden, which felt longer than she remembered. Each step was an ordeal and by the time she reached the compost container, she'd broken out in a cold sweat. She picked up the lid with her left hand, noting its considerable weight before wedging it back on. It was locked in place and although she was doing her best not to succumb to paranoia, there was no way the gentle breeze in the garden could have shifted the lid on its own.

She lifted the knife again and turned in a circle, glancing up at her neighbours' windows in case they were watching her paranoid dance. Her heart was hammering but she refused to succumb to panic. She moved to the back gate and double-checked it was locked, albeit with an insubstantial cross bolt.

From the wrong end the garden looked twice its normal size. To a neutral bystander the setting would seem tranquil, lacking in danger, and, despite her panic, Julie could hear early evening birdsong in the trees. But to her, danger was lurking everywhere. She had the undeniable feeling she was being watched, and that if she did creep back towards the house, she would be attacked.

She put her paranoia down to the considerable amount of wine she'd been drinking these last few days, but still she didn't move.

Come on, Julie, she mouthed under her breath.

Gritting her teeth, willing herself onwards, she placed her left foot forwards. It started as a walk – her eyes closed for the first couple of seconds – and then she was sprinting for the back door. Time slowed down, the garden stretching endlessly before her, as she ran against an invisible force, and by the time she was back inside the kitchen, her whole body was shaking.

She locked the back door, before repeating the process through the house, making sure every window, door and curtain was shut until she was cocooned inside. Having imprisoned herself in her own house, she let out a deep breath. She hated feeling this way, loathed having succumbed to the invisible threat of the narrow-eyed man outside the police station. But with Patrick missing, what else was she to think?

She took her laptop to the living room and collapsed on the sofa, eyes glancing at the wine rack. Trembling as she opened her social media pages, she looked at her Twitter account only to see there were no more messages from the mysterious sender.

Julie had joined a number of missing people forums in the last few days only to discover that she was far from alone. She'd had no idea how many people went missing in the country every year from all walks of life. She turned to the forums now, reading notices of people who'd been waiting for years for their loved ones to return, wondering if that was what her future held in store.

The glare of the screen stung her eyes but she didn't want to go to sleep yet. Despite putting her earlier paranoia down to her alcohol consumption, she found herself opening a new bottle of wine.

Two glasses in, she did something she had promised herself she wouldn't do and called Derek.

Chapter Seventeen

Louise spent the night at Thomas's, enjoying the heat of his body next to hers. She'd told him about the conversation with her mother, and he'd seemed relieved that she'd finally told her.

When she woke in the morning, the bed was empty next to her. Light pierced the curtains she'd inched open during the middle of the night, as the smell of coffee rose from the kitchen. She showered before heading downstairs, spending a few moments on her knees by the toilet bowl as she successfully fought the morning nausea to make it downstairs without having been sick.

'Don't get used to this,' said Thomas, placing a cup of tea before her as she sat at the kitchen table. 'I won't be able to do it when I'm back at work.'

'You'll be fine,' said Louise. 'You'll be up all night with the baby anyway.'

Thomas scrunched his eyes. 'About that,' he said, cracking some eggs into a pan.

She knew the indecision about their living arrangements was frustrating Thomas, but she was reluctant to commit to anything until after the scan. 'We can discuss that after tomorrow,' she said, her mind already cramped with the investigation.

'Of course,' said Thomas, placing a plate of scrambled eggs and toast in front of her. 'My special recipe.' He smiled.

'What, eggs, butter and milk?'

'Don't forget the salt and pepper,' said Thomas, sitting opposite her. 'You know it's all going to be OK, don't you?' he said.

'You say that, but remember you were much younger when you had Noah. You're with an old lady now.'

'Hardly. And what does that make me? I'm a year older than you!'

'I'll need to speak to Robbo; for all we know he'll transfer me,' said Louise, trying to steer the conversation away from tomorrow's scan.

'You know that won't happen. That said, I can't imagine you being behind a desk.'

'I'm trying not to,' said Louise, taking a mouthful of eggs, her thoughts already turning to the Aisha Hashim investigation. She ate in a rush, Thomas watching in pretend shock as she demolished the scrambled eggs and toast in minutes. 'Don't wait up,' she said, kissing him on the head as she grabbed her coat and left.

Tracey called when she was on the motorway. 'I've found some-one to talk to us,' she said as Louise answered, 'about the Hashim investigation. It's over in your old neck of the woods, actually.'

Louise had lost her train of thought, and asked Tracey to repeat herself.

'Clifton. Where you used to live, remember?' said Tracey. 'Anyway, if you pick me up, we can go straight over there.'

'Is this to do with the Hashim investigation?' said Louise.

Tracey laughed down the line. 'Everything OK, hun? You don't sound at your sharpest this morning.'

Louise shook her head, dragging herself into the present. 'Don't worry about me,' she said, crossing the Avonmouth Bridge. 'Pick you up in twenty minutes or so.'

Twenty minutes turned into forty as Louise was forced to pull over on the Clevedon Road, succumbing to the morning sickness she'd tried to fight off earlier. She rested in the car for five minutes, her bout of vomiting zapping her energy, and stopped at a local petrol station to buy some mints before continuing to the station where Tracey was waiting.

Her colleague was a bundle of nervous energy as she got into the car. Hair at maximum frizz, she smelled of nicotine and perfume, and Louise was forced to buzz down her window to keep her nausea at bay. 'Who've you found?' she asked.

Tracey buzzed down her own window, as if offering moral support.

'A young lady by the name of Helen Norrell – you must have heard of her,' said Tracey with a hint of a smirk.

'I'm afraid I'm not down with the kids like you.'

'Well, that is true,' said Tracey. 'Helen is a growing star on Your Eyes – I presume you've heard of that?'

Louise knew little about the website beyond the fact that it was some type of subscription model. People would pay others, sometimes minor celebrities, to perform various acts, many of which were sexual in nature. It had grown in popularity over the last few years, and wasn't short of controversy.

'I don't subscribe to it, but, yes, I've heard of Your Eyes.'

'Apparently, Helen's a bit of a rising star. I got wind of her in one of the forums. I was chatting to her last night.'

'What does she do?' said Louise, turning her head to the window, trying to suck in fresh air without alerting Tracey.

'Basically men, or mostly men, pay her to take her clothes off . . . and you can imagine the rest. However, there's a specialism that hopefully will be of interest to us.'

'What's that?' said Louise, a bead of sweat dripping down her brow as her stomach rumbled.

'She performs some of her acts in confined spaces. I had a quick scan through last night. I think she has some sort of studio in her flat. All a bit weird for me, but she has hundreds of paid subscribers.'

'I don't suppose any of her videos come from a shipping container, do they?' said Louise.

'If only it were that simple,' replied Tracey.

Louise passed her old flat as she drove to the address they had for Helen Norrell in Clifton. It had been years since she'd lived there, and her life of singledom in the heart of the city felt like a lifetime ago. The place was currently rented out to a young professional couple who were expecting their first child, and, rent money aside, the flat no longer felt as if it was hers.

'Here we go,' said Tracey as they pulled up outside a quaint Victorian building in the back streets of the area.

As Louise left the car, she felt the nausea returning, and for one horrendous moment thought she was going to be sick in front of Tracey.

'Are you sure you're OK, Lou?'

Louise leaned her arm against the doorframe of the car. 'I'm fine, just had a couple too many gins last night with Tom.'

The lie felt unconvincing, Louise's fear confirmed by Tracey's sideways glance. 'You can just wait here and I can go up,' said her colleague.

'I'll be fine,' repeated Louise, composing herself as she pushed away from the car and up the steps to the front door of the property where Tracey pressed the video doorbell.

They were buzzed inside and walked up a beautiful mahogany staircase to the penthouse flat where a young woman in a light blue cotton tracksuit was waiting for them.

'Helen?' asked Tracey. 'I'm DI Tracey Pugh and this is my colleague, DI Louise Blackwell.' They withdrew their warrant cards. 'Obviously you can call us Tracey and Louise,' said Tracey, flashing the woman a smile.

Helen returned the smile, revealing a set of impossibly white teeth. Louise was shocked by how young the girl looked – at the most in her early twenties. With her baggy tracksuit she looked frail, almost emaciated, her long hair more white than blonde. 'Come on through,' she said, leading them to a large open-plan living area which in itself was at least twice as big as Louise's apartment. 'Let me get you something to drink – tea, coffee, water, soft drinks?'

'Tea would be lovely,' said Tracey.

'Water, please,' said Louise, with a smile.

'I'm in the wrong business,' Tracey said under her breath, as Helen moved off to the kitchen area, glancing over at a baby grand piano that took pride of place in the centre of the room.

Helen returned, bringing their drinks as they all took seats on sofas surrounding a large glass coffee table. Louise was struck again by how young the woman looked. She wasn't wearing make-up, and her skin was perfectly smooth, her eyes glowing as she poured the tea.

'Thank you for seeing us,' said Tracey. 'I mentioned last night the reason we wanted to speak to you.'

Helen nodded. 'That's why I agreed to meet. I heard about that girl at the docks. I admit it freaked me out a bit. I'll do anything I can to help.'

'I'm sure you can appreciate why we'd want to reach out to you,' said Tracey. 'How long have you been in your line of work?'

Helen smiled, Louise noting a hint of defiance in the gesture. 'Online for three years now. I moved here from London. Knew a few girls in the business and thought I'd give it a go.'

'Your specialism?' said Louise.

'My specialism?' repeated Helen, leaning towards Louise. 'That was something I just stumbled upon. I was doing some general requests one evening – show me this, show me that, you know how it is – when one of the punters asked me to go under the table. This table, in fact,' she said, pointing to the glass coffee table, 'and from there it just escalated. He asked me to do some other places – wardrobes, behind the sofa, even under the kitchen sink,' said Helen, with a chuckle. 'I thought he was nuts, then he started telling his friends and I knew I'd stumbled on to something.'

'Why do you think they ask you to do those things?' said Louise.

Helen shrugged, brushing her long silver-white hair over her left shoulder.

'I try not to be judgemental, you know? I know people don't approve of what I do but let me tell you, it's a hell of a lot safer than being out there,' said Helen, pointing to the window. 'I'm not going to judge these punters, and that's why they feel comfortable asking for the things they do. I try not to think about it. They pay me, and that's all I really care about.'

Louise wondered if the punters enjoyed seeing Helen in positions of vulnerability or peril, and whether sites like these could act as a gateway to something more sinister.

'Do you always work out of the apartment?' asked Tracey.

'Most of the time. I've had requests to do things away from here. One guy liked to have me touch myself in various toilet stalls. Go figure on that one.'

'If you don't mind us asking, and I'm sure it's a long shot, but did anyone ever ask you to go to the docks, or into a shipping container?' asked Louise.

Helen pursued her lips as she shook her head, long fingernails raking over her left hand. 'I've been thinking lots about that, ever since we chatted last night,' she said, looking towards Tracey. 'Never had anything as specific as that. Do you think whoever did that to that poor girl might come after me?'

Tracey inched closer to the young woman. 'I'm so sorry, Helen, we didn't mean to scare you. We don't even know for sure how the victim died. It could have been a game that got out of hand, or she could have chosen to place herself there on purpose. I don't think you're in danger, no.'

Helen smiled but the gesture seemed forced.

'Have any of the punters ever asked to meet you?' asked Louise.

'All the time. I get some fantastic offers but for me it's not worth it, although I know a lot of the other girls do.'

'Anyone ever freak you out?' asked Tracey.

'Any weird requests?' added Louise.

Helen laughed. 'Weird,' she said, with eyebrows raised. 'It's all weird. Someone paid for me to buy a coffin once. I didn't enjoy that. I had to get some friends round here while I filmed myself inside. In the end I told him I wasn't going to do it any more.' Helen glanced up towards the ceiling. 'There's a guy who pays to watch me sleep through the night. That was a bit weird to begin with.'

'How often does he pay for that to happen?' asked Louise.

'He offers to pay for me to do it every night. The problem is he will only do it if I sleep in a very small space. It ends up hurting too much so I only do it once or twice a week for him.'

'I don't suppose you have a name or contact details for any of these punters, do you? That last guy in particular would be of interest to us.'

Helen shook her head. 'It's all supposed to be anonymous. A few of them have given me their numbers in the past. I don't really want to give you that information though. If they know I've given out their information they won't subscribe to me any more and the knock-on effect could take me out of business.'

'Of course not,' said Tracey. 'We understand.'

Louise wasn't finished. 'The guy who films you sleeping . . . has he ever asked to meet you?'

'Yes,' said Helen, 'but I'm strict about it. I think they all under-stand now.'

'I don't suppose you've got any contact details for him, do you?'

'Afraid not. Only his username and that was freaky enough for me not to want to meet up with him.'

'Can you share that with us?' asked Louise. 'It might help us match with our records and there's no way he would know it would be linked to you.'

'It's not the username as such that freaked me out, actually,' said Helen. 'That's just a combination of letters and numbers . . . more what he always makes me call him.'

'And what's that?' asked Louise.

Helen shivered. 'It'll make your stomach crawl, but he always makes me call him Father.'

Chapter Eighteen

The second she heard Derek ring the doorbell, Julie realised she'd made the wrong decision, but still she'd let him in. At some point during the evening, he made a move on her and she'd had to fend him off a few more times before he finally got the message. It wasn't his clumsy advances that had left her reeling, or his total disinterest in Patrick's disappearance and her well-being. What had really annoyed her, and had her fuming still, were his parting words.

No wonder he left you.

What she'd ever seen in the man, she didn't know. It had all been a terrible miscalculation, a temporary misappropriation of taste, and she couldn't believe it had taken her this long to see him for what he truly was. At least it had given her some sort of closure. She was certain she would never meet up with him again, and after locking the front door – and checking every window, blind and curtain in the house – she'd continued the steady job of drinking herself into oblivion.

Now here she was the following morning, fully dressed, lying on the sofa, open laptop still by her feet. How could it be that it was already Thursday, yet no one seemed to care about Patrick? Shuffling herself into a sitting position, Julie eased her body off the sofa and moved towards the curtains. She opened them only to be attacked by the sun's glare, and pulled them shut again.

Although she'd locked herself in as a way of escaping the attentions, imagined or not, of the narrow-eyed man, she had to concede there was a certain comfort in being so enclosed. She retrieved a blanket from upstairs and returned to the sofa, wrapping herself in the material as she opened her laptop and looked through the latest horde of messages that had piled up for her during the evening.

She hated herself for reaching out to Derek, hating him more for his parting words, but feared he was correct. One way or another, Patrick had left because of her. They hadn't been getting on well for months and she had to shoulder at least half of the blame. She'd pulled herself away from him after the IVF had gone wrong, had withdrawn into herself as she'd conducted the affair with Derek. And hadn't she driven him out of the house that night? Maybe if she'd been more patient, had better articulated her concerns rather than issuing what was essentially an ultimatum, he might never have left.

But there was nothing to be gained from blaming herself. She still had the chance to rectify her mistakes. Despite her throbbing headache and shaking hands, she was determined to persevere. Patrick was out there, and she would find him.

After a couple of hours of scrolling through the messages, Julie began to feel hungry and ordered some takeaway lunch from the local Chinese restaurant. She jumped when the doorbell rang and glared through the window before opening the door for the driver, half expecting it to be the narrow-eyed man. She shut the door without thanks and plated up the food, eating in silence at the dining room table.

The food didn't make her feel any better, a fine film of sweat coating her body from the effort of eating. Without bothering to clear away, she returned to the sofa and her laptop. The machine was becoming something of a crutch. With Derek gone and Alistair having all but dismissed her, the laptop was her only link to the outside world and Patrick's disappearance.

As if determined to prolong her misery, she turned to the missing persons forums and began reaching out to those on the sites. Each story was tragic, and as she read about the lives lost and the families torn apart, she felt like an intruder. What right did she even have to be on the site, when here was a mother talking about the day her teenager went into the city for the day, never to return, or the woman whose husband had gone for a walk in the local woods and had never been seen again?

Deciding she had no right to compare herself to these unfortunate souls, she slammed her laptop shut. Seconds later she heard her mobile phone ping – a high-pierced alert tone she'd never heard before. She picked up the device to see she had a text message. Her heart hammered as she read:

It's not only you we're watching.

The message was followed by a link, which she clicked without thought, then found herself gripped by the image that appeared on her screen.

She peered closer at the photograph, disbelieving at the sight of her husband dressed only in his underwear. Patrick was crammed into a tight space, his knees pulled up to his chin as he looked pleadingly into the camera.

Julie screamed and dropped the phone.

By the time she'd composed herself and returned to the screen, the image of Patrick had been deleted.

Chapter Nineteen

Tracey and Louise had tried to convince Helen to hand over her laptop, but she'd been steadfast in her refusal. Louise couldn't blame her. She'd been risking her livelihood by talking to them and Louise was appreciative of the insight she'd given.

As they were leaving the apartment, Helen had relented and given them two usernames from the site. One for the client who'd arranged for her to buy the coffin, the second for the client who liked to watch her sleep, the man who called himself *Father.*

It was late afternoon, and she was sitting in CID with Tracey and Simon Coulson. 'Do you think you can do anything with those usernames?' she asked the IT consultant.

'I think we're going to be very lucky to get anything out of this,' said Simon, his eyes downcast. 'We would need a warrant to get any information from the company. And even if we did, security checks are not going to be the most stringent. I would say it's highly doubtful these users would have used their real name or address to sign up.'

'And the *Father* moniker? Would that help us track him down in any way?' asked Louise, more hopeful than expectant.

Simon frowned. 'There's no shortage of family porn perverts out there. It would be far from a unique username.'

'What about the religious aspect?' said Tracey.

'It crossed my mind,' said Louise, 'but it feels a little bit too on the nail.'

Her first proper investigation in Weston involved a number of ritualistic killings involving the local Catholic congregation. A priest had been murdered during that period, and another had come under investigation. Although the culprit had eventually been brought to justice, the legacy of the killings still resonated through the community.

The truth none of them was admitting was that these potential leads were at best marginal. The laptop in front of them had downloaded images from Helen Norrell's Your Eyes account. Sexual explicitness aside, the images were reminiscent of how Louise imagined Aisha's final moments had been spent. There was a coldness in seeing Helen prone in these confined positions, and her death stare towards the camera.

Even the ones of her sleeping looked unnatural, her body cramped into something akin to a foetal position. Louise was grateful the young woman had been happy to share these images to help them, but it made her wonder what sort of mind would be aroused by such sights.

'Did Aisha have a Your Eyes account?' she said, the thought springing to her mind.

'I can run through the names,' said Simon. 'But Helen doesn't use her real name. If Aisha was on the site, she'd probably have used a pseudonym.'

'There must be another way of checking. They get paid through the site, don't they? So they would have their bank details.'

'I'll call them now,' said Tracey. 'With a potential murder victim, I'm sure they'd be more willing to play ball.'

'I could also run some facial recognition software on the site,' said Simon. 'I could do with some more images of Aisha. I can run them through the system and see if there are any matches on the website.'

'I've a folder here from the Hashims,' said Louise. 'I'll email them over to you now.'

◆ ◆ ◆

With the scan tomorrow morning, Louise wanted to catch up with as much work as possible before leaving the office. Her focus recently had been on Aisha's murder but she had a number of outstanding investigations that needed to be updated. She spent the next couple of hours going through the laborious duty of updating her paperwork on the system and making calls. She wrapped up by 8 p.m., and was about to leave when Greg called.

'Hi, Greg, I forgot you worked here,' she said to the DS who was still in Huddersfield.

'Apologies, I'm still living the high life up north. Have you ever slept two nights in a row on a motel mattress?'

'No, thankfully not.'

'Well, I wouldn't recommend it. Anyway, this call is brought to you from a caravan site in Skipton.'

'You really are on holiday then?' said Louise.

'If it wasn't pissing down with rain, and I could see the scenery properly, then I'd say it was an upgrade on where I'm staying. At the moment it's a bit of a coin toss. I've located Malcolm Knotsford,' he added, cutting the frivolity.

'Maybe you should have opened with that, Greg. Do you have eyes on him?'

'Looking at him now in a static caravan, we believe with two other IC1 males.'

'Got backup with you?'

'A couple of lads from Huddersfield CID and a team from Skipton. Thought you'd want to know before we went in.'

Louise's phone pinged, an image appearing on her screen of Malcolm Knotsford sitting in the caravan drinking from a can of lager.

'I'm sending you a feed now,' said Greg.

Louise clicked on to her laptop. A blurred image from what she presumed was Greg's bodycam loaded on to the system. It was the breakthrough they'd been waiting for and adrenaline rushed Louise's blood stream. 'Good luck,' she said, hanging up.

She could only see from Greg's point of view as the team converged around the static caravan. Battering rain blurred the camera lens, but the caravan came closer and closer into view. Greg stepped towards the door and knocked. Louise sensed the tension despite only being able to see the outside of the caravan.

The door slowly opened, a close-up of Malcolm Knotsford appearing on her screen. They weren't going to arrest the man at this instance unless he refused to talk.

'What's this about?' Knotsford said, after Greg had explained his reasons for being there.

'It would just be easier if you came with us now, sir,' said Greg.

'Not until you tell me why – I know my rights,' said Knotsford, as a second face appeared behind him.

'What the fuck is this?' said the other man, a few inches shorter than Knotsford, but broader in body shape.

'Just take a step back,' said Greg. 'Nothing to worry about, Mr Knotsford, we're just here to question you in relation to the death of Aisha Hashim, your ex-girlfriend.'

Even through the grainy image on her screen, the panic in Knotsford's eyes was obvious. He looked behind him at his still furious-looking friend, as if debating whether to run at Greg. In the end, he agreed to go, Greg and his team leading him away to a waiting patrol car in the pouring rain.

◆ ◆ ◆

Greg Farrell sat in CID in Huddersfield waiting for Malcolm Knotsford to be processed for interview. The woman he'd met on the first day in the city, Detective Constable Nancy Williams, handed him a cup of tea. 'Yorkshire's finest,' she said, with a smile.

Greg, who had been wrapped up in the investigation and had suffered two uncomfortable nights in the local hotel, had noticed the odd glance coming his way from Nancy. *It's a shame we live three hundred miles apart*, he thought as he accepted the tea. 'Don't have coffee machines up here then?'

Nancy frowned, feigning confusion. 'That's just for fancy folk,' she said, broadening her usually light Yorkshire accent. 'Be ready soon,' she added.

Greg, wondering if Nancy was expecting him to say more when she hesitated before turning away, sipped at the strong tea. He called Louise as he waited for it to cool down. 'Still at work, boss?' he said, when she answered.

'I'm not going to miss this.'

'I half expected you to catch a flight up here,' said Greg.

He'd been working with Louise for the last few years, ever since she first arrived in Weston-super-Mare. He'd been a DC then and their relationship had been uneasy to begin with. That had soon changed when he'd come to understand the type of officer and person she was. He couldn't recall coming across anyone so diligent and hard-working in his time with the police, and he knew first-hand the type of shit she'd had to go through; particularly with the now disgraced former DCI Tim Finch, who had once tried to take him under his wing.

'I'm sure you've got everything in hand,' said Louise.

'Anything in particular you'd like me to push him on?' said Greg.

'I'd certainly like to know where he's been these last few days to begin with. But I'm sure you know how to play it. Leave the story the Hashims told us about finding him and Aisha in the eaves of the house until last. Apart from that, it's all yours.'

Like Louise, Greg had seen some troubling things in the past, but Aisha's death had struck an uneasy chord with him. The prolonged suffering bothered him the most; that she'd endured days in the dark confines of the container without an inch to move while some dumb sick fuck of a killer watched at a safe distance. If Knotsford was responsible, he would throw everything at him. 'OK, boss. The camera's all set up so you should be able to watch.'

'Go do it, Greg,' said Louise, hanging up.

'You can take your brew in with you,' said Nancy, returning to the office. 'They're ready for you now.'

Again, he caught a sense of hesitancy from the DC; an awkwardness between them that he was enjoying. 'Nancy, wish me luck,' he said, walking to the interview room.

The head of the department had offered to accompany him in the interview but with Louise watching via video link there didn't seem any need. At present, Knotsford was little more than a suspect and Greg planned to keep the chat as friendly as possible until he saw an opening.

Greg introduced himself again to Knotsford and told him their conversation was going to be recorded. 'You're not under arrest, and can leave at any time,' he said. 'I'd like to remind you that you're free to have legal representation, if you like?'

Knotsford shook his head. 'No need,' he said.

'I need to point out you're being recorded by video as well,' said Greg.

Greg had hoped for some reaction at the mention of a camera, but the suspect didn't respond. He sat slouched on his chair, arms folded, his face peering down into his lap. He was supposedly only twenty-six years old but looked like he was in his late thirties. His skin was pocked with acne scars, his patchy hair receding. In the glare of the neon light in the interview room, Greg saw dark bags under his eyes which he hadn't noticed at the caravan site.

'Thank you for agreeing to speak to us, Malcolm,' he said, the suspect shrugging in response. 'We've been trying to get hold of you for the last few days. Any reason you haven't been picking up?'

'Off my phone,' said Knotsford, not making eye contact.

'You haven't been at any of the addresses for you. No one's seen you for days on end. That's where you're shacked up now, the caravan park over in Skipton?'

'Just staying with some mates for a few days.'

'A man of no fixed abode. How's that working out for you?'

Knotsford shrugged, his bottom lip jutting out.

'You know why we wanted to speak to you, I presume?'

Knotsford continued ignoring him, so Greg changed tack. 'The body of Aisha Hashim was found in a shipping container on Sunday. I'm sure you've heard that, haven't you, Malcolm?'

His eyes flickered, but he still refused to make eye contact.

'I need a response from you, Malcolm. Your ex-girlfriend died under suspicious circumstances. For the record, can you tell me if you are aware of that fact?'

'I heard,' said Knotsford.

'How did it make you feel, Malcolm?' said Greg.

For the first time since Greg had stepped into the interview room, Knotsford made eye contact. 'What are you, a kind of trainee psychologist? It wasn't the best news I've ever heard, was it?'

'You were together for some time?'

'I guess so, on and off.'

'On and off since she was about sixteen from what I understand.'

'That a crime?'

'No, of course not, I'm just trying to establish what relationship you had with Aisha.'

Knotsford sat up straighter, thrusting his hands out. 'Jesus, what is this? She's my ex-girlfriend, big deal. I'm not the only one – far from it.'

'Are you saying she had other boyfriends?' said Greg.

'If you like. I wouldn't say they were exactly boyfriends, but yes.'

'What do you mean by that?' said Greg.

Knotsford looked at Greg as if in disbelief. 'She slept around. What the hell's wrong with you?'

'I see. Is that why you split up?'

'Jesus, that was a long time ago. I don't care. We used to argue all the time. It meant nothing to me.'

'So, when was the last time you saw her?' said Greg, trying to spring the question on Knotsford while he was talkative.

'I don't know.'

'A year ago? Half a year ago?'

'Just before she went to London. That's why she went. I dumped her and she couldn't take it. She upped sticks. Good riddance,' said Knotsford, before closing his eyes and grimacing. 'Sorry, I didn't mean that. I'm sad she's died. I'm sad she died in that way,' he added, his face going slack.

'You know how her body was found?'

Knotsford nodded.

'So we're clear: she was found in a shipping container in a tightly confined space. She would have been barely able to move. Does that mean anything to you?'

Knotsford shifted in his seat. 'No, why should it?'

'There was a camera set up in that container. She was being watched.'

Knotsford lifted his arms again, the gesture overdramatic. 'So?'

'You like cameras, don't you, Malcolm?'

'Man, you are weird,' said Knotsford, looking around the room with a gormless grin on his face.

'Maybe I'm mistaken, but weren't you involved in an up-skirting racket?'

The grin faded. 'No charges were made,' said Knotsford.

'That's OK then. But you were questioned about it, weren't you? Illegally using your phone to take images of unsuspecting women. And now you're back here because your ex has died while being filmed. You can see the connection, Malcolm?'

'What the hell is this?' said Knotsford, his face drained of colour.

'Just asking questions,' said Greg. 'You're free to go whenever you want. It will make things a lot easier on all of us if you just tell me what you know without any trouble.'

'Ask me a question then,' said Knotsford, as if he thought Greg was stupid.

'Here's the thing, Malcolm. We had a very interesting chat with Mr and Mrs Hashim after we had to tell them the devastating news about their daughter. They told us about an incident at their house. Can you figure what that may have been about?'

Heat rose in Knotsford's face, his pitted scars flashing into colour. He shook his head, his mouth open as if dumbstruck.

Greg read from his notebook, relaying the story about Knotsford and Aisha being discovered in the eaves of the Hashims' house. 'Mrs Hashim thinks you'd been there for at least two, maybe three, days. I've seen the space there, Malcolm. Let me tell you, I didn't much care for it. It felt claustrophobic just looking inside. When I was in there, it was all I could do not to run out screaming.'

'That's on you, man, isn't it?' said Knotsford.

'Exactly. Some of us can deal with tight spaces, some of us can't. You and Aisha obviously could. Know what that space reminded me of?' said Greg, leaning closer across the desk at the suspect whose face was now bright red. 'What it reminded me of, was last Sunday morning. When I was led to a shipping container that contained Aisha's withered corpse.'

The room fell silent as the defiance faded from Knotsford's eyes, as if the enormity of his situation was finally hitting him. He appeared shell-shocked. His mouth hung open, his skin still flushed with colour. 'I don't know anything, man, I promise,' he said. 'She was into weird things and so was I, but that doesn't mean I had anything to do with her dying.'

'You admit you stayed two or three nights in the eaves of her parents' house?'

Knotsford shrugged.

'Who instigated things, Malcolm?' That the pair had this particular kink was of no interest to Greg, but he needed to know if Aisha had been coerced.

'No one *instigated* it, man,' said Knotsford, who was now more talkative than ever. 'We met online, chatted about things a long time before we met up.'

'You talk about being cooped up together? How does that type of conversation go?' said Greg.

'We were on specialist sites, obviously,' said Knotsford. 'We would hang around and chat in forums and then break off into private conversations. I'd been speaking to her for a few weeks. We got chatting and found out we lived quite near to each other. After a while we hooked up. It was all above board. We met out in public. Didn't even try anything for months.'

'I need to see details of these sites,' said Greg.

'You can have anything you want, man, it's not as if it's dark web or something. It's all out there. We're not monsters.'

'When did you last see her?'

'I told you. We broke up and then she left to go to London.'

'And why did you break up?'

'We'd been having arguments for ages. Her dad's a control freak nutcase. After he caught us that time, he never let me back into the house. That's when things started to go downhill. It's one of those things. We broke up, she left for London. In a way, I was pleased for her. She's got more brains in her little finger than I have in the whole of my body. She could do things with her life. Living here was holding her back. I'd hoped she'd make a success of it but she wasn't talking to me. I swear I haven't seen her since.'

'What about Bristol?' asked Greg.

'What about it?'

'Why would she go there?'

'I've no idea,' said Knotsford. 'Maybe she found someone else on the forums, I don't know.'

'These sites you visit. Have you heard of anyone who goes by the handle, *Father*?' said Greg.

Knotsford squirmed as if he'd said something unpleasant. 'No. Why, is that relevant?'

Greg ignored him. 'What happened to Aisha, being in that shipping container, was it something she would have readily agreed to?'

Knotsford gazed towards the ceiling. 'Honestly, man, I don't know. We never did any of the voyeurism stuff but she was always up for trying new things.'

It was only then Greg realised Knotsford had looked away because he was crying. 'She didn't have any death wish, I know that,' he said through sobs. 'I told you, she's not stupid.'

'OK, Malcolm, one last question. Then we're going to get you in to have your fingerprints and DNA tested, is that OK?'

Knotsford nodded, all the fight now evaporated.

'I'm sorry I have to ask this, but did Aisha ever talk of suicide?'

Knotsford stopped and wiped his eyes. The last remnants of the cocky tough guy he'd pretended to be had vanished. 'She wasn't always the happiest of people, thought she'd messed her life up, but there's no way she would have done that. No way at all.'

Chapter Twenty

Thomas was still awake when Louise returned from the station at around 2 a.m. He was used to her working late nights, after having been in the police himself, but she could understand his concern. 'You know the scan is at nine,' he said. 'That's seven hours, and you haven't been to sleep yet.'

He didn't mean anything by it, but it was a pointless observation. 'Of course I know, Tom,' she said, 'but I had to work late.' She wanted to tell him about Greg's interview with Malcolm Knotsford but was struggling to keep her eyes open. 'I'm sorry you waited up but I need to go to sleep.'

Thomas sighed. 'Sorry. You know I'm not being overprotective, don't you?'

It was an awkward situation for both of them, but ever since she'd told him she was pregnant he'd treated her slightly differently. Again, she could understand his concern but she didn't necessarily agree with him. 'I know. If I could have got back any earlier, I would have. I don't want to be getting up in a few hours either. I should've called but there was a . . . We found one of the suspects in the Aisha case and we needed to question him tonight.'

'You don't need to explain,' said Thomas.

'Sounds like I do though, Tom?' If she had one concern about their relationship, it was the way they occasionally crept around each other's feelings. She suspected Thomas was angrier than he was letting on and was being too appreciative of her feelings to say anything.

'What does that mean? I'm sorry I was worried that you're out until two a.m. when you have a scan in the morning.'

'It's not just that though, is it?' said Louise, the first of them to raise her voice. She didn't know where it was coming from, and she knew she was making something out of nothing, but she couldn't resist prolonging the argument. It was as if she wanted to get a reaction from him.

Thomas stared at her. She could almost see his brain ticking over. He didn't deserve this, and she wanted to back down, but she also wanted to see how he would react.

'You're not my boss any more, you know,' he said, a hint of a smile defusing the situation in the way she'd seen him do so many times in the past at work.

Why she'd wanted to get into an argument, she didn't know, but she was glad he'd stopped it before it got out of hand. She was exhausted, her head was thundering and all she wanted to do was sleep and put the day behind her. 'I am still your boss,' she said, with a wink. 'But I agree that we should get some rest.'

She crashed asleep, her dreams alternating with thoughts of Malcolm Knotsford and Aisha naked in the eaves of Aisha's parents' house, with imagined images of her unborn baby in her womb. She hadn't given too much thought to the scan, but had a vague idea of what to expect. For now, it just felt like another step – a milestone that needed to be completed – and she'd hoped to have been a little more excited by this point.

Her sleep was interrupted abruptly: Thomas opened the bedroom curtains and placed a cup of tea by her side. Louise felt a rumbling in her stomach and was about to succumb to another bout of vomiting before the feeling relented.

'We should get going if we're going to miss the traffic,' said Thomas.

The scan had been arranged at St Michael's Hospital close to the centre of Bristol. She had chosen this option, rather than Weston, due to a specialist she'd met in the department through work. Thomas wasted no time on the motorway, and they arrived with thirty minutes to spare. 'You OK?' he said, as they sat together in the waiting room. 'You look worried.'

Louise had to remind herself that this wasn't a new experience for Thomas. He'd been here before and he'd been treating it like it was the simplest thing in the world.

'You know how to make a girl feel special,' said Louise. 'I'm just tired. I realise this should be some amazing adventure but at the moment I just feel a little weary.'

Thomas held her hand and they sat in silence until her name was called out ten minutes later. 'Come on,' said Thomas, easing her to her feet as if she was full-term. 'It will all seem so much more real after this. It is an adventure, an amazing one,' he said, mirroring her words.

Louise appreciated the enthusiasm but couldn't quite match it. Maybe it was the exhaustion creeping up on her, but at that moment it didn't feel like an adventure. If anything, it felt like a reckless mistake. Here they were, planning to bring a child into the world, while at the same time she was working on an investigation into a woman who had effectively been starved to death in captivity. She thought about Aisha's parents. They would have gone through this same moment, would have pictured a wonderful future for their daughter, and now they were left with nothing but pain and memories. She thought too about her own parents, and the trauma they'd endured with Paul. Were either of them ready for the responsibility that was coming their way?

She held on to Thomas's hand as they were guided into the small consultation room where the midwife went through a number of questions before asking Louise to lie down on the bed. All of sudden, everything felt very real as the cold gel was placed on to her stomach and together they watched the fuzzy images forming on the screen. Thomas held her hand throughout, the smile never leaving his lips as the midwife busied away taking measurements of the foetus Louise could barely see.

'You can pull your clothes back on now, Louise,' said the midwife, a few minutes later, offering Louise a roll of purple paper to clean herself up with. 'If you'd like to take a seat in reception, I'm going to arrange for one of our consultants to have a quick word with you.'

Louise was attuned to the nurse's words and glanced at Thomas for clarification, noting his smile had faded. 'No issue, is there?' he asked.

'Definitely nothing to worry about at this stage, but there are a couple of things the consultant will need to talk to you about. Nothing to worry about for now, OK?' said the midwife. 'At the most, he'll ask you to do a couple more tests. But please go through to reception and we'll call you when he's ready.'

Louise felt insubstantial as Thomas led her away. She'd heard that kind of talk before from medical professionals, had even used similar words herself when she'd needed to placate worried individuals at crime scenes. The midwife may have been speaking the truth, but Louise's mind kept turning to worst-case scenarios. The midwife had mentioned hearing a heartbeat, but Louise hadn't been able to see anything on the screen. What if it had stopped beating? What if it was already too late?

'Did this happen with Noah?' Louise asked Thomas, as they sat back down in the reception area. She barely heard the words leave his mouth, as she prepared herself to receive the worst news imaginable. The room felt smaller than before, as if the walls and ceiling had somehow contracted since their departure. She wanted to escape, to run outside into the fresh air and pretend none of this was happening.

'Not that I remember. The midwife told us not to worry. It must be hard to get these measurements right. I'm sure the consultant will give us a clearer picture,' said Thomas, his palms sweaty as he took hold of her hand once more.

The consultant, Dr Burchet, called them in a few minutes later. He was all smiles, his bedside manner practised to perfection. He spent the next few minutes discussing the measurements they had taken. 'Two issues we need to address,' said Burchet. 'First is a potential blocked bowel. Baby isn't cooperating, so we can't get as good a look as I would like. Basically, we'll have to run a few extra scans over the next few weeks until we get a clearer picture.'

'And if it is blocked?' asked Louise.

'That will depend. We may need to do surgery when Baby is born, or there could be other complications.'

'We could lose the baby?' said Louise.

'It's far too early to be thinking along those lines. This isn't an uncommon situation. We will monitor Baby's development. As I said, it will simply mean we will need to get you back in for some more scans until we have a better handle on things.'

Louise felt as if all the air had been knocked from her. She gripped Thomas's hand as she remembered how to breathe, already longing for the ignorance of earlier that morning.

'Linked to this is the measurement we took for the nuchal fold. It appears to be slightly thicker than we would expect. This could be a sign that the baby has Down's syndrome. However, due to the potential complication with the bowel, it could also mean that the baby has other conditions. In particular, I am concerned about a risk of Edwards' syndrome. Have you heard of this before?'

Louise and Thomas shook their heads, both listening in silence as Dr Burchet explained the condition. Louise heard something about chromosome 18, her focus drawn more by the high expectancy of miscarriage and early death for babies born with the condition.

'I'd like to run a CVS on you, Louise. This involves collecting a sample from the placenta and is a combined test for genetic and chromosomal conditions such as Down's, Edwards' and Patau's syndrome. It is not without its risks. There is a one in one hundred chance of miscarriage, and also a risk of infection. I'm one of the leading practitioners in the world for CVS, but it is totally up to you if you would like to proceed.'

'Can we do that now?' said Louise. Everything was happening so fast, but she needed to know. She hadn't considered any of this before, and couldn't start thinking about raising a child with any of these conditions without knowing for sure what she would be dealing with.

'Once you're ready, we can do this today. I'll let you both go and talk in the waiting room. In fact, you stay in here, I'll go out. Let me know when you're ready.'

Louise felt punch-drunk, the energy drained from her body. Even Thomas looked subdued. His earlier enthusiasm vanished, his face pale.

'What do you think?' said Louise.

Thomas sighed. He looked like he was on the verge of tears. 'It's your decision, of course, but from what the consultant said I think we need to do it.'

'He seemed sure about his own ability,' said Louise.

'The world's leading practitioner, no less. What do *you* think?'

Louise gripped his hands. 'I think you're right,' she said. 'Let's get him back in here before I change my mind.'

Chapter Twenty-One

Sweat dripped down Julie's brow as she sat waiting in the airless reception room at the local police station. She was the only one there, but had been waiting for nearly an hour for PC Jackson to see her.

She'd turned up yesterday evening at the station after Patrick's image had flashed on her screen, but the station had been closed. She'd considered calling 999 or 101 at that point, just to have someone to speak to. Everything had finally got on top of her, and she'd been at breaking point. But what could she have told them? That an image of her estranged husband had appeared on her phone and disappeared within an instant? They would have thought her insane – without proof, she realised everything sounded so far-fetched – and even though PC Jackson knew her backstory she thought he would probably feel the same way.

One thing she was sure of: she hadn't imagined it. Patrick had been on her screen as sure as she could see the sullen desk officer now through the glass partition. He'd been confined, his eyes pleading to the camera. The image would forever haunt her, that helpless look burned on to her retinas.

She'd spent the evening on various IT forums trying to find a way of getting the image back. Every time she clicked the link, it sent her to a blank page. The advice varied from those telling her to restart the phone and try again, to those suggesting her phone had now been hacked and to destroy it. After that, she'd cancelled all her bank cards but was still using the phone in case Patrick was able to reach out to her.

It was another fifteen minutes before PC Jackson arrived. 'Mrs Longstaff, please excuse me for the time you've spent waiting.'

Julie looked over at the young police constable, whose apology had been laced with weariness. She wanted to scream at him, 'What have you been doing for the last hour?' but instead got to her feet, not wanting to give him any more reason to think that she was crazy. He led her to an interview room that was somehow even smaller than the reception area she'd been trapped in for the last hour.

'Thank you for coming in,' said PC Jackson, as if she was there because of an invitation. 'Your husband's case is with our missing persons team. They sent me an update this morning. We are doing everything we can, you can rest assured on that.'

'That is comforting,' said Julie, trying to hide her sarcasm. 'Someone has taken him, I'm sure of it,' she said.

Jackson smiled as if he were placating a toddler. 'What makes you say that?' he said.

'A number of things,' said Julie, turning her phone over to him where the original Twitter message was on the screen.

We are enjoying watching you.

'When was this sent to you?'

'Two days ago, but that's not all,' said Julie. She paused, trying to form the best way of telling him about the text message from yesterday evening. In the end, she blurted it out. She heard herself telling the constable about Patrick being in his underwear, and the pleading look he'd given her from his confined position.

To his credit, Jackson heard her out. 'Do you have this image on your phone?'

'It disappeared,' said Julie. 'The link no longer works.'

'But it was on your phone?'

'Yes, but it disappeared before I could save it—' said Julie, insistent as she leaned towards the PC.

'What time did the message arrive?'

'Late afternoon.'

'I have to ask you this, Mrs Longstaff, but have you been intoxicated in any way in the last couple of days?'

Julie bit down on her lower lip, her eyes boring into the constable. 'I've had the odd glass of wine. Who can blame me?' she said. 'But I wasn't drunk when that message arrived and I didn't imagine it. It was Patrick. He was trapped and somebody wanted me to know that he was trapped. He was looking up at the camera as if he was looking at me. I know what my husband looks like.'

The constable nodded. 'Sometimes when people are enduring extreme moments of stress . . .' he began.

'Spare me your cod psychology bullshit,' said Julie, interrupting. 'I'm stressed but I wasn't imagining it. That's why they sent the image this way. They didn't want me to have proof. They're playing games with me.'

'Why do you think they're doing that?' said the constable.

'How the hell should I know? Maybe Patrick pissed somebody off. Anyway, that's not the point.'

'You must see it from my point of view, Mrs Longstaff. I believe you believe what you're saying is true but all I can go on is what you can show me. The message on Twitter must be very concerning, but I'm afraid it could just be people messing around with you. You have a very big social media following about your husband's disappearance, and I'm afraid some sickos like playing games on there. If I was to guess, the same person who sent you that message on Twitter sent you the text message and probably deep faked your husband in that position.'

Julie shook her head. 'He was all but naked. There's no way someone found an image of him like that. It was really him. You must believe me,' she pleaded.

'I'll certainly speak to my CID team. I'll do everything I can, I promise.'

'Maybe I should be speaking to them?'

'That can definitely be arranged,' said the constable, 'but they're not going to be able to give you any more answers than I can at this moment. I can suggest two things. I can take your phone and get my tech team to look at it. They may be able to trace the source of this message, though from what you're telling me, I think that is unlikely. Alternatively, you keep hold of the phone and if another image appears, you need to record it. Do you know how to take a screenshot on your phone?'

Julie glanced around the small interview room. Part of her wanted to find something to smash, preferably over the unhelpful policeman's head. She couldn't understand how he could remain so composed when presented with everything she was telling him. It was clear to her that he didn't believe her, and that she was wasting her time, so she stood up. 'Yes, I know how to do that,' she said.

PC Jackson stood with her. 'I'll do everything I can,' he said, repeating himself, but she was no longer listening.

◆ ◆ ◆

She walked home in a daze, glancing around every few seconds as if she was being followed. Everyone she saw became a potential suspect. PC Jackson had promised to pass the information on, but what good was that to her when Patrick was in peril and someone was toying with her? None of it made sense. For the life of her, she couldn't think of anyone who would want to hurt her or Patrick in this way.

All she wanted now was to get back home and lock herself away. But as soon as she opened the front door, she sensed something was wrong. There was a tinge to the air that didn't feel right. She almost stepped back over the threshold, but refused to be cowed by whoever was doing this to her.

She went through the house room by room, checking the windows and making sure that the curtains were still shut. This was her refuge and she needed it to remain so. She walked back downstairs, the banister slippery beneath her touch, into the living room where she saw her laptop on the dining table. She stood, rooted to the spot, staring at the machine. For the life of her she couldn't remember placing it there. But that didn't mean she hadn't. She was out of sorts, struggling to remember one moment from the next.

Maybe PC Jackson had been right. Maybe some sad, lonely teenager was playing games with her. Deep faking images of Patrick on to another man's body and sending her anonymous messages. She wasn't sure which alternative she hated the most. The one where her husband was out there and they had no leads to his whereabouts, or the one where he was being held in captivity.

Either way, she wasn't going to rest on her laurels. The social media campaign was going well but she needed to keep it updated, needed everyone to know the despair she was in so they could act upon it. She made herself a tea and carried it to the dining table where she lifted the lid of the laptop. The keyboard felt slimy to the touch, and as she typed the password she realised that her palms were coated in sweat. A pinging sound left the laptop as it sprung to life, and Julie sat dumbfounded at what appeared on the screen. It wasn't a photo image this time, it was a video stream and the time ticking away in the bottom right-hand corner seemed to be live.

Remembering what the constable had said, and not remembering how to take a screenshot on her laptop, she scrambled for her phone ready to take a picture of the video feed before it disappeared. She was transfixed. It was the same image she'd seen before: Patrick in his underwear, unable to move, eyes pleading towards the camera. He was so still that only the occasional twitch in his features made her realise she wasn't looking at a photograph.

As she raised her phone camera, she caught a reflection in the screen, and turned to see a figure walking towards her. He was wearing a mask, but she knew who it was. She could see his blue eyes through the narrow slits in the mask. The man who'd been watching her outside the station.

'Close the laptop, Julie,' the figure said. 'I think it's time for you to get a little closer to your husband.'

Chapter Twenty-Two

As Thomas arrived at the car park at headquarters, he tried to persuade Louise once again to come home with him. The CVS procedure had been a success, the specialist successfully taking the necessary sample from the placenta. Although it had been obtrusive, the consultant had remained calm and professional throughout and had assured Louise that everything was fine, at least for the time being. Initial results would be with them in a few days – when they would potentially have to face a life-changing decision – but they could be waiting much longer for the potential bowel obstruction to correct itself.

What was she supposed to do with that information? Thomas had wanted her to go home, suggesting they sit together and watch old films and eat popcorn, but that would only give her mind a chance to wander. Far better to be back at work, doing the one thing she was good at.

'You can pick me up at six,' she said to Thomas, as he parked up outside the main entrance. 'I need to do some work before the weekend.'

'You won't be going in tomorrow?' asked Thomas, with a resigned laugh.

'That's to be determined. But I'm not going to sit around moping. The baby's fine, the procedure was a success. All we can do now is wait. Let's not spend the next couple of days worrying,' said Louise, doubting her own words as she said them.

'I'll be here at six,' said Thomas, as Louise left the car.

'Best call me first,' she replied with a grin, shutting the door before Thomas had the chance to argue.

◆ ◆ ◆

Greg arrived at the office at the same time as Louise, having driven back from Huddersfield that morning. He looked ashen-faced, his eyes red, his usually smooth-shaven face pitted with stubble. Even his suit, which would normally be perfect, looked ruffled, the top button of his shirt undone.

'Those northerners been keeping you up all night, have they?' said Louise.

'Something like that,' said Greg. 'Our contact up there will be keeping an eye on Knotsford for the next few days. We've told him not to stray too far.'

'You're just in time for a debrief. Round up the others and grab me a cup of tea. I'll meet you up in the incident room in ten minutes,' said Louise, excusing herself as she walked over to the downstairs toilets. A heavy scent of bleach hit her as she entered, and she locked herself in one of the cubicles, unsure whether she wanted to cry or be sick.

She was still tender where the specialist had taken the DNA sample. 'It's over and done with now,' she told herself. 'And you're still with us,' she said, placing her hands on her belly, which felt no different from twelve weeks ago. There was nothing she could do until they processed the DNA samples. She'd read some of the literature around Edwards' syndrome on the way back, and even if she didn't miscarry, making it through to birth, the life expectancy of a baby with Edwards' reaching five years or more was only ten per cent. And that was before all the considerable health issues were taken into account. In her wildest nightmares, she'd never thought she would have to face something like this and although she wasn't religious, she offered a prayer to anyone who might be listening that her baby would be OK.

She sent Thomas a quick message. He'd be worried too and had probably not wanted to spend the afternoon alone. Even though she still saw him on a daily basis, she missed working together. In the long run, it would probably have turned out problematic, but for now she missed being able to steal an occasional look at his smiling face.

Taking deep breaths, tuning herself in to her body, she tried to fight her nausea. All she wanted was to know that her baby would be OK. Hopefully that news would arrive soon. Until then, what she had told Thomas was true: she couldn't afford to dwell on the prospect of losing the life growing within her. She needed to treat her pregnancy no differently to before, and to focus what energy she had left into her outstanding investigations.

Greg had found Tracey and Simon Coulson, and the trio were waiting for Louise in the incident room. A hot cup of tea had been placed in her spot, and she tried her best to hide her distracted thoughts as she sat down with her team – her three closest allies in the station. She was about to speak when she caught sight of DCI Robertson leaving his office. He glanced over, giving her a brief nod before looking away.

In the strictest sense, she was duty-bound to tell him of her pregnancy today, but with the added complications she felt justified in keeping the information from him for a little bit longer. There were no strict rules about declaring pregnancies, but as soon as she did procedures would be put into place that could curtail her activity in certain circumstances. The last thing she wanted was special treatment, and she definitely didn't want to be taken off the case.

'I've been working on the website Malcolm Knotsford gave us,' said Simon Coulson, nodding at Greg, who looked even more dishevelled under the glare of the incident room's neon lights. 'Easy enough to sign up with a fake name and email. There's lots of information in the group chats, all open to the public. I've downloaded everything over the last year. I've tried the obvious search terms: "Aisha", "Malcolm Knotsford" and "*Father*". I'm hoping I can isolate Aisha's handle, given that we already have Malcolm Knotsford's identification. From that I'll be able to see who else she was chatting to in the group chats and maybe see who she's arranged private chats with.'

'Even though the chats are encrypted?' asked Louise.

'Yes. Well, we should be able to gather some information, if nothing else, but you'll have to leave it with me.'

Greg updated them on the interview with Malcolm Knotsford from the previous night, which Louise could already recall verbatim. 'I got the feeling that he's more of a follower than a doer. I think he was going along with Aisha's demands more than anything. At least, that was the impression he gave off.'

'He'd been on the site before he knew her?' asked Tracey.

'Oh, he's definitely into it all. I just get the feeling she was the driving force in their relationship.'

'I agree,' said Louise, sighing. The site Knotsford had given them was promising, but aside from that the investigation felt as if it was stalling. All the staff from the docklands and the linking shipping companies had been interviewed and there was still no significant suspect beyond Malcolm Knotsford. They could potentially get a hit from the DNA testing at the docks, but with no direct suspects, and an unconfirmed cause of death, it would only be a matter of time before they would have to shelve the investigation. She could already see it being passed on to the coroner who'd possibly judge it as death by misadventure. It wouldn't be satisfactory for any of them but it was sometimes the way investigations went. 'OK. Simon, if you can get on with that as soon as you can. Let's reconvene before we leave this evening,' she said, wrapping things up.

She spent the afternoon trawling through her open cases, her thoughts alternating between her baby and Aisha. She called Thomas at 5.30 p.m. and told him she could borrow a pool car to get home.

'No need, I'm waiting in the car park,' he said.

'Did you ever leave?' asked Louise, with a laugh.

'I did, and presuming you wouldn't be ready on time, I came back now.'

'Taking the decision away from me?' asked Louise.

'I think in this circumstance I'm justified, don't you?' said Thomas.

'OK, I'll be done in five minutes,' said Louise.

Later that evening, they sat on the sofa together watching a silly disaster movie while sharing a tub of salted popcorn. The escapism worked for a time but Louise's thoughts kept oscillating between the baby and finding Aisha's killer, if such a person existed. She hadn't been prepared for the brutal reality of not being in control of her pregnancy, and kept finding her hands on her belly as if they'd been pulled there by some magnetic force.

'I'm going to go up and read for a while,' she said to Thomas.

'But we're getting to the good bit,' he replied.

Louise pushed the popcorn over to his lap, and kissed him on the forehead before heading upstairs. It had only been a white lie. Loading up her laptop she checked for any recent updates from Simon Coulson, before logging on to Helen Norrell's Your Eyes account.

She took a sharp intake of breath as her screen loaded with images of the young woman lying asleep in a tiny, restricted space. Helen had given her full access to her channel and this was a private feed for one client in particular. Louise was unable to add comments but she could see every time *Father167* added anything on to the screen.

She wondered how Helen could sleep in such a restricted position, knees pulled tight up to her chest, her elbows hunched in to her body. She was either a very good actress or was indeed asleep. She watched for another thirty minutes, transfixed by the all but unmoving image before any text was added to the screen. The message that appeared was short and simple. Immediately, Louise wondered about its significance.

Father167: we're both enjoying you sleeping, beautiful lady.

Chapter Twenty-Three

Louise had still been awake when Thomas had come to bed. He hadn't been best pleased to find her on her laptop after he'd thought she was going to sleep. She had still been thinking about the message *Father167* had sent, and had slapped the screen down as Thomas appeared in the bedroom, offering no explanation. Thomas had frowned before moving off to brush his teeth and they hadn't spoken much since. They sat at the dining table together reading Saturday's papers, Louise nibbling on some lightly buttered toast.

'I was hoping to go and see Emily later,' she said, trying to ease the tension in the room. 'Fancy popping along? I need to speak to my parents about the scan anyway.'

'That'd be nice,' said Thomas, as Louise's phone rang.

Both of them fell silent, the piercing sound filling the space between them. 'Better answer that,' said Thomas, rolling his eyes.

Thomas, more than anyone, understood how her role wasn't simply nine to five. She could understand that he was concerned over the pregnancy, and a part of her resented the weary acceptance in his voice.

'It's Simon Coulson. I need to take it,' said Louise, picking up the phone and moving to the living room.

'Simon.'

'Sorry to bother you on the weekend, Louise. I was wondering if you were coming into the office today?'

'I hadn't planned to. Is there anything urgent you need to show me?'

'In a way, yes,' said Simon. 'Can we meet for a few minutes? I don't mind coming over to wherever you are.'

She'd worked with Simon on a number of investigations over the last few years, and he had a work ethic that outshone everyone in the department. He was also acutely professional and would never have bothered her had it not been important.

'I'm at Thomas's. I'll ping you the address,' said Louise, hanging up.

'We have a visitor coming,' she said to Thomas, returning to the kitchen.

'You were supposed to be taking it easy,' he said, filling the dishwasher.

'Nothing has really changed, Tom,' she said. 'I'm still only three months pregnant. We have to wait for the DNA samples, so we need to just get on with our lives as best as we can. Moping around won't speed anything up and I'm far from being an invalid. Look, I'm not even showing,' she said, lifting up her blouse to reveal the smallest curve of her stomach.

'Put that away,' said Thomas, beaming with happiness.

'Yes, sir,' said Louise.

◆ ◆ ◆

Coulson arrived thirty minutes later.

'Good to see you, Simon,' said Thomas, showing him through the front door. 'Welcome to Chez Ireland,' he added, shaking hands with his former colleague. 'As this is police business, I presume you want me out the way?' he added, looking at Louise.

'I really don't mean to disrupt anything,' said Simon.

'You aren't, Simon. Come on in,' said Louise. 'I'll just be a few minutes,' she whispered to Thomas, as Simon walked through into the living room. 'And then we can go and see Emily, OK?'

Thomas nodded, but they both knew that the rest of the day was dependent on whatever Simon was about to tell her. It felt so odd shutting the door on Thomas when what she wanted was to get his opinion on everything that was happening. She'd never questioned his decision to leave the force. He'd grown considerably unhappy with the mounting bureaucracy, and had considered that his career had reached a natural conclusion. But she hated him being on the outside. She was only thankful that he had his new job to focus on.

Simon was sitting on the sofa when Louise entered the living room. He stood up as she entered, as if he'd done something wrong.

'Everything OK, Simon? You look a little jittery,' she said. 'Would you like a tea or coffee?'

'I'm fine, Louise, I'll get out of your hair as soon as I can.'

'OK, what is it you have to tell me?'

'I wanted to tell you face to face. I may have done something a bit naughty.'

Louise couldn't help but grin. It was hard to imagine Simon being involved in anything untoward. And the straight face he'd used to deliver the message made her want to chuckle. 'A bit naughty?' she echoed.

'I was looking through the website last night.'

'The one Malcolm Knotsford led us to?' said Louise.

'Yes. I began seeing patterns in the conversations and ran a few routines until I discovered the handle Aisha was using.'

'Well, that sounds positive,' said Louise, sitting down next to him.

'Yes, definitely. I recorded the conversations she had with Malcolm Knotsford on the main forum and then I noticed her interaction with another member, so I did a little more digging.'

'And by digging you mean . . . ?'

'I managed to find a way into the private conversations. The website's not supposed to have done so, but they've kept all their records on their servers.'

'And I take it you're not supposed to access this information,' said Louise.

'Personally, I'd say that's a grey area,' said Simon, 'but I didn't want to make it official before I'd spoken to you.'

'And what was the information you uncovered?'

'Aisha was chatting to someone who shared the same interests. It looked like a randomly generated username, but in the private conversation things changed slightly. I've printed off the main conversation points for you,' he said, pulling out a sheet of paper from his laptop bag.

Louise glanced through the exchanges.

'It goes on for pages and pages. The user calls himself *Jason* in the conversation,' said Simon. 'I've downloaded everything and there's no way of tracing it back to me.'

'And when was this conversation taken from?' asked Louise.

'That's the thing. The conversation started about three months before Aisha's body was discovered, and the last interaction was six weeks before we found her. You'll read it yourself, but someone, it's not clear who, had suggested Aisha make contact with this Jason person. And they agree to meet, two days after their last interaction, which would have been the twenty-seventh of July.'

'Where had they agreed to meet?' said Louise, scanning through the document until her eyes alighted on the location at the end of the page.

Simon let out a deep breath. 'A place called Rosie's Café in Avonmouth Docks,' he said.

Thomas wasn't going to like it, but this changed her plans for the weekend. This was a definite lead. If they could find someone who had seen Aisha in this location during that period, then they might be able to find the killer. Louise didn't know how long she had left on the case, but she needed to do everything in her power to find out who was responsible for Aisha's death before the investigation was taken away from her. She thanked Simon and showed him to the door.

'I guess our plans are on hold?' said Thomas, when she returned. He was smiling, but the disappointment was evident in his eyes.

'Forgive me?' said Louise, still unsure what his reaction would be.

'There's nothing to forgive. You go sort out what needs to be sorted out. I've got enough to occupy me for the time being.'

Relief flooded through Louise at Thomas's understanding, and she kissed him goodbye. With everything that had happened with the scan yesterday, it felt strange and awkward leaving now, but it couldn't be helped. Harder still was the call she then made to Emily. She'd promised to spend the day with her and her niece's easy acceptance stung hard. Louise was thankful that Thomas would be there for Emily today, but it was still hard to say goodbye. After hanging up, she returned her focus to the case. She had to put everything else to the side for the time being, however painful it was to do so. She owed it to Aisha, and to Aisha's parents, and there was no other place she could possibly be at that moment.

Chapter Twenty-Four

Julie kept her eyes closed as the thudding in her head intensified. She didn't know how much she'd had to drink last night but her body was suggesting it was too much. All she wanted to do was will herself back to sleep and escape the agony assaulting her body, but bitter experience told her that sleep couldn't be forced. Even her eyelids hurt as she tried to face the day. The room was dark, and she shifted uncomfortably where she lay. It was only when she tried to manoeuvre herself out of bed that she realised she wasn't at home. Panic gripped her as she relived the experience from last night: the feed she'd seen on her laptop screen and the mirror image of the man as he'd moved towards her.

She was hemmed in. There were walls to either side of her, but not enough space for her to stretch out her arms. She moved her head backwards, and her skull hit another wall. A couple of metres in front of her, a red light winked at her. She was nauseous, and gripped by panic, but managed to struggle herself into a kneeling position. As she eased towards the blinking light, her pathway was blocked by a fourth wall, this one made of glass.

The reality of her situation was difficult to grasp. She sensed her sanity fading as she recalled the image of Patrick in the same predicament. This couldn't be happening to her. She screamed, the sound reverberating around the tight cubicle. She couldn't tell how but she was certain the sound hadn't escaped her makeshift prison.

'Can you hear me, you bastards?' she screamed at the flashing light of the camera.

We're enjoying watching you.

They were watching her now, there was no doubt about that. But who they were and why they were watching she didn't know. What could she have possibly done to warrant such a retribution? She'd made mistakes in her past but she'd lived an almost blameless life – certainly nothing that justified her imprisonment.

Trying to keep in the present, she took in deep breaths through her nose and out through her mouth like a yoga teacher had once taught her. She began to calm, her pulse rate dropping. She closed her eyes and thought about last night – and the man with the mask. She rubbed her neck where the syringe had entered, her flesh tender to the touch.

A horrible thought crossed her mind that she wanted to banish. Maybe this was all down to Patrick. Who else would want to hurt her so? He'd always been a gentle man, and this was perverse whatever way you looked at it, but his was the only life she'd ever wrecked. What if he'd been behind this all along? Had his disappearing act been a ruse to worry and then entrap her for some reason?

No. She shook her head. It just couldn't be. Asking for a divorce was no justification for this. Patrick simply wasn't that type of man. He couldn't be.

She tried to think. She'd watched enough horror movies in her time to know that the only people who got out of these situations were those who didn't panic and could think logically. She ignored the nagging feeling inside of her, telling her that most people never

155

got out of these situations, but it was hard not to despair. Who was coming to her rescue? Maybe the authorities would believe her now that she'd disappeared too. Surely the police constable would follow up with her at some point soon and realise she was gone? If not him, there were the hundreds of followers on social media. Failing that, her mother, or even Alistair. Someone would realise she was missing and put two and two together, and then the police would be forced to take her seriously. She only hoped she'd left enough clues for them to find her, though that felt unlikely as she had absolutely no idea where she was.

She lay back on the mattress, which was little more than a yoga mat, and began to study her surroundings. The wall behind her was brick, as was the one to her left. The wall to her right was glass, like the one in front of her, but she couldn't see through it as some type of curtain was draped over it.

Julie struggled to turn in the confined space and had to bend her body to face the wall behind her. She ran her hands over the crumbling plaster, looking for a seam, something that could aid her way out of here. There was a way into her prison, so there must be a way to get out. She shifted herself around again, so that she was facing the glass front wall and the camera.

She peered through the glass. The camera appeared to be two metres away, behind another wall of glass, the gap in between empty. To the bottom right of the front wall, there was a rectangular opening. She lent down, her head pushed between her knees, the slightest breeze billowing through the gap, and tried to reach through the tiny opening but her hand wouldn't fit. Her body ached all over, her muscles tight. She tried to stretch but there just wasn't the room. She lay back again on the mattress, trying to think positively as light began flooding into her little cell, the curtain on the right wall slowly falling.

Julie sat upright, a sharp pain running through the length of her spine as the room next to her gradually came into focus. She screamed when she saw what was there.

It was a cubicle the same as hers. On the floor next to her, close enough to touch if it hadn't been for the glass, lay Patrick.

Only, his eyes were closed, and Julie didn't think he was still breathing.

Chapter Twenty-Five

Louise was the first to arrive at the department on Monday morning. She'd managed to spend some time with Emily yesterday, following a difficult conversation with Robertson during which he'd eventually agreed to a door-to-door campaign in and around the Avonmouth Docks, which was due to start today.

Alone in the incident room, Louise studied the crime board. Aisha's picture was centre of the screen, a cascading tree of suspects and interested parties beneath her. Directly below Aisha was a photograph of Malcolm Knotsford, and two blank spaces with the names *Jason* and *Father167*. Beneath those were images of everyone Louise or her colleagues had spoken to: the Hashims, Raymond Atkinson and his colleagues from the docks, the warehouse manager at the shipping company in Chipping Sodbury, Aisha's old flatmate in London, even one of Helen Norrell who'd been so helpful in regard to the Your Eyes site. It was one of the least convincing crime boards Louise could recall, and for the moment only served to remind them how far off they were.

Simon Coulson was the first to arrive, thirty minutes later. Judging by his dishevelled appearance, Louise suspected he hadn't had much sleep. 'I've been working all night on the site,' he said. 'The only conversation I can find involving *Jason*, at least using that handle and IP address, is the one with Aisha. Of course, it's more than possible he used other aliases – and other IP addresses, for that matter. I'm all but certain he was using a VPN – his location with the conversation with Aisha was Liberty Island in New York.'

Tracey and Greg arrived, glancing up at the crime board as if hoping for new information, before Tracey placed a cup of tea on the desk in front of Louise. They talked through the case, Louise allocating each officer specific duties for the questioning that would take place later.

Louise's heart skipped as Robertson walked into CID and headed directly for them. Although they'd talked a few times on the phone over the weekend, she'd yet to tell him about the pregnancy and had no intention of doing so yet.

'The troops have arrived,' said Robertson, sticking his head through the incident room doorway. He didn't meet Louise's eyes and she wondered again if their relationship would ever return to normal.

'You two OK to head things up for a time at the docks while I have a quick word with Robertson?' said Louise, when the DCI had left.

'Sure thing,' said Tracey. 'Ready, Greg?'

'Let's do it,' said Greg, following Tracey out of the door.

'I'll keep trying,' said Simon, getting to his feet as if he didn't want to be left alone with her.

Louise nodded and waited for him to leave the incident room before slowly making her way to the toilets where she was sick for the first time since she'd had the scan. The only saving grace was that no one was in the bathroom to see it happen.

Robertson was waiting by her desk. 'Everything OK?' he asked.

Louise moved her hand, which had been resting on her belly. 'I'm heading off to Avonmouth now,' she said.

'Well, good luck with it all,' said Robertson, in his Glaswegian brogue.

Louise was convinced the pregnancy was making her paranoid. She felt sure Robertson knew, and it felt like a betrayal keeping the news from him. She wondered if he thought differently of her now. It wasn't like her to be so insecure, but he'd seen her place a gun towards the head of a suspect, and despite him shrugging it off as a necessary evil, she couldn't help fear he'd lost his respect for her. What if her keeping the pregnancy from him was the final straw? She couldn't quite bear the thought that the relationship she'd developed over these last few years could be destroyed so easily.

'Thanks, Iain,' she said, the pair of them standing awkwardly in silence before Louise moved off to the exit.

◆ ◆ ◆

It was raining by the time she reached Avonmouth. The uniformed officers she'd managed to second from the local police stations were busy at work, questioning residents close to Rosie's Café. The procedure was hit and miss at best. Although more people tended to work at home nowadays, not everyone was willing to open their door, especially to a police officer. But all it took was one decent sighting and everything could change.

The skyline was dominated by the bridge spanning the river; everything else dwindled in its presence. The bridge gave her something solid to focus on. Louise felt her attention drawn more and more to the giant structure, as if it held secrets to the investigation, only for a feeling of light-headedness to come over her and drain her energy.

Louise waited for the wave of tiredness to subside, before making the short walk to Rosie's Café. The small greasy spoon was empty, save for one elderly man nursing a cup of tea as he read a tabloid newspaper.

'Yes, love,' said the woman behind the counter.

Louise displayed her warrant card. 'DI Blackwell. Are you the owner?' she asked.

The woman was in her twenties, a thick layer of make-up applied over a fake tan. 'Actually, I am,' she said, folding her arms.

'Can I help you?' A second woman appeared from the kitchen; a slightly older version.

Louise displayed her warrant card again, before showing the pair a photo of Aisha Hashim. 'You've obviously heard what happened to her?' said Louise.

The photo seemed to placate the pair, the older one saying, 'Poor girl,' as she shook her head.

'Long shot, I know, but did you ever see her? Aisha Hashim? Perhaps she popped in for something to eat one day?'

The women looked at each other, both shaking their heads. 'Sorry, no,' said the older one. 'We're both here every day.'

'We're sisters. Rosie was our gran,' said the younger one.

'It's a family business, and a very local clientele. We would have remembered if we'd seen her. Pretty thing, wasn't she?'

'Perhaps you could ask around,' said Louise, leaving the pair her card before leaving, where she was attacked by a sudden downpour as she made her way to her car.

'DI Blackwell?' Louise turned to see a woman in her twenties with long curly blonde hair running towards her. 'Constable Ellie Smith, ma'am,' she said, breathless.

Louise nodded. 'Everything OK, Ellie?'

'I think there's someone you may want to speak to. He lives in a block of flats further down the road. My colleague's with him now. He thinks he saw Aisha.'

Louise wasted no time following the constable to the flats. 'Where are you based out of?' she asked, as they walked briskly down the road, the rain subsiding.

'Weston, ma'am.'

'Weston nick?'

'That's right, ma'am. You're a bit of a legend there, if you don't mind me saying.'

'I'm not sure about that,' said Louise, dismayed that she didn't know one of the officers from the station. 'How long have you been there?' she asked.

'Six months, ma'am,' said Ellie, looking away as if she'd done something wrong.

'I need to pop in a bit more often,' said Louise, as they reached the block of flats – a decrepit building three storeys high. Beside another officer she didn't recognise stood a nervous-looking man smoking a roll-up cigarette.

'This is Paul Dawson,' said Ellie.

'Mr Dawson, DI Blackwell. My colleague says you may have some information for us.'

The man puffed on his cigarette, his hand shaking, his head moving as he struggled to focus on Louise. 'That's right. I feel bad for not telling you lot earlier. It never really crossed my mind. I saw that girl in the papers, of course I did. I don't always think that good, you understand? I didn't put two and two together.'

Louise held her hand out in front of her. 'Slow down, Mr Dawson, it's OK. When do you think you saw Aisha?'

'The twenty-seventh of July,' said Dawson, dropping his cigarette to the floor and stamping on it with his threadbare shoes.

'How can you be certain it was the twenty-seventh?' said Louise, wondering if the two officers had disclosed the information about Aisha's potential meeting with *Jason* scheduled for that date.

'The wife's birthday,' said Dawson.

'The twenty-seventh is your wife's birthday, Mr Dawson?' said Louise.

'That's right. I'd forgotten, hadn't I? I was making my way over to the newsagent's to get her something. That's when I saw them.'

'Them? What specifically did you see?'

'I thought nothing of it to begin with. She was a pretty young thing and he looked a little bit older than her. That's probably why I looked longer than I should have. I knew they weren't father and daughter, but age-wise they could have been.'

'How did you know they weren't related?' asked Louise.

Dawson opened his arms wide, his hands trembling. 'Well, I could be wrong, I guess,' he mumbled, 'but they both had different colour skin, if you know what I mean. She was . . . I don't know how to put it . . . of Asian heritage – India, Pakistan, perhaps. He was as white as a ghost. It was then I noticed he was gripping her.'

'Gripping her? In what way?' asked Louise.

'Her left shoulder was tight against the side of his body. His arm was under her armpit. I stopped then and looked more closely. The man didn't react but the young girl . . . she smiled at me. I presumed everything was OK.'

'Did you see where they went after?' asked Louise.

'Yes, I did,' said Dawson. 'Another fifty yards or so along there,' he added, pointing down the road. 'There was a white transit van. He opened the passenger door, she got in. Then he got in and they drove off.'

'A white transit van?' asked Louise, her heart already sinking. The ubiquity of white vans in the UK meant it would be impossible to track without more details. 'Did you see what make the van was? Or get a look at the number plate?'

Dawson shook his head. 'I'm afraid my eyesight's no longer that good.'

'Why didn't you come forward with this information before?' asked Louise.

Dawson hung his head, his hands fumbling inside his pockets for another roll-up. 'I'm stupid, I know. I don't pay that much attention. I heard about what had happened over in the docks but I just didn't put two and two together,' he said, repeating himself. 'If I'd known it was her, I would have called you straightaway, I promise.'

'If you saw the man again, would you be able to recognise him?' asked Louise.

'Of course,' said Dawson, lifting his head and meeting her eyes. 'As I said, she was a beautiful young woman, so, yeah, I'd know her. As for him . . . there was something about him. His eyes . . . they were odd.'

'Odd how?' asked Louise.

'I can't quite put my finger on it. It was as if they were wrong.'

'You need to explain a bit more than that, Mr Dawson.'

'They just didn't look right to me. I don't want to get all heavy on it, but they looked soulless.'

'I need you to come back to the station, Mr Dawson. See if we can put a photofit together of this man. Would you be willing to do that?'

Dawson shrugged, the roll-up cigarette now between his lips. 'Maybe, I don't know much about that sort of thing.'

'We'll help you through it.'

'OK. I'll have to tell the missus first.'

Tracey arrived as Mr Dawson was being eased into a patrol car. Louise told her about the possible sighting of Aisha, and the unknown man.

'Could have done with a better vehicle,' said Tracey.

'I've got the witness in for an E-Fit session,' said Louise. 'We know that we're looking for a white male, fifties to sixties, soulless eyes,' said Louise, raising her eyebrows.

'I know a few of them,' said Tracey.

'The dates match. Aisha agreed to meet someone here on the twenty-seventh, and we have a sighting.'

'If they met here, it's possible they went straight to the docks,' said Tracey. 'The white van may have had direct access.'

'I think you're right,' said Louise. 'I think it's time we paid Mr Atkinson and his friends another visit.'

Chapter Twenty-Six

It was far from concrete evidence, but the fact they had a witness placing Aisha and an unknown male in the vicinity of the docklands on the twenty-seventh of July was a step forward. In Louise's mind it solidified her feeling that they were working on a murder investigation, and for now the presumption had to be that the man with Aisha that day was the person they'd identified on the group forums as *Jason*.

The docklands' head of operations, Raymond Atkinson, was sitting in the office with his head of security, Bradley Davis, when Louise and Tracey arrived. 'Good to see you again, DI Blackwell,' he said, his voice devoid of enthusiasm as he remained in his seat.

'Mr Atkinson, Mr Davis, this is my colleague, DI Tracey Pugh,' said Louise.

'How can I help you both?' said Atkinson, who was wearing a different suit to the last time she'd seen him – this one a tailored pinstripe number that put Louise in mind of bankers from the eighties.

'We've had a sighting of Aisha Hashim in the local vicinity on the twenty-seventh of July,' said Louise.

'That's good, I guess,' said Atkinson, gesturing to two empty chairs on the other side of his desk.

'You're correct, it is good,' said Louise. 'Hopefully it will help us narrow down our search. Did you happen to be working on the twenty-seventh?'

'Me?' said Atkinson, raising his eyebrows. 'If there's a D in the name of the day then I was working. I don't remember the last time I had any time off, isn't that right, Davis?'

Louise turned to the head of security, who looked over from the bank of screens towards his boss. 'That's right, you're very hard-working,' he replied, with a droll wit.

'I'd like a full itinerary of events from the twenty-sixth to the twenty-eighth,' said Louise. 'All deliveries, all personnel working, shift starts, shift ends, etc.'

Atkinson lowered his eyes. 'It can be arranged. You'll need to give me some time, though.'

'I need it today,' said Louise, 'and, Mr Davis, video footage from that period as well, please.'

The head of security stopped what he was doing. He smiled, but there was little humour behind the gesture. 'I'll get to work on it now.'

'Thank you,' said Louise, noting Davis's eyes were a dark brown colour, soulless or not.

'Aisha Hashim was seen getting into a white transit van,' said Tracey. 'Near Rosie's Café, less than a mile from here.'

'Do you have a number plate?' said Davis. 'Our system makes a note of every number plate that comes in and out of this place.'

'No.'

'What type of vehicle was it?'

'I'm afraid "white transit van" is all we have.'

Davis frowned. 'You may have noticed we have a few hundred of them in our car parks, waiting to be shipped.'

'It's not those we're interested in,' said Tracey. 'Do you make a note of the vehicles that come in each day?'

'We don't have a specific register of the type of vehicles. If I gave you a list of number plates, I presume you could cross-check them.'

'It would be very handy,' said Louise, getting to her feet. 'Thank you both for your cooperation.'

'Anything for the police,' said Atkinson, offering the pair of them a mock salute as they left his office.

In the main area, forklifts and cranes were busy moving containers on the two ships docked at port. Louise couldn't tell if these were new additions from the last time she'd been there or not. Tracey walked with her towards the waterline, a red shipping container currently floating mid-air, the crane it was attached to seemingly unmanned. Louise pictured Aisha inside, and again wondered what her last moments would have been like.

'What do you think of the head of security?' she asked Tracey.

'Bradley Davis? If I had to sum him up in one word it would be *smug*,' said Tracey, brushing her billowing hair from her face. 'He sounded like a particularly petulant child explaining technical things to a parent.'

'Yeah, I got that vibe too,' said Louise. 'What do we have on him?'

'His record's clean. As I recall, he's single. He lives alone in the marina in Portishead. Why, what are you thinking? Soulless eyes?'

Louise chuckled. 'Nothing much. I'll do a bit more digging when we get back. I suppose if anyone has the means to do this it would be him.'

'Why would you bring your dirty laundry to work?' said Tracey.

'The thrill of it?' said Louise. 'I don't know either but I'd love to know if he's driven a white transit van any time in the last month or so.'

◆　◆　◆

Back at headquarters Louise met with Simon Coulson. 'I need you to take control of the situation, Simon. Everything we have from the docks from the twenty-sixth to the twenty-eighth needs to be assessed. The shipping company are going to email a list of all number plates that came in and out over that period. I need you to cross-reference them.'

'What are we looking for?' said Simon.

'Don't snigger, but a white transit van.'

Simon grimaced. 'We can look for number plates that are registered to vans. There can't be that many vans that went in over the three days.'

'Thanks, Simon. Listen, I know it's a million-to-one chance, but have you ever come across that guy?' she said, pointing to a small image of Bradley Davis at the foot of the crime board.

'Not before this investigation, no,' said Simon. 'I've spoken to him a few times since though. Been pretty helpful, actually. Sending over files and answering queries almost immediately.'

'Too helpful?' said Louise, more hopeful than expectant.

'I wouldn't say that. Why? Do you think he might be involved?'

'Only in so far as he's in charge of all security on site. He'd have access to the cameras.'

'He won't be the only one, of course,' said Simon. 'They have nightshift workers manning the cameras. Obviously, he's going to have to leave the site at some point.'

Louise already had a list of the other security personnel who'd all been questioned. 'Would it be possible to tamper with any of the cameras without someone like Davis finding out?'

Simon glanced upwards, momentarily in thought. 'Depends on the type of guys he's hiring. All it takes is some tech wizard. I'm sure there's a way to tamper with the images, track what they're doing. If I had a more specific timeline, I could look into it for you a bit more.'

'A three-day period.'

'It would take me weeks, if not longer.'

'That's fine. Good to know, Simon. I'll take another run through with his colleagues.'

The incident room door opened and DCI Robertson stepped in. 'Thanks, Simon,' said Louise, an uneasy silence descending as Coulson gathered his stuff together.

'So, we have a potential suspect,' said Robertson, walking towards the crime board as Simon shut the door behind him.

Louise stood up next to her boss. 'If you count an IC1 male aged forty to sixty, driving a white transit van as a suspect, possibly called Jason, then yes we do,' she said.

Robertson grinned. 'It's a start.'

'I guess so,' said Louise, feeling a slight tremor in her stomach.

'They moved him today, you know,' he said, not looking away from the crime board.

'Who?' said Louise.

'Milner,' said Robertson.

Louise closed her eyes at the mention of the bomber that had terrorised Weston-super-Mare earlier in the year. 'Somewhere nice and secure, I hope,' she said.

'Cat A, naturally, and nice and far away from here.'

Louise glanced down to see her hand was resting on her belly once more, the fluttering feeling now more acute.

'Is there anything you need to tell me, Louise?' said Robertson, turning towards her.

For a panicked moment, she thought he was going to ask about the baby and wondered again if she was showing more than she'd realised. She hesitated before deciding she couldn't let things between them continue the way they had been. 'We did the right thing, didn't we, Iain?' she said.

'With Milner?' asked Robertson. 'I've put all that stuff behind me. We saved hundreds of lives that day, Louise, and I'm not feeling guilty about using a little bit of force to have achieved that. I hope you're not either?'

Robertson was right but she still couldn't overcome her unease, recalling holding Milner's loaded weapon and pointing it directly at him. At first, Milner had been holding Robertson by the throat, a steel wire placed to his neck. She'd had no qualms about pointing the weapon at him then. It was what had happened next that haunted her. Milner had let Robertson go, but still she'd kept the gun pointed at him as she'd decided whether to fire or not.

She grimaced as her stomach cramped. If Robertson noticed, he chose to ignore it. 'And, anyway, I think we can both agree he was one hell of an arsehole, wasn't he?' he said.

'That he was,' said Louise. 'Is there anything else you need from me, Iain? I need to pop to the loo,' she added.

'Be my guest,' said Robertson. 'Just remember it's over and done with. He got what was coming for him. We didn't hurt him in any way and now he's where he belongs. I know you well enough to understand you're likely to dwell on such things, but it's over. Have we reached an agreement on that?'

Louise nodded. 'Yes, sir,' she said, moving towards the door, trying to conceal her desperation to get to the toilet.

There were only three people in the outer office, but Louise felt as if they were all staring at her as she made her way across the room to the toilets. The cramping had intensified and it was taking all of her concentration to keep walking straight.

Once inside, she ran to the cubicle and sat down on the toilet, the cramping making her double over, the pain so intense that she bit down on her hand. If this was an insight into what she was to expect over the next six months, she wasn't sure she'd be able to go through with it. The pain was dizzying, shooting up from her belly to her chest. She kept her teeth clenched on to her hand until she tasted blood, and stayed that way for an indeterminate time until finally the pain subsided. Cold sweat dripped from her brow and she knew she couldn't wait too much longer before telling Robertson.

She left it for another five minutes before standing. Pulling up her skirt, she was about to pull the flush when she noticed spots of blood in the toilet bowl.

Chapter Twenty-Seven

Julie banged on the divide until her fists were numb, but Patrick didn't stir. Every inch of her ached, her imprisonment forcing her body into unnatural positions, straining muscles she didn't even know she had.

Her predicament mirrored the way Patrick lay in his own cell. He was in a type of foetal position, the resting pose enforced by the lack of space in his cell, which appeared smaller than Julie's. She placed her eyes up against the glass but couldn't see any movement from Patrick's chest. How long had he been this way, and why?

Lacking the strength to manoeuvre herself into a different position, she continued staring at what might be Patrick's corpse. Was this to be her destiny? Left alone in a glass prison, until her body finally gave up? Panicked, she began beating the glass again, screaming expletives into the air, hoping that someone was listening.

She didn't know how long her rant continued but, at some point, she found herself face down on the cold, tiled floor, breathless. Beating the glass and shouting expletives wasn't going to get her out of this spot. She had to think logically, had to banish the thoughts of mounting panic that threatened to overcome her.

There had to be a reason why first Patrick, and then she, had been targeted. She tried to think who would have a grudge against Patrick. Maybe it was some business associate Patrick had pissed off at some point. Maybe it was Derek, or even Alistair, but she couldn't imagine anyone hating Patrick this much that they would do something like this to him. The simple fact was Patrick was too nice for anyone to want to take such drastic action against him. In part, that was why their marriage was in such a state. She wouldn't say exactly that he was boring, but he was far from being a dynamic character. He wasn't prone to anger and there was little to no hatred in him, so she couldn't quite understand why someone would want to harm him and especially in such a horrific way.

The thought didn't make her feel any better. Somehow, it felt so much worse, if it was all random. Could Patrick have been at the wrong place at the wrong time? Had she become an accidental victim too due to her relationship with him? If that was true, then she struggled to see any room for hope. If the abduction was random, how would anyone even know where to begin looking for them?

'Stop it, Julie,' she said to herself, as, in the adjoining cell, Patrick remained perfectly still. Trying to put everything into some kind of logical order, she replayed events in her head: the last time she'd seen Patrick and the ensuing argument where she demanded a divorce, returning to the house on the Monday only to find Patrick not there, the subsequent meetings with Alistair and the young police constable, the social media campaigns, and the messages on her phone.

There was an unreality to the whole situation that she was struggling to get past.

Closing her eyes, she allowed her breathing to return to normal. Flickers of the last few weeks played through her mind, and her subconscious alighted on a memory from the other weekend. An article in the papers not long after Patrick had gone missing. A body had been found in a shipping container in the Avonmouth Docks. A young woman, a possible stowaway, had been trapped in an airless container, in a confined space similar to the one she was in now. Was this all linked? Now that she thought of it, it seemed impossible for it to be a coincidence. And although it raised more questions than it answered, at least it was a starting point and gave her mind something to consider.

She couldn't believe she hadn't thought of it before. Patrick worked in marine insurance. Maybe the narrow-eyed man who'd abducted her in her own living room was part of that world too. Whether or not that information would help her in the long run she didn't know, but it felt good to know it. She'd thought before that she'd seen the stranger at one of those boring conventions. Maybe when he next appeared, she could strike up a conversation with him, somehow manipulate him into letting her go.

She screamed in agony as she manoeuvred her body into a sitting position, straining her lower back with the effort. Lying against the cold wall, she thought about what she would say to her captor if she ever got the chance.

Hours may or may not have drifted by, and she was about to fall asleep when the small area outside her cell was flooded with light. A man dressed all in black emerged from the opening, wearing the same mask as last time. 'I know you, don't I?' Julie cried out.

The man didn't answer, bending down in front of Patrick's prison where he pushed two packages through the tiny opening at the foot of the cell. He did the same for Julie, and she grabbed the bottle of water and the cling-film-wrapped sandwich. She began devouring both before realising she should pace herself, having no idea when she would next be fed, as the man retreated.

To her amazement, Patrick was beginning to stir. His movements were slow and awkward, as if he was only just realising how to move his body. He stretched for the bottle of water, fumbled the screw cap and allowed the liquid to trickle into his dry mouth.

'Patrick,' she screamed, banging on the side window again, light momentarily blinding her when the man in black left.

'Patrick, look at me,' she said. Knuckles bleeding, she rammed them against the glass in a steady beat only to be ignored by her husband.

'He can't see or hear you.'

Julie looked around, searching for the source of her captor's voice that reverberated against the ceiling of her prison cell.

'It's mirrored glass,' said the voice.

'You can see him, but he can't see you,' said the voice. 'At least, not yet.'

Chapter Twenty-Eight

Tracey stopped Louise as she was packing up her stuff from her desk. 'You OK?' she asked, her obvious concern etched into every crease on her face.

'I'm fine,' said Louise, doing everything in her power to keep things together when all she wanted to do was scream through fear of losing the baby.

'You don't look it,' said Tracey.

'When I'm looking for some moral support, I'll know where to come to,' said Louise, mustering a smile.

'Seriously, Lou, what's the matter?'

'Just feel a bit peaky. I told you earlier I thought I was coming down with something. I'm going to go home and get some rest. Call me with any developments.' Part of her wanted to blurt out about the pregnancy to her friend, but it felt too late. Everything was all messed up, and she needed to get out of there; needed some time alone to sort out the array of feelings threatening to overwhelm her.

Tracey nodded, but didn't move.

'I'm fine,' said Louise, a little louder than intended. 'I'll give you a call later,' she added, heading for the door and not looking back lest she break down.

She waited until she was in the car before calling the midwife, telling her what had happened. After answering a few brief questions, she was instructed to return to St Michael's. Louise was so used to being in charge of situations and was thrown by her current predicament. Even when investigations were not working out as planned, there was always a different approach to take, more people to question. Now she felt completely helpless. For all she knew, the life within her was dying and there was nothing she could do about it beyond driving as fast as possible to Bristol.

She called Thomas as she drove, trying to keep the panic from her voice. He went briefly silent when she told him what had happened, and she hoped for both their sakes that he would be able to remain strong.

'I'm leaving now. I'll meet you at the hospital,' he said. 'It's going to be OK.'

Louise nodded to herself, trying to believe his words. 'See you there,' she said, hanging up.

She arrived at the hospital before Thomas. After checking in, she sat in the waiting room, pretending to focus on the out-of-date magazines. She considered calling her mother, but worrying her wasn't going to help anything. She did some internet research on spotting, cherry picking the most optimistic diagnoses.

Thomas arrived and almost sprinted towards her, embracing her before she had a chance to say anything. All she wanted to hear from him was reassurance and thankfully that was what he offered. There was no questioning, just a gentle arm around her shoulders. She allowed herself a brief cry, her head nestled into his chest as her name was called out by the same midwife who'd seen her last time – the smiling young woman who'd told her she needed to speak to the consultant.

'Come on through,' said the midwife. 'You can wait outside, Dad, if you like, until we're ready to do another scan?'

Thomas looked at Louise, who nodded before allowing herself to be led into the airless consulting room that felt smaller than before. She felt dizzy and the midwife placed her hand on her shoulders. 'Here, take a seat. Let me get you some water,' she said.

Louise did as instructed, closing her eyes and willing the dizziness to subside. The midwife handed her a beaker of water, the cold liquid like nectar as it trickled down her throat.

'So, tell me what happened?' said the midwife.

Louise explained about the cramping and the spotting in the bathroom. 'With everything that happened last time, and the CVS test, I thought it was best to call,' she said.

'You did completely the right thing, Louise. If you're ever concerned, you always call us and let us take a look.'

Louise felt her heart thudding against her chest as she lay down on the bed. The next few moments were hellish as the midwife examined her, Louise trying her best to remain positive when the midwife stopped and washed her hands. 'Everything feels fine. We'll do another scan. Shall I call in the father?'

Louise shuddered at the word *father*, distraught to be reminded of the investigation when she was about to have the scan. 'Yes, that would be great,' she said. 'You can call him Thomas.'

Thomas looked pale as he entered the room, offering Louise a hopeful smile that she matched.

'OK, it's just going to be the same as before,' said the midwife, spreading the cold liquid over Louise's belly before running the probe over her.

The jeopardy of the situation made it so much more real than last time. The midwife was reassuring, but Louise understood she had to face the possibility that something was wrong.

'There,' said the midwife, pointing to the screen, 'it's the baby's little heartbeat.'

'Does that mean everything's OK?' asked Thomas.

'Everything seems the same as before. The measurements are near identical, which is unsurprising seeing as you were here only a few days ago. So, yes, I'd say everything is fine. Now, Mum, you just need to monitor yourself closely. If anything like this occurs again you call us immediately.'

The wave of relief running through Louise was like nothing she'd ever experienced before.

'I'll give you a second,' said the midwife, as Louise grabbed hold of Thomas and began crying with an intensity she hadn't experienced since she was a child.

She didn't know if it was the relief, or baby hormones, or simply a release from all the tension over the last few days, but the crying proved cathartic, and as Louise drove back to Weston she called Tracey for an update on the investigation.

'I thought you were going home,' said Tracey, ever the detective.

'I'm on my way now,' said Louise, 'but I'm feeling much better, thank you.'

'That's something, I suppose,' said Tracey. 'Mr Dawson has managed to put an E-Fit together for us. I'll send it through to you now.'

Louise's phone buzzed and she clicked on the image Dawson had compiled of the man they were calling *Jason*. She snuck glances at the face as she drove, particularly the narrow blue eyes. 'This makes him look older than I'd pictured,' she said.

'I was thinking along the same lines. But Dawson is quite adamant that it's a good likeness.'

They'd have to decide whether they would make the E-Fit public. It could prove a positive input, but as soon as it went public they would be inundated with calls, which would test their manpower.

'Let's get this in front of all the major players first,' said Louise. 'Starting with everyone at the docklands, everyone we've interviewed. Especially those working during the period of the twenty-sixth to the twenty-eighth. See if anyone recognises this person.'

'Already on it,' said Tracey. 'Tell me how you're feeling?' she added.

'I told you, I'm fine,' said Louise. 'Just arrived back home now,' she lied, as she crossed the Avonmouth Bridge. 'I promise I'll get some rest, but I'll be back in first thing tomorrow,' she added, before hanging up.

At Thomas's, Louise ate the pasta dinner he'd prepared, her left hand never leaving her belly. They ate all but in silence, both coming down from the adrenaline rush at the hospital. Thomas cleared up. She knew he wanted to say something to her and eventually she had to coax it out of him. 'Say it,' she said.

Thomas drew in a large breath. 'Look, you know I'd never even try to tell you what to do, but you are going to take off a few days now, aren't you?'

'I wasn't planning to, no,' said Louise.

Thomas pursued his lips, a new gesture she'd noticed of late when he wasn't sure what to say. 'I'm worried for you, and the baby,' he said.

'I'm not going to put the baby in danger, Tom.'

'I do know how stressful these things are, Louise. Don't forget that I was a copper too.'

'I haven't forgotten. And it is stressful, but what would be more stressful would be me sitting here at home watching the clock until this thing comes out of me. Sorry, Baby,' she added, tapping her belly.

'At least take tomorrow off.'

'We've had some developments on the case. We have an E-Fit for a potential suspect. We're going to do another door-to-door, tomorrow mostly likely.'

'That's fine, but you don't need to be there for that, do you? Tracey can handle it from her end and can update you on the results. It's not going to make any difference you being on site.'

Louise didn't want to argue. After what had happened at the hospital, she felt closer to Thomas than ever and didn't want to ruin it. 'I'll think about it,' she said, edging herself off the seat and stretching.

Thomas moved towards her, and placed his hands around her waist.

'*I'll think about it*,' he said, smiling. 'I think I know what that means.'

'Shush,' said Louise. 'Just tell me everything will be OK, Thomas.'

Thomas gave her a mischievous grin and said, 'Everything will be OK, Thomas.'

Chapter Twenty-Nine

Of course, it had to rain. For the second day running, PC David Jackson was in Avonmouth going door-to-door with the E-Fit of the suspect in the Aisha Hashim case, and for the second day running it had started to rain. At least he'd been partnered with Ellie, a colleague he'd known for the last few years.

Ellie worked out of Weston nick, and they'd trained together a few years back. If he was being true to himself, he'd been nursing a crush ever since their first meeting. Unfortunately, he wasn't the only one. Ellie was so far out of his league it was laughable, but as she smiled at him, brushing rain off her sleeve, he thought that maybe today he would try his luck.

'There's better things I could be doing with my Wednesday,' he told her, as they moved to the next two households.

'Such as what, drinking lukewarm tea in that tiny hovel of a police station you work at?' said Ellie, knocking on her front door before he had time to respond.

David laughed, and with a heavy heart knocked on the door in front of him.

Inspector Baker, who was coordinating the door-to-door search, had insisted they return again today, having been displeased with the lack of response they'd received yesterday. David thought it was a waste of time. Even as the front door opened, he knew the type of response he would get as soon as the person within clocked his uniform.

'PC Jackson, ma'am,' he said, to the harassed-looking woman holding off a growling pit bull with her right hand. 'We're currently doing a door-to-door search in the area. We're trying to see if anyone has seen this man in the last few weeks?' he said, showing the woman the E-Fit picture on his tablet.

'No,' said the woman, shaking her head, not even bothering to look at the screen.

'Ma'am, if you could take a closer look.'

'Is this to do with the body they found in the docks?' she added. The dog was up on its hind legs now, the woman's arm tensed as she struggled to hold it at bay. She frowned and glanced at the screen. 'Odd-looking guy, isn't he? I'd have remembered if I'd seen him. I haven't.'

'Thank you, ma'am,' said David, the door shutting before he'd managed to finish his words.

'Shall we sneak off to the bar?' he said to Ellie, who'd had a similar response from her property.

'You don't have to work with Baker, I do,' said Ellie, as they both crossed the street in the pouring rain. 'He was pissed off yesterday. I know for a fact he'll be checking every single house has been accounted for.'

David felt his pulse quickening and couldn't believe what he was about to do. 'How about we go for a drink later instead, after our shifts finish?' he said, forcing the words before he bottled it.

Ellie stopped in her tracks and turned to face him with a look of curiosity. 'Are you asking me out, David?' she said.

David wasn't sure if she was incredulous or just surprised. His heart was beating in time to the rain dripping off his hat. 'I guess I am,' he said, matching her smile.

'I see,' said Ellie, opening the gate to the next property on the list, David doing the same in the neighbouring house. She knocked on the door before adding, 'It's taken you some time. Sure, we can go out for a drink. You can pick me up at eight.'

David did his best to hide his delight as he knocked on the door and went through the same routine with a woman who must have been at least in her eighties, receiving exactly the same response. All of sudden, the rain didn't bother him as he walked the streets with Ellie. He was already counting down the minutes to later that evening.

'What have they got you working on at the moment?' said Ellie, as they rounded a corner and walked towards a large block of flats.

David shook his head. 'Man, I need to get out of there soon. No one told me police work could be so boring. A civilian officer could do the work I'm doing. The most interesting thing I've had in the last week has been a missing persons case and that's just some guy leaving his wife after she told him she wanted a divorce.'

'I'm sure Baker would always welcome you to the Weston team.'

'I think the sea air would do me good, actually,' said David.

In truth, his professional intentions were focused elsewhere. He wanted a place in CID out of headquarters in Portishead, though it felt like such a distant dream at that moment. He was hoping to make a good showing of the door-to-door searches to help get his name better known, but that was all down to luck, and it felt like securing a date with Ellie had taken up his share of that for the day.

He glanced at the E-Fit as they took the lift together to the top of the building. He focused on the man's eyes, remembering what that woman – Julie Longstaff – had told him about her husband disappearing and subsequent messages she'd been receiving on her phone. She mentioned something about a man following her from the station and had described his eyes as being narrow. Were they similar to the man in the E-Fit?

David dismissed the thought as quickly as it had appeared – though, as the day progressed and he showed the E-Fit photo to tens of other people, he began to wonder about Julie Longstaff.

He hadn't heard from her since Friday, but prior to that she'd been in contact by email on a daily basis. She'd shown him a private message on Twitter from someone claiming to be watching her. He'd all but dismissed that out of hand, and his mind hadn't changed when she'd claimed to have been sent an image of her husband that had been conveniently deleted. He'd seen it so many times before, people trying to gain attention by inventing elaborate lies. But what if she'd been telling the truth?

Late that afternoon, back at home, he looked up Julie Longstaff on his social media accounts. She'd been gathering quite a lot of momentum with a number of extra followers since her husband Patrick had disappeared. Messages from well-wishers were still appearing on her timeline but, scrolling through, he noticed she hadn't posted anything since Friday lunchtime. An hour or so before she'd met him at the station. Before showering, he decided to give her a quick call, but it went straight to answerphone.

He had a day off tomorrow and he was about to go on a date with Ellie Smith, but he made a note to contact Julie Longstaff first thing Friday morning. He even made a note of her address, thinking that it might be worthwhile showing her a copy of the E-Fit image.

Chapter Thirty

Friday morning, four days after Louise's scare, she was back in the incident room with the rest of the team, each member going through their most recent updates. The cramping sensation she'd endured on Monday hadn't returned. She was hopeful that it had just been an anomaly, though her stomach fluttered every time she thought about the hospital appointment arranged for later that day with the consultant at St Michael's.

Tuesday and Wednesday had been spent conducting more door-to-door searches in the Avonmouth area trying to get a match for the E-Fit photograph of the suspect known as *Jason*. Most of those leads, which had been questionable at best, had been followed up and the decision had been made last night to release the E-Fit photo to the wider public.

It was due to go into the local papers later that day and had already hit some of the nationals who'd agreed to run the story. Extra call staff had been assigned to deal with the anticipated influx of calls, and pressure was already filtering down to her from on high about additional costs. It was close to make-or-break time. If there was no response to the wider E-Fit campaign over the weekend, then they would be forced to scale the investigation back. Although such campaigns often brought with them significant leads, there was always a lot of dross they had to wade through and dismiss, so it would be important to keep on top of all the information that came their way.

Tracey was going through the updates on the latest door-to-door searches when Simon Coulson arrived, carrying a large bundle of paper and looking flustered. 'I've all but finished anyway,' said Tracey, taking a seat.

Simon blushed and moved towards the crime board. 'Last night I was given a lead about a second claustrophilia site, this one hidden within the general populace. I've managed to gain some traction in the community from my earlier work, and spent last night going through it.'

'It looks like you haven't had any sleep,' said Greg, swinging on his chair, his polished shoes making circular patterns in the air.

'I haven't,' said Simon. 'I think I've found a second handle for Aisha. I cross-referenced repeated phrases, spellings and such and came back with a ninety-two per cent match. Because this site is harder to access, I think some of the participants have their guards down. Though, of course, it would be impossible to trace anyone – they're all using pseudonyms and false IP addresses, as you'd expect. However, I've managed to track a conversation I believe Aisha was having from eighteen months ago. It's all mundane to begin with. Over days of chatting, there was talk of their shared experiences.'

'Do you have a name for the person she was talking to?' asked Louise, wanting Simon to get to the point.

'Aisha calls herself Sarah in the chat. The other user goes by the name of Rachel.'

'Go on,' said Louise.

Simon held the ream of paper in front of him. 'This is just the first printout,' he said. 'There are literally hundreds of pages to go through. Maybe there's something in it,' he said, placing the documents in front of Louise.

'Thanks, Simon, I'll begin going through that later,' said Louise, noticing her hand was resting idly on her stomach.

◆ ◆ ◆

By mid-afternoon, calls from the articles in the national newspapers were already causing a jam on the phone line. Six additional operatives were working flat out but already some missed calls were being dropped and Louise was desperately trying to get more reinforcements.

Simon had forwarded the correspondence from *Sarah* and *Rachel*. In between everything else, Louise was trying to make progress through the transcript. As Simon had suggested, the conversation between Sarah and Rachel was mostly mundane but every word had to be accounted for. It was the only conversation Simon had managed to find where Aisha, under her alias, had been so forthcoming.

The pair tiptoed around one another for the first few days, gradually getting to know about their shared interests. Louise had already read through the first fifty pages and had only reached the first two weeks of their correspondence. She pictured Aisha sitting behind a laptop somewhere, typing away to the stranger, and wondered how it was that people would give away such intimate details to people they'd never seen or met.

Glancing around, she noticed the office manager's hand was in the air, and she looked over towards her. 'Call for you,' said the manager. 'Tania Elliot.'

Louise shook her head. Tania was a former local journalist who'd hit the big time on the back of a number of Louise's investigations. After the Milner case, Louise had stopped speaking to the journalist and had no intention of resuming their relationship just because the journalist had spotted the E-Fit in the nationals.

Instead, she continued reading through the transcripts with no idea of what she wanted to see – though a mention of shipping containers would certainly have piqued her interest. She'd only read through another twenty pages when the office manager called over once more.

'Sorry, Louise, we have someone in reception to see you. PC David Jackson?'

Louise leaned back in her chair. The name sounded familiar but she couldn't quite place him.

'He was one of the officers despatched to do the door-to-door searches in Avonmouth,' said the office manager. 'He's out of Henleaze nick. Asked to speak to you directly.'

Louise ran a hand through her hair. She'd skipped breakfast that morning and was now suffering hunger pains. 'Put him in one of the interview rooms,' she said. 'I need to grab something from the canteen.'

The police constable stood as she entered the interview room ten minutes later, having demolished a triple chocolate muffin on the way back up. 'PC David Jackson,' he said, hints of colour in his cheeks.

'Hello, David, take a seat,' said Louise. 'You wanted to speak to me?'

'Yes, ma'am. Bit of a strange one, really. I had the day off work yesterday and just got back in today. I was going to go to my sergeant first, but he's off sick and we're down to the bare bones at the station.'

'Henleaze, aren't you?' said Louise.

'That's right, ma'am.'

'I'm surprised you guys are still open,' said Louise. The whole constabulary had been restructured over the last few weeks, and many local stations had closed or were manned by community officers.

'Well, we're not very often, especially at the moment.'

'What were you going to speak to your sergeant about?'

'That's the thing, ma'am. I wouldn't have bothered you if I didn't think it was important, and it might not be, but I thought I had to tell you anyway,' said Jackson, clearly ruffled.

'Calm down, David, let's start at the beginning. Tell me what you have to say and then I can judge if it's important or not.'

Jackson smiled. 'Yes, ma'am,' he said. 'I'm not sure if you know, but I was doing the door-to-door searches on Tuesday and Wednesday this week in Avonmouth.'

Louise nodded, not saying anything and hoping the young constable would get to the point.

'I kept looking at the E-Fit we had of the possible suspect. It made me think of a missing persons case I've been working on. A woman came into the station just over a week ago, Julie Longstaff. She'd had a row with her husband, Patrick Longstaff, over the weekend. There'd been talk of divorce and he'd disappeared after going on a bender. Nothing out of the ordinary there, but she kept bothering me every day and she started a large social media campaign to try to find him.'

'And you've heard nothing from the husband?'

'No, and I didn't think much of it until Julie Longstaff came back to the station and said she'd received an anonymous message on Twitter.'

'What did the message say?' said Louise.

'*We're enjoying watching you,*' said Jackson, reading from his notebook. 'Even then, ma'am, I'll be honest, it didn't mean much to me. Mrs Longstaff claimed she'd seen someone outside the station on the day she'd reported her husband missing. He'd been staring at her, apparently. But with only that, and an anonymous message on Twitter, it was hardly anything to go on.'

'Of course not,' said Louise. 'So why are you here?'

'Mrs Longstaff came back a couple of days later, and claimed to have been sent a photograph of her husband by text message.'

'Go on.'

'She claimed she'd received a photograph of her husband in his underwear, and that he was being held captive. However, the photo had supposedly been deleted remotely and . . . I don't wish to be unkind, but she was stinking of alcohol when she reported it. Anyway, I put it to the back of my mind. Then we did the door-to-door, and I kept looking at the E-Fit of the suspect. The man she'd described looking at her had the same colour eyes as the suspect in the E-Fit. Mrs Longstaff had been quite adamant about the detail – his *narrow blue eyes*,' said Jackson, reading from the notebook again. 'Sinister-looking, whatever that means. Again, I didn't think anything of it, even when I was going door-to-door, but when I got back in – this was Wednesday evening – I thought I'd give her a call anyway. There was no answer. I noticed she hadn't been active on social media since she'd seen me on the Friday.'

'OK,' said Louise.

'Yesterday was a day off, which I'm sure you're aware of now. So then, this morning I tried her again, her phone still goes straight to answerphone, so I decided to pop round.'

'Her house?' said Louise.

'I just wanted to be thorough. There was no answer from the front door. All the curtains were closed. I called the station to see what I should do. They didn't give me authority to take things any further so I had a quick look around the back before I left. It was then I saw the back door was open. I called the station to see if they would give me permission to search the house but they refused. So I went back to the nick.'

'What, and you're here to get permission from me to search her house?'

'The thing is, when I got back, I did a little bit more digging. When Julie Longstaff came to the station and reported her husband missing, I did the assessment risk, usual thing. The wife claimed he was a suicide risk and I checked up and followed the procedures. I tried his phone, spoke to his work colleagues and family members, bank checks, that sort of thing. There was no official record of attempted suicide but it was agreed that he was a medium-to-high risk.'

Louise knew that missing persons could often be the bane of police work. People went missing all the time and quite often they didn't want to be found. In this instance, the man PC Jackson was talking about was in his forties, and had argued with his wife about divorce and subsequently got drunk. Such disputes happened all the time, and not making contact with his wife didn't warrant a full-blown investigation. The supposed previous suicide attempt would have warranted a more stringent response, but with over three hundred thousand people reported missing nationwide each year, it was impossible to dedicate full resources to everyone, despite the perceived risk. 'And you've found out some more information since?' she asked.

'I called his work again. Taylor & Taylor Insurance. I spoke to his boss. Obviously, they're concerned he hasn't shown up for work since that first day. But here's the thing I hadn't realised at the time.'

'And what's that?' said Louise.

'Taylor & Taylor Insurance specialise in shipping insurance, and having spoken to Longstaff's boss, I understand that part of their business was insuring consignments inside shipping containers.'

Chapter Thirty-One

Louise was conscious of the time when she arrived with Greg at Taylor & Taylor Insurance Brokers. PC Jackson's information was potentially useful, and Louise had arranged to speak to his employers while asking Tracey to arrange a warrant to search the man's house. Greg was unusually quiet, and she asked him if he was still in contact with Huddersfield CID as they entered the high building in the centre of Bristol.

'I spoke to one of their officers this morning. They've still got eyes on Knotsford.'

'That's something,' said Louise. 'I have an appointment not far from here at four thirty. If things take longer than necessary, I might have to leave,' she said.

If Greg was curious as to where she could possibly need to go in such a rush, he kept his thoughts to himself. 'You're being quiet,' she said, as they walked over to the reception desk.

'Just thinking about the case,' said Greg, straightening his tie before he spoke to the receptionist.

They both waited in reception for ten minutes, until a young woman in a sharp business suit came down and introduced herself first to Greg. Louise suppressed a smile, noticing the keen eye the woman ran over Greg's appearance before it dawned on her that Louise was the more senior of the pair. 'Mr Wetherby is ready to see you,' she said, her attention now focused on Louise before turning and moving towards the lifts, her high heels clicking on the marbled floor.

Lyle Wetherby's office was situated on the penthouse level of the office block, with impressive views over the city. He stood as the young woman led Louise and Greg into the office. He was as immaculately dressed as Greg – maybe more so. His three-piece suit was perfectly tailored, his smile practised as he shook hands with Louise and Greg before asking them to sit. Despite his courtesy, the mood was changed by his opening sentence. 'It's nice to finally see someone from the police,' he said, as Louise eased herself into the cushioned seats opposite.

'I believe it was Mrs Longstaff who reported Patrick missing, isn't that right?' said Louise.

'That may be so but we'd have thought we'd have warranted a visit at the very least. Patrick is one of our top workers,' said Wetherby, the same painted smile stuck firmly on his face.

It was clear Wetherby wasn't concerned about Patrick's disappearance on a personal level. 'I'm presuming you haven't heard anything from Patrick since his disappearance?' she asked.

'No, of course not,' said Wetherby, indignant.

'These things happen, Mr Wetherby. As an employer you wouldn't be required to inform Mr Longstaff's wife if you had been in contact with him. So the question isn't as obvious as you may think it is.'

Wetherby was nonplussed. He glanced at Greg as if he somehow expected support from Louise's colleague before shrugging his shoulders and saying, 'Either way, he's still missing. You've done nothing about it.'

Louise didn't immediately respond. She considered explaining to Wetherby how common it was for people to go missing but there was no point. 'What can you tell me about Mr Longstaff?' she asked.

'A damn fine guy and we miss him around here.'

'And what exactly is it he does for you?' asked Greg.

'Business development. He works mainly with existing clients, though we put him in front of potential clients as well. He's a very sociable guy, wins us lots of business.'

'Likes a drink?' asked Louise.

'Goes hand in hand with the role, but he hasn't got a problem, if that's what you're suggesting.'

'When did you first realise Mr Longstaff had gone missing?'

'It was that morning, when his wife called Alistair.'

'Alistair?' asked Greg.

'Alistair's one of our junior BDMs, works directly for Patrick. Patrick's wife called him that morning and then we realised he hadn't turned up for a meeting he had over in Bath.'

'Is Alistair in the office at the moment?' asked Louise.

'He's out at a meeting, covering Patrick's clients,' said Wetherby, shaking his head.

'What did you do when you found out Patrick was missing?' asked Louise.

'Obviously we phoned round everyone to see if they'd heard from him, and then Alistair spoke to all his clients, and I know he's been in contact with Julie ever since.'

'Has Patrick done anything like this before?'

'Not at all,' said Wetherby. 'He's a company man, always has been.'

Louise took out a notebook and pretended to read from the empty page. 'You provide maritime insurance, is that correct?'

'That's correct,' said Wetherby.

'And what exactly does that entail? What are you insuring for?'

'We cover everything from small pleasure cruisers to oil tankers. We're one of the leading brokers in the country.'

'How about shipping containers?' said Greg.

Wetherby opened his mouth to speak. Louise could almost see the gears turning in his head, as if a memory had alighted in it. 'Why would you ask that?'

'You heard about the body found at Avonmouth Docks?' said Louise.

'Surely you don't think that has anything to do with Patrick?' said Wetherby, with a chuckle. 'Of course we insure for shipping contents. It's a major part of our business. It's not as if Patrick has access to them. He's a bit far removed from all that. More face-to-face with senior management.'

'He must visit ports and docks?'

'Of course, Patrick would show his face all over, but it's not where our deals are conducted.'

'Patrick wouldn't have access to a shipping container?' said Greg.

'Of course not. What is this?' said Wetherby.

'But some of his clients would?' said Louise.

Wetherby shook his head, smiling at her as if he were humouring a child. 'I don't think you understand the people Patrick works with. He deals with our major clients. We're talking CEO level, not the sort of guys who lock up shipping containers at night.'

Louise nodded, waiting for the condescending expression to disappear from Wetherby's face. 'Can you think of anyone who would want to hurt Patrick?' she said.

'I told you, he's the salt of the earth as far as our clients are concerned.'

Louise wrote the words in her notebook – a memory teasing her, just out of reach. 'Surely at this level of business you're bound to make enemies,' she said, playing to the man's ego.

'Naturally you have competitors. What are you thinking? That someone's come for Patrick like they did for that woman they found? I think that's patently ludicrous,' said Wetherby.

'Why do you think he's gone missing then?' said Greg.

'You're the detective, you tell me.'

Louise ended the interview, the conversation going nowhere. She left Greg to talk with the rest of Patrick Longstaff's colleagues and made the short walk to the hospital where Thomas was waiting for her.

◆ ◆ ◆

'Sorry I'm late,' she said, out of breath by the time she arrived.

'Did you run here?' said Thomas, as they walked along the antiseptic corridors of the maternity ward.

'I walked very briskly, I'll have you know,' said Louise. 'Greg drove me to the city centre. We had to interview someone about the Hashim investigation.'

'Any good?' said Thomas.

'We may have a couple of missing people to go along with the murder,' she said, knocking on the consultant's door.

'You're going to leave it there, on that cliffhanger?' said Thomas, incredulous as the consultant called them in.

Louise smiled. 'I couldn't tell you any more even if I wanted to,' she said, opening the office door.

It was the same consultant as before, Dr Burchet, and if he had bad news to tell them he was hiding it well beneath his welcoming smile. 'Louise, Thomas, please take a seat,' he said, the smile never leaving his face.

Louise's stomach lurched as she sat down, and she wondered if the baby was getting nervous awaiting the announcement of its fate.

'I'll get straight to the point,' said Dr Burchet. 'The tests have come back, and the news is very positive. The chances of Edwards', which was my main concern, are very slim. Roughly the same as you would expect for any pregnancy at your age. Same for Down's and Patau's syndromes.'

Louise grabbed Thomas's hand. Her relief resonated through every cell in her body. It was like the other day with the midwife times ten. She didn't want to look at Thomas in case she began to cry but caught sight of his red eyes before she turned her focus back to the consultant.

'The other complication?' said Louise.

Dr Burchet's smile faded briefly. 'As I said before, we still hope that will rectify itself in time. We're going to do another scan now for you and then we'll see about scheduling another one. I just wanted to put your mind at rest about the CVS results.'

It was another hour before one of the midwives was able to scan her again. The same issue remained, the baby stubbornly refusing to move position to let them fully judge its development.

'Let's leave it for another ten days,' said the midwife. 'Give the baby a chance to move and we can take a better look.'

'Is this a common thing?' asked Thomas.

'Relatively,' said the midwife. 'Obviously I don't want to get your hopes up either way. As the baby moves, we'll be able to tell you more. I'm pretty sure the little thing will have shifted by the time you next come here,' she added.

Despite the lack of certainty, Louise felt a surge of renewed energy as she left the hospital.

'I'm starving,' said Thomas. 'Should we grab something to eat before we go back?'

All Louise wanted to do was to go back to the office and continue work on the Hashim investigation, but it was late and it felt unfair on Thomas after all they'd just been through. 'We can go to that bistro on Gloucester Road,' she said just as her phone began to ring.

'Why do I feel like those were famous last words?' said Thomas.

'Hi, Tracey,' said Louise, answering the phone.

'Hi, Lou, everything OK? Greg said you had to rush off for a meeting.'

'It's nothing. What's up?'

'I managed to speak to our legal team – we've got a warrant to search Julie Longstaff's house.'

'That came quick.'

'I'm heading that way now,' said Tracey. 'Shall I meet you there?'

'OK,' said Louise, hanging up.

'Change of plan?' said Thomas.

'Kind of,' she said, placing a hand on his shoulder. 'We can still get something to eat but it's going to have to be a takeaway. And if you don't mind, I need you to drive me to Henleaze.'

Chapter Thirty-Two

It was dark before they reached the Longstaff house in Henleaze, Louise having demolished a McDonald's Big Mac meal on the drive over – something she hadn't done in years. Thomas joined her outside the quaint, detached building, which had a beautiful front garden lined with trees. Tracey and a group of uniformed officers were waiting for them, including PC David Jackson. Thomas walked over with Louise. 'It feels like ages,' Tracey said, wrapping Thomas in a bear hug. 'When are you coming back to work for us?' she added, breaking her hold.

'Well, I do miss these late nights. Is it OK if I watch, DI Blackwell?' said Thomas, exchanging a knowing look with Tracey.

'As long as you stay out of the way,' said Louise, pretending to push him away from the scene.

Together with Tracey, Louise walked along the pebble-dashed driveway to the front door. The curtains were drawn at the front of the house, no lights on within. Louise knocked on the door and waited thirty seconds before sending the uniformed officers to the rear of the property.

'Why is Thomas here?' asked Tracey, as they waited to hear what the situation was at the back of the house.

Louise was desperate to tell Tracey where they'd just been, and the positive news they'd received, but the potential complications made that feel impossible. She didn't want to be congratulated on the baby by everyone, even Tracey, until she knew for sure that all the risks had been eliminated as far as was possible.

'Thomas had a doctor's appointment. I said I'd go with him.'

Tracey frowned, and Louise wasn't sure if it was through concern over Thomas or because she'd seen through the lie. 'It's nothing,' said Louise. 'Anyway, he has the all-clear so it's all good and he doesn't want anyone to know about it,' she said, hating herself for the white lie.

PC David Jackson returned from the rear of the house. 'Ma'am, I think you should come round the back. I tried the door again, and it's still unlocked.'

Louise and Tracey followed the constable down a side path to the back of the house. A beautiful, manicured lawn gently sloped upwards away from the property, illuminated by two parallel rows of night lights. It must have been at least a hundred and fifty yards in length and was surrounded on both sides by three-metre-high hedges. Tracey and the rest of the team had spent the day trying to reach Julie Longstaff, and despite the unlocked back door, Louise had to wonder if they were making too much of the situation.

Large concertina glass doors spread across the width of the house and, to the left-hand side, one of the doors was slightly ajar from where PC Jackson had tried it again.

'Curtains are all drawn,' said Tracey, glancing up at the second-floor windows.

'Mrs Longstaff,' said Louise, knocking on the door before stepping over the threshold into the kitchen. The air was thick and musty. In the sink were unwashed dishes from a few nights' worth of dinners, the ceramic island in the middle of the room populated by empty wine bottles.

'Mrs Longstaff,' she called out again, the sound reverberating in the high ceilings of the kitchen area.

The same musty smell lingered in the air as she moved with Tracey further into the house. What appeared to be blackout curtains were drawn in each room and Louise switched on lights as she went, calling out Mrs Longstaff's name. She checked every room before she let the rest of the team in for a more thorough investigation.

'No sign of forced entry,' she said to Tracey, as they stood outside the concertina doors at the back of the house.

'Enough wine bottles to knock out an elephant though,' said Tracey. 'Maybe she's just gone on a massive bender like it sounds like her husband did the weekend before.'

As they waited, Louise checked Julie Longstaff's social media profiles. As PC Jackson had suggested, she'd been busy over the last week or so – her campaign to find Patrick attracting hundreds of messages and considerable interest. Julie's public desperation to find her husband didn't sit well with a woman who wanted a divorce. Her posts on social media were so heartfelt that Louise found it difficult to believe Julie didn't still have strong feelings for her husband.

It began raining, small droplets landing on the dry lawn. Louise had stepped inside, where officers were fingerprinting the discarded wine bottles, when the doorbell rang. Everyone stopped what they were doing as Louise moved through the house to the front of the property. The threat level was minimal – emergency vehicles were parked outside, and the house was swarming with officers – but still Louise opened the curtains to see who was calling before answering the door.

An older woman, possibly in her late sixties, was staring ahead at the front door. Even in the poor light, Louise could see she was partly in shock as she opened the door. 'DI Louise Blackwell,' she said, 'may I help you?'

'Where's Julie?' said the woman, her voice strong, more determined than Louise had expected.

'And you are?' asked Louise.

'I'm her bloody mother. Now where the hell is she?'

Louise led Julie's mother, Vanessa Haydn, to the living room where Tracey gave her a cup of tea. Vanessa lifted the cup to her mouth, her hand shaking as Louise explained why they were at the house. 'When was the last time you spoke to your daughter?' she asked, after the woman had taken a sip.

'A week or so ago, I guess. All this stuff about Patrick.'

'What stuff?' asked Louise.

Vanessa frowned as if lost in thought. 'Why are you here again?' she said.

'We're investigating your son-in-law's disappearance,' said Louise.

'What disappearance?' said Vanessa.

'Julie never told you he was missing?'

'What is this? Where is Julie?'

'We're not sure. We came here to speak to her about Patrick.'

Louise glanced at Tracey. Reluctantly she told Vanessa about the reason for Patrick's disappearance, the divorce demands Julie had given him the previous week.

Vanessa squinted her eyes, assessing the information. 'I know about the supposed divorce demands,' she said. 'That will all die down. Julie can blow things out of proportion. Believe me, she was already regretting her words on Sunday morning when her hangover kicked in.'

'Do you know why Julie asked her husband for a divorce?'

Vanessa sighed. 'From what I understand, it was an argument that got out of hand. They had IVF treatment some years ago but it never took. Julie was reminded of that fact over the weekend, and it made her dwell on things. She can be restless at times.'

'And Patrick? How do you get on with him?'

'Patrick's a good man, drinks a bit too much, I know that, but she'd be mad to divorce him – I mean, look at this place. She would never have got anything like this on her own.'

Louise was surprised by the comment, finding it strange that Julie's mum would believe her daughter would be happy in her relationship just because of material comforts.

'You said he drinks too much. Has that been a problem for him for long?'

'Julie's no angel herself, let me tell you that. I've been here for the odd Sunday dinner, and they both knock it down as if it were water.'

'Did Patrick ever become violent towards her?' asked Tracey.

Vanessa shook her head. 'No. I think I would have known if he was being violent to my daughter.'

Louise doubted that was the case. The woman clearly had an uneasy relationship with her daughter, and Louise found it unlikely that Julie would confide in her if the last few minutes were anything to go by.

She took a deep breath. 'This is probably going to be difficult to hear, and even harder to answer,' Louise began to say, before changing her mind. She was going to ask Vanessa if she thought Julie and Patrick had any fetishes about being in small spaces, but decided they hadn't reached that stage yet. Instead, she said, 'Can you think of anyone who'd want to hurt Patrick or Julie, or both of them perhaps?'

Vanessa squinted her eyes, as if the enormity of the situation was finally hitting home. 'Has something happened? Are they in trouble?' she asked.

'We don't know, Vanessa,' said Louise. 'All we know for sure is that Patrick went missing nearly two weeks ago and your daughter went missing possibly the end of last week. It's a strange enough coincidence for us to get involved.'

'No, no,' said Vanessa, shaking her head. 'There must be more to it than this. Why are you all here? You haven't found a body, have you?'

Tracey got up and sat next to Vanessa, putting a hand round her shoulder. 'Nothing like that, Vanessa, this is just routine in this type of situation. We need to know if anyone would hurt them so that we can eliminate potential suspects.'

'I don't know, I don't know,' said Vanessa, her whole body shaking as the colour drained from her face.

Tracey looked up at Louise who nodded, ending the informal interview for the time being. Louise left Tracey to console Vanessa, and walked to the kitchen area where she was stopped by PC Jackson.

'Ma'am, we just found this,' said the constable, handing Louise a plastic evidence bag that contained the latest iPhone model. 'There's a picture of Mrs Longstaff on the lock screen,' said Jackson.

Putting on protective gloves, Louise clicked on the side of the phone. The display showed there were fourteen missed calls and over twenty notifications.

'Make sure you get this back to headquarters as soon as possible,' she said. 'This has to be Julie Longstaff's phone.'

Chapter Thirty-Three

In spite of everything that had happened over the last few days, Louise had the best sleep she'd had in ages, waking in the early morning and nudging Thomas awake.

'What time is it?' said Thomas, blinking his eyes as he looked at his watch.

'Seven a.m.'

Thomas stretched and sat up. 'Isn't it Saturday morning?' he said.

'It is, but there's no rest for the wicked,' said Louise, getting out of bed.

'Maybe not, and I understand why *you're* getting up – because you've got to go to work – but why exactly did you wake me up?'

'Baby's hungry, of course.'

Despite her new-found energy after yesterday's positive news, a surge of melancholy hit Louise as she showered. For the second time in as many weeks she had cancelled on Emily. It reminded her that they'd yet to resolve what would happen when the baby arrived, though anything but having Emily move in with them would feel like a betrayal. She'd called her mother last night to give her the news about the DNA tests, only to hear the disappointment in her mother's voice as she told her she would have to postpone seeing Emily this weekend.

And what would happen if Emily moved in with them? Would Louise have to rely on Thomas to look after the children when she went to work on Saturday mornings, or would something in her role have to change?

'I've made a bit of everything,' said Thomas, as she headed downstairs, the kitchen foggy with smoke as fried food sizzled on the hob.

Louise could hardly believe her appetite as she devoured everything Thomas placed before her. Loading her fork with bacon and egg, she looked up to see Thomas smiling at her. 'Amusing you, am I?' she said, her mouth full.

'It's just good to see you eating,' said Thomas. 'I was thinking, I'm going to see Noah today and take him to the beach. I was wondering if I could take Emily too? Perhaps we could go to the pier.'

Louise balked at the mention of the pier, the place where the IED had been planted by Bryce Milner only three months ago. She'd been back a number of times since to follow up on the investigation, but somehow it didn't seem right allowing Emily to go there. 'That would be lovely, she'll be so pleased,' she said, after a pause, fighting her insecurities. 'Do you want me to give my mum a call?'

'No, I can do it. You get yourself to work. It would be good to spend some time with you this evening though.'

'I'll try to get back as soon as I can,' said Louise, heading out the door.

◆ ◆ ◆

Louise was still thinking about the conversation as she sat in the incident room in Portishead an hour later with Tracey, Greg and DCI Robertson. This would be the first time Thomas had looked after Emily without her, and although she saw it as a positive sign, it made her feel neglectful for not being there herself.

The crime board had been altered: images of Julie and Patrick Longstaff were now below Aisha Hashim, and the E-Fit of *Jason* took prominence on the suspect list.

Robertson stared hard at the images as if he could somehow will them to reveal their truths.

'We have a meeting arranged with Alistair Whitehall this morning,' said Louise. 'He's Patrick Longstaff's right-hand man at Taylor & Taylor, though he seems to be taking over a lot of his role in Patrick's absence.'

'That's motive enough for me,' said Robertson, deadpan, just as Simon Coulson knocked on the glass door and walked in.

'You're loving these dramatic entrances, Simon, aren't you?' said Louise, recalling the other day.

'I've been working on Julie Longstaff's iPhone,' said Simon, connecting his laptop to the white screen. 'The link she claimed led to the images of her husband is defunct, but we have uncovered some tracking software. My guess is the link she clicked on installed some malware. However, the phone still works and we've been tracing her contacts and have identified a number of people she was in contact with last week, including her mother, PC David Jackson at the Henleaze office, and Alistair Whitehall. But I think what will be more of interest is this,' he said, clicking a button on the laptop. 'Messages between Julie Longstaff and a man we've identified as Derek Watson.'

Louise read through the messages, which were explicit in nature. 'Now we know why their marriage was on the rocks,' she said.

'They agreed to meet last week. Two days before we think Julie Longstaff went missing,' said Simon.

'Good work, Coulson,' said DCI Robertson.

'I don't suppose you have an address for us?' said Louise.

Coulson smiled. Too humble to be triumphant, he clicked another button, revealing Derek Watson's address.

'Right, what are you waiting for?' said Robertson.

◆ ◆ ◆

Louise drove with Greg to the address they had for Derek Watson – a small farmhouse in Longwell Green to the east of the city. They pulled up outside the property, the smell of manure ripe in the air as they walked along the gravel path to the farmhouse door.

The man who answered appeared to be a cliché of the farming look. He was wearing a green tweed suit with a buttoned-up waistcoat and matching flat cap, his smile fading as Louise displayed her warrant card.

'Mr Derek Watson?' said Louise.

'That's correct,' said Watson, 'how can I help you?'

'We're here to talk about Julie Longstaff,' said Louise.

Watson stepped away from the front door, shutting it behind him. 'What the hell are you doing at my house?' he said, under his breath.

'Are you aware that Mrs Longstaff has gone missing?' said Greg, emphasising the *Mrs*.

'No. I know Patrick had gone missing, but I didn't know anything about his wife. Why are you asking me about this?'

'How well do you know Julie Longstaff?' asked Louise.

'You're not serious?' said Watson, his arms wide in exasperation.

'We have significant evidence suggesting you and Mrs Longstaff were having an affair,' said Louise.

Watson shook his head. 'My wife and children are inside there. How dare you come to my house and spread these ridiculous rumours.'

Louise took out her phone and showed the man the messages from Julie Longstaff's phone.

Watson's face turned ashen in response. 'Down here,' he said, leading them along the driveway as he nervously glanced back at the house. 'How did you get those?' he said, his brusque manner fading into a more cooperative tone.

'That's not important now. What is important is that Julie Longstaff is missing and she went missing shortly after you agreed to see her,' said Louise.

'Did you meet up with her on the evening in question?' asked Greg.

'Listen, can we go somewhere else and talk about this?' said Watson, his eyes darting from Louise and Greg back to his house.

'If we leave here, you'll be coming in the car with us and going back to the station,' said Louise. 'So please, Mr Watson, answer the question.'

Watson rubbed his forehead. 'Yes, I saw Julie that night. I was there for less than an hour. She was in a right state and it was a mistake to have gone over. It was a mistake from the beginning, if I'm honest.'

'How did it all happen?' said Louise.

'We met at a work conference. We were both a little bored, and a little drunk, and one thing led to another. It only lasted a couple of months and I broke it off five or six weeks ago.'

'You broke it off?' asked Louise.

Watson curled his lip. 'I don't know who broke it off, but it's over.'

'Yet you came to see her again last week,' said Greg.

'I shouldn't have done so, but she caught me on the hop. She called and asked if I would come over. So shoot me.'

'I take it your wife doesn't know about this?' said Louise.

'Of course bloody not,' said Watson, through gritted teeth.

'Tell me what happened when you last saw Julie. You said you were there for less than an hour.'

Watson sighed again, shifting from one foot to the other, as if he were walking on hot coals. 'She was in a state over Patrick, if you must know. You lot were doing nothing about it, despite all the social media attention she was getting. I guess she just wanted someone to talk to, but she was pissed out of her mind by the time I arrived and all she wanted to do was argue. I knew then it was a mistake and I got out as soon as I could.'

'What was the house like when you arrived?' asked Louise.

'I don't know,' said Watson, throwing his arms up in the air. 'All the curtains were drawn, I know that. What do you think's happened to her?'

'There's been no communication from Julie since Friday afternoon, so I was hoping you could tell us.'

Watson was incredulous, his eyes shifting from Louise to Greg and back again, as if he was searching for someone to blame. 'I really don't understand why you're here. Do you think I've abducted her or something? I couldn't have got out of that house quick enough and I certainly didn't go back to see her.'

'Do you know Patrick Longstaff as well?' said Greg.

'Sort of, we're in the same industry, but I've barely talked to the man before.'

'Yet you had no qualms sleeping with his wife,' said Greg.

Watson shook his head, dismissing the question. 'I really think that's irrelevant, Officer,' he said. 'Do I need to call my solicitor?'

'If you think you need your solicitor, that's fine with us,' said Louise. 'Why don't you step back inside your house and call them now?' She gave him a moment to consider. 'We'll wait outside to take you back to headquarters,' she added, calling his bluff.

'Listen, it's not the biggest industry in the world, you bump into people. I know Patrick Longstaff. I own a haulage firm. Sometimes we work with the shipping companies, and I've used him as an insurance broker. I don't know what's happened to him and Julie, but it has nothing to do with me. It's the first time I've seen Julie in six weeks, I've told you that.'

'Is there anything she said to you that might help us locate her?' said Louise.

'I don't know, she was rambling. She said on the day she'd reported Patrick missing she thought someone had been following her and reckoned the same person had sent her a message on Twitter,' said Watson, repeating what Julie had told PC David Jackson. 'If you ask me, she was paranoid. She'd been drinking every day since Patrick had disappeared by the looks of it. There were empty wine bottles everywhere. I think it was all getting a bit too much for her and she'd convinced herself she was being followed.'

'And did she have any idea who was behind it?'

'No. She said something about a man with blue eyes, for all the use that was.'

Louise showed Watson the E-Fit image they had of the man who'd been seen with Aisha near to the docks. 'Do you recognise this man at all?'

Watson stared hard at the image, as if trying to impress on Louise how serious he was taking this all now. 'I'm afraid not.'

'Think carefully, Mr Watson,' said Louise. 'Maybe at one of your shipping conferences, someone who may have worked for you?'

'I'm sorry. I have a good memory for faces and I just don't recognise this man. Now if you please . . .' he said, as the front door opened and a woman in an outfit similar to Watson's stepped out.

'Everything OK, Derek?' said the woman, walking over towards them.

Louise handed Watson her card. 'If you think of anything, contact me immediately.'

Derek fumbled in his pocket and handed Louise his own business card back. 'Please call me on this if you need to speak to me again,' he said, as his wife approached.

'Everything OK, Derek?' repeated Mrs Watson, smiling at Louise and Greg in turn.

Derek matched his wife's smile. 'Just helping DI Blackwell and her colleague here. Nothing to worry about.'

Louise smiled at the woman. She was tempted to continue questioning Derek in front of her, but that would serve no purpose. Instead, she thanked the man and walked back to her car, wondering what excuses Watson would give his wife for their presence there that morning.

'I think you went quite easy on him, boss,' said Greg, as they drove back to headquarters.

'Maybe, but we've planted the thought in his mind now. He'll have had to tell his wife some made-up story and will fear us coming back again to see him. If he does know more than he's letting on, then I think he'll get in contact,' said Louise.

She was surprised to find herself hungry again so soon after the full English breakfast Thomas had cooked for her. They stopped at a petrol station, Louise buying a meat pasty, to Greg's surprise.

'I've had nothing to eat all day,' she said by way of explanation.

'I'm not sure I'd consider that food,' said Greg, buying a bottle of water.

Back at the station, Louise signed off on a few investigations she'd been neglecting through the week, her time taken over by the Hashim case. She assigned as much of the work as best she could before returning to the second set of transcripts Simon Coulson had provided her with. As she read through the mundane conversation between *Sarah* and *Rachel* – possibly between Aisha and someone as yet unknown – her thoughts turned to Julie and Patrick Longstaff. After what she'd witnessed at Aisha's crime scene, it was all too easy to imagine the married couple somewhere in shipping containers, enduring the fate that eventually killed Aisha. If it had happened, at least this time they had a chance to intervene, though it felt as if time was running out.

She reached the end of the transcript, the conversation abruptly ending three weeks before Aisha left Huddersfield for London. Coulson had said that the security settings on the site had tightened around that period so it was possible the conversation had continued beyond that date. Louise glanced up at the crime board before she began reading the transcripts again from the beginning. She thought about the major players in the investigation, from Aisha, Julie, and Patrick downwards. Malcolm Knotsford, Aisha's parents, Raymond Atkinson and his head of security at the docklands and everyone else she'd interviewed along the way, including Derek Watson this morning.

As she reread the conversation between Sarah and Rachel, she tried to place *Rachel's* tone of voice and match it with each person involved in the investigation. It proved all but impossible until she caught one phrase. Five weeks before Aisha had left Huddersfield, she'd been talking to *Rachel* about locations. *Rachel* had mentioned her landlord, who she'd described as being 'the salt of the earth'. It was a common enough phrase in the West Country. Louise had only highlighted it because she recalled Lyle Wetherby using the same phrase yesterday to describe Patrick. Louise had thought nothing of it at the time, but now she realised it had jarred her subconsciously and she recalled where she'd recently heard it.

She ran through the transcripts again, this time with a different person in mind. She pictured *Rachel* – Aisha's female correspondent – as being Aisha's former flatmate in London, Meryl Gatwood, and all of a sudden the transcripts came alive. It was the cadence of the sentences that reminded her of the short, sharp way Meryl had spoken to her when they'd been there and there was that phrase again: *salt of the earth*.

It was rather a specific phrase. Not totally uncommon, as demonstrated by her meeting with Wetherby, but unusual enough for her to take notice. Maybe she was making connections that weren't there, but Aisha had been talking to *Rachel* about landlords three weeks before she left for London, and *Rachel* had used the same phrase as Meryl Gatwood. It was enough for Louise to want to speak to Meryl again, and twenty minutes later she was on her way to London.

Chapter Thirty-Four

Tracey and Greg had been away from their desks, so Louise had notified Robertson before departing. He knew better than to question her decision, even if it did involve going to London on a Saturday afternoon. She called the DC she'd met in London, Stephen Brown, to notify him she was on her way. She could have called ahead to check with Meryl, but the risk of her absconding was too great. It was imperative she be met face-to-face, and Louise had to be the one to speak to her.

Thomas called as she was crawling along the M4 close to Reading. Louise heard the wind and the squawk of the gulls as he told her he was in Sand Bay with Noah and Emily.

'How's Emily been?' asked Louise.

'She's fine. Came along with me no problem. They've been having a great time together. In fact, here she is. Do you want to speak to her?'

Before Louise had time to answer, Emily was on the phone. 'Aunty Louise,' she said, 'I'm at the beach with Noah and Thomas. Thomas took us to the pier earlier and we got some sweets and ice cream.'

Louise didn't know if it was the baby hormones, but she found herself welling up as she listened to her niece excitedly telling her all about her day. 'That sounds fantastic,' she said, masking her melancholy. 'You make sure you're a good girl for Thomas, won't you?'

'I will, Aunty Louise,' said Emily, before Thomas came back on the line.

'So what time are you going to be home?' he asked.

Louise hesitated before answering. 'Not for a while. I'm on my way to London.'

Thomas went momentarily quiet. 'I'm sure there's a good reason for that,' he said, after the pause, the disappointment evident in his tone.

'I'll tell you all about it when it's over,' said Louise, hankering after the days when Thomas used to work with her and she could share everything with him.

'It's fine,' he said. 'I'm going to take Emily for tea and then drop her back to your parents, if that's OK?'

'Of course it is,' said Louise. 'I really appreciate you doing this, Tom.'

'Well, she's family now, isn't she?' said Thomas.

Louise struggled to reply, mouthing a quick goodbye before hanging up and viciously wiping the tears from her face. 'Pull yourself together, there's no time for this,' she said out loud, her mind making things worse by presenting her with images of Aisha Hashim's emaciated corpse, and Patrick and Julie Longstaff in captivity.

The south London traffic was gridlocked as she left the M25 sometime later. DC Stephen Brown called as she headed through Croydon city centre, en route to the block of flats in Sydenham.

'Thanks for calling back on a Saturday,' said Louise.

'You're OK,' said Stephen. 'I had a quiet day planned, anyway. What time are you arriving?'

'ETA is still forty minutes. I've never seen traffic like it,' said Louise.

'I'm just around the corner from the block of flats,' said Stephen. 'I can go in and question her?'

'If you don't mind, I'd like to do that myself,' said Louise.

'Understood. I'll go there now, keep an eye out for her coming or going,' he said, hanging up.

The sky was darkening by the time Louise arrived nearly an hour later. She'd been caught in more congestion and had been forced to take a diversion along small side streets with a seemingly endless supply of speed bumps.

DC Brown was waiting outside the flats, sitting on the wall like the first time she'd seen him. 'No sign of her since I've been here,' he said.

'Let's go up then, shall we?' said Louise.

The same musty smell greeted them as they entered the block of flats. Louise drummed her fingers against the side of the lift as it made its way to the eighth floor, fighting thoughts of the lift breaking down and being trapped within. She wasn't sure what she was hoping to achieve by coming here, but she needed to look Meryl in the eye to determine if she was the one who'd been in correspondence with Aisha before she'd moved to London.

Noise blasted from the apartment building as they walked along the corridor, the music – some form of death metal – lowering in volume as Louise knocked on the door. The young man she'd met last time – the owner of the giant flat-screen television – answered in his dressing gown, an unlit cigarette drooping from his mouth. 'Yes?' he said, a quizzical look on his face as looked from Louise to DC Brown.

'Sebastian, isn't it. Do you remember me?' said Louise, displaying her warrant card.

The man looked nervous, pulling his dressing gown across his chest. 'Do you need to come in?' he asked.

'We're here to see Meryl. Is she in?'

Sebastian furrowed his brow, glancing again at each of them in turn as if he thought he was somehow being tested. 'Meryl?' he said. 'Don't you know? She's left.'

'Left?' said Louise. 'When did she leave?'

'She packed up and left that day.'

'That day?' said DC Brown.

'That day you both came to visit. A couple of hours after you left, she'd packed her bags and said her goodbyes. Haven't seen her since.'

Chapter Thirty-Five

Louise was immediately on alert. Coincidences happened, but Meryl had given no indication she was planning to leave the last time she'd been there. Nothing in her room had been packed, and the fact she had left a few hours later was more than suspicious.

'Can we come in?' she said to Meryl's former flatmate, Sebastian, who was now holding firmly on to the lapels of his dressing gown.

Sebastian stood aside. 'Sure, sure, come in. It's a bit of a mess,' he said.

Louise needed verification before she did anything else, but every passing second increased her concern about Meryl's disappearance. 'Can you show me Meryl's room?' she asked.

'I can but someone's in there. Sadie.'

Sebastian led them to Meryl's old room and knocked on the door. A young woman, dressed in a tight black dress, her face coated in make-up, answered. Meryl had told Louise about the high turnaround at the flat so it wasn't a surprise that her room was already occupied. She questioned Sadie but the young woman had never even met Meryl.

Sebastian led them to the living room, the giant TV still pride of place on the wall. 'So did you see her before she went?' asked Louise.

'Yeah, it wasn't long after I saw you and you asked me about that television,' said Sebastian. 'She must have called Bob, and the next thing I know she was packing all her stuff up.'

'And Bob is?' said Louise.

'The landlord. Do you want his number?'

Louise nodded. 'How was she acting as she packed?'

'I didn't really pay any attention. She knocked on my door before she left. All her stuff was in a number of rucksacks, and she said goodbye. I didn't really know her, to be honest.'

'And you didn't think it was strange she left the day we interviewed her?' said DC Brown.

'Not really. This whole place is full of different people from when I moved in. People come and go.'

Louise called the number for the landlord and left a message when it went to answerphone. 'Do you have an address for him?' she asked Sebastian.

'For Bob? He lives over in north London,' said Sebastian, finding the address on his phone.

'Great,' said Louise. 'When was the last time you saw him?'

'The day I moved in. He showed me around, took all my cash off me and I haven't seen him since.'

'What happens when you need something done in the flat?'

'We call that number. To be fair, Meryl used to sort all of that. Thankfully there's been no need to call him since she left.'

Louise drove with DC Brown through central London to West Hampstead in north London where the landlord, Bob Lashbrook, lived. Throughout the journey, she grew more confident that Meryl was *Rachel* in the online conversation when Aisha had been *Sarah*. Initially, Louise had made the connection on little more than a turn of phrase. The transcripts Simon had unearthed had ended before Aisha left for London, and there was no way to know for sure if

Meryl had directly invited her – though it seemed more than feasible that Meryl had lured Aisha in from the beginning.

But if Meryl was the reason Aisha had relocated to London, why had she coerced her into moving? Had the overall goal from the beginning been to kill her? And what, if any, was the connection to Patrick and Julie Longstaff?

Lashbrook lived in a narrow-terraced road, off West End Lane. The lights were out in the house and no one answered when DC Brown rang the doorbell. They tried the neighbours on both sides of the property, the elderly couple to the left of Lashbrook's house giving them the lowdown on the landlord. Lashbrook was married with three teenage daughters. The neighbours thought he may have been away for the weekend but they couldn't be sure.

Louise left another three messages on Lashbrook's phone before giving in for the night an hour later.

'We try again in the morning,' she said to DC Brown.

'You're not heading back to Bristol, are you?' said the DC.

'No, I'll check into some hotel nearby. Are you OK to meet me back here in the morning?'

Brown nodded. 'You're welcome to stay with me if you like. I've got a sofa you can crash on. Far from ideal, I know.'

Louise smiled. 'Thanks for the offer, but I'll catch you tomorrow.'

She called DCI Robertson before booking herself into a chain a couple of miles from Lashbrook's house. She updated Robertson about Meryl's disappearance and although the evidence against her was flimsy, they agreed to put a wanted notice on the woman.

Louise ordered a takeaway and ate it alone in her hotel room. She felt a bout of loneliness as she watched the Saturday night television. The feeling was unusual for her. She spent so much of her time alone that she thought she'd grown accustomed to it. Perhaps she was just at the wrong place at the wrong time. She wanted to be back with Thomas, with her family, and again she was reminded that they'd yet to put in place a proper plan for their future together.

She struggled to sleep, her mind wandering between thoughts of Thomas and Emily, the baby growing within her, Aisha in her metal tomb, Patrick and Julie Longstaff, and the missing Meryl Gatwood.

At some point she fell asleep, and was woken by the piercing screech of her mobile phone, which she'd turned to maximum volume. She answered the unknown number, a hesitant voice introducing himself as Bob Lashbrook. 'I'm really sorry to bother you on a Sunday morning, I've only just got your messages about Meryl. We were away for the evening,' he said.

Louise rubbed her eyes, trying to gather her thoughts. 'You at home now, Mr Lashbrook?' she asked.

'We're just on our way back. I didn't check my phone. I'm sorry.'

'That's fine. When can I come round and see you?'

'In an hour?'

'See you then,' said Louise, calling DC Brown before showering and getting ready for the day.

Bob Lashbrook was reverse parking his car outside his house when Louise and DC Brown arrived an hour later. He looked a little worse for wear as he left the driving seat, his pale face bloated, his lips dry and blistered as Louise introduced herself and DC Brown to him and the rest of his family.

'Come in,' said Lashbrook, leading them through to a home office as the rest of the family disappeared upstairs. 'I keep records of all my tenants – everything's up to date, I promise,' he said, as

Louise and DC Brown sat down in two of the office chairs in the small room.

'Here, here we go,' said Lashbrook, pulling open a drawer containing Meryl Gatwood's file. 'She's been a great tenant. I couldn't believe it when she left. She must have been there five or six years,' he said, handing Louise a paper envelope.

'Did she have a deposit on her rental?' asked DC Brown.

'She did. I explained to her I couldn't give it back due to the short notice of her leaving,' said Lashbrook, looking sheepish, 'but she didn't care.'

'Did she give her forwarding address?' asked Louise.

'She told me she was going away, abroad. Look, it's none of my business. I did ask her a couple of times for a forwarding address, in case she left something behind, you know? But I can't demand it from them.'

Lashbrook was acting defensively, and Louise wondered if he was hiding anything. 'How well did you know Meryl?' she asked.

'Not that well. This is my whole business. I used to have a shop on the high street but after Covid I gave it up. I work from home and meet people at the properties.'

'When did you last see Meryl?'

'About three months back. There was a light fitting that needed to be changed. I try to do all that myself – cut down costs, you know?'

'But you've known her for five or six years, you think?'

'Yes, it should be in that file when she first moved in. But as I said, I just knew her to speak to. We only met when there was an issue at the flat or when a new person would come in.'

'You have quite a high turnover of renters, at least that's what Meryl said.'

'It's true. We ask for a three-month deposit and then it's a rolling one-month contract. It appeals to a lot of people, especially those new to the city.'

Louise opened the file. There was a contract dated five and a half years ago and a bank statement from that time. 'No references?' she asked.

'Can I see?' said Lashbrook, taking the file from her. 'We usually get references. I'm digitised now. We ask for proof of funds but as they pay three months in advance it's not that big an issue for us. We just ask them to leave if they refuse to pay.'

'But would you have taken references?'

'I think so,' said Lashbrook.

DC Brown shook his head. It was clear the whole enterprise needed auditing but that wasn't Louise's concern. 'Did you have any indication she was going to leave?'

'None at all.'

'And do you know about Aisha Hashim?' said Louise.

Lashbrook stopped, as if having to consider his answer. 'She was that girl found in the shipping container? I read about her, yes.'

'Did Meryl ever mention anything to you about her?' asked Louise.

Lashbrook shook his head, his furrowed brow suggesting he had little idea of where the conversation was heading.

'Did you know we questioned Meryl on the day she left?'

'No, I didn't know that,' said Lashbrook. 'What is this all about?'

'Do you have emergency contacts for your tenants?'

Lashbrook grimaced. 'Everyone that's been digitised, yes. Sometimes people are reluctant to give out that information. All I have for Meryl is what you have there.'

Louise looked at the contract, at Meryl's scrawling signature and again at the bank statement. She frowned. 'What name do you have for Meryl?' she asked.

'How do you mean?' said Lashbrook.

'What full name do you have for Meryl?'

Lashbrook looked confused, glancing at DC Brown. 'Meryl Gatwood,' he said.

Louise turned the bank statement around so he could see it. 'Then why does it say something different just here?'

Chapter Thirty-Six

Julie was in a strange mental and physical hinterland, reminiscent of the worst type of hangover. She couldn't remember the last time she'd moved, having adjusted herself into a foetal position so she was facing Patrick through the mirrored glass. Time drifted by. Occasionally, light would filter through from the outer area, but hours seemed to pass in a hazy darkness where all she had were her thoughts. She must have slept at some point, but it was impossible to tell if she was having nightmares or if her mind was actively taunting her with the enormity of the situation.

More and more, her thoughts returned to the woman's body that had been found in the Avonmouth Docks. It seemed clear to her now that what had happened to that woman – wasn't her name Aisha? – was somehow linked with her current predicament. She hated herself for doing so, but she wondered how much Patrick was to blame. He worked in maritime insurance. What if he'd had something to do with that poor woman's death? Aisha. Yes, it was definitely Aisha. Aisha Hashim. Julie hadn't seen any photographs of her, but had read that her body had been found shrivelled up in one of the shipping containers that Patrick probably insured.

Julie wondered how long it would have taken for her to die. How many hours she'd spent alone in that container. Whoever was holding them captive was still giving them food and water, but those occasions seemed to be rarer in nature and the quantities were diminishing – the last meal she'd had being a small plastic bottle of water and a slice of dried bread.

She tried her best not to move, her body in agony every time she tried to stretch a muscle. Even if she was freed from her prison, she doubted she would be able to escape. Her muscles only seemed to exist now to cause her pain.

As for Patrick, he was like a ghost next to her. Every now and then she would panic, fearing he'd stopped breathing, only to be rewarded with his eyes blinking, or his mouth hanging open.

On cue, light spilled into the room as the outer door opened. Julie felt the damp, warm feeling, alerting her that she'd once more soiled herself, as her captor approached, pressing his masked face up against the glass so he was looking down on her. Julie tried to retreat to the back of her prison, but even the slightest movement sent waves of pain through her joints and muscles.

'What do you want?' She wasn't sure if she'd said the words or thought them. Either way, the man responded by doing the one thing she hoped he wouldn't do: removing his mask.

Julie blinked away tears. She couldn't be sure, her eyes all but useless due to the prolonged darkness, but her captor appeared to be the man she'd seen in the car outside the police station. Only, he looked a good twenty to thirty years older than what she'd remembered, and for some inexplicable reason he appeared to be crying.

It was this more than anything that provoked her to move. Ignoring the extreme cramping in her back and legs, she retreated the few inches to the rear of her cell and pulled her knees up to her chest. 'What is it you want?' she said, this time hearing the words leave her mouth.

The man bent down so that he was at eye level, and through the glass she saw his frailty. His papery skin was chipped with wrinkles, his tears running through the rivulets, clear even in the faint light from behind him, and as he pressed a button to open the door, she could see his hands were trembling.

The divide parted and it was as if time stood still, the only things left in the world Julie and her captor. This might be her one chance. If she could just mount the strength, she could charge at him and knock over his weak, frail body, escape and get help. But it had taken the last of her strength to retreat to the back of the cell, and as the man crawled in next to her, she couldn't do anything except shiver as he put a leathery hand tight across her wrists and began pulling her out.

She struggled as best she could but it was pointless. Her body wasn't designed for such restriction and despite his apparent age and infirmity, the man had a wiry strength to him that she found impossible to fight. He dragged her into the outer area and, for a short while, she was in a room which, although only five by seven, felt as vast and wide as any room she'd ever inhabited in her life.

'Why are you doing this?' she said.

The man just stared at her, the narrow blue eyes she'd seen before withered and lost. It appeared to Julie that he had no better idea than she did. Again, she considered running at him but it was taking all of her strength just to remain in an upright position. The man pressed a button on his mobile phone and a partition next to Julie eased open.

'Patrick,' she said under her breath.

The man nodded. 'That's right,' he said, dragging her again by the wrist to Patrick's cell. 'I thought it was time you and your husband became reacquainted,' he added, pushing her into the small cell where Patrick lay dormant, and shutting the glass partition behind her.

Chapter Thirty-Seven

The statement found at Lashbrook's house from when Meryl moved in had showed her surname as being Hutchinson, not Gatwood. Louise called it in immediately, recalling how Meryl had cleared an identity check after Louise had last returned from seeing her in London.

Information trickled in on Meryl Hutchinson as Louise returned from London on Sunday afternoon. It was believed Meryl Hutchinson had created her alter ego, Meryl Gatwood, when she'd arrived in London seven years ago, although it hadn't been done by deed poll. It was still easy enough for people to forge documents and open fake bank accounts if they had the necessary will and it appeared Meryl had done so. The only anomaly was why Lashbrook had a statement with Meryl's real name on it. At this stage, Louise thought that Meryl had mistakenly shown Lashbrook an account with her old name when she'd registered with him. From what she'd seen of Lashbrook's system, it was more than conceivable that he hadn't done due diligence on the woman beyond taking her three months' rent in advance.

Meryl was a former Bristol schoolgirl, having attended private schools in the area. She had two older siblings – Neil and Jacqueline – and her parents had passed away when she was ten.

From what Louise and her team had uncovered so far, it appeared that Meryl hadn't worked, or paid any tax, during her period in London. However, she had received a monthly donation to her bank account from an as yet unidentified source.

Although they had no address for the woman, they did have a location for Meryl's former family home – a detached property on the Bath Road. Louise was currently making slow progress to the house on the outskirts of Bath, and every passing minute felt wasted. She was convinced Patrick and Julie's lives were on the line and she drummed her fingers impatiently on the steering wheel as the vehicles in front of her inched ahead.

The sky had darkened by the time she arrived, rain pitting against her windscreen. The full team were waiting for her as she pulled up next to the flashing blue lights of two patrol cars. Greg, Tracey and Robertson were standing outside the Victorian property in deep conversation.

'No one's at home,' said Robertson, as she left the car.

'It appears no one's been at home for a long time,' added Tracey. 'We talked to the neighbours. No one's lived in the house since the parents passed away – some thirty years ago – though apparently someone comes and looks after it once a month.'

'Do we know how the parents died?' asked Louise.

'Old age is the official cause of death,' said Tracey. 'Though they both died within a day of one another. No more information as of yet.'

'And Meryl's siblings?'

'We have addresses for them. Neil and Jacqueline Hutchinson. One in Norfolk, one in Birmingham. We've sent local plods there but haven't been able to get hold of them as yet.'

'So can we go in?' asked Louise.

'I've been on to legal,' said Robertson. 'We're presuming there's a chance that Patrick and Julie Longstaff are being held captive, so that's enough.'

'What are we waiting for then?' said Louise, summoning one of the uniformed officers who was standing waiting with the enforcer – the battering ram used by the police to gain entrance.

The front door splintered open after one strike, Robertson stepping inside first as Louise tried the lights, which were working.

'It's like a museum,' said Greg, as they walked through the house. The décor – all browns and flowered wallpaper – suggested it hadn't been changed since the sixties. It felt as if the Hutchinson family were keeping the house as a memorial to their parents. A musty smell hung in the air, the numerous ornaments and sides covered in more than a thin line of dust. The net curtains in the living room had browned with age. As Louise lifted them up, she saw mildew on the window frames. No one had lived here in a long time and it was apparent Meryl hadn't returned to her family home.

'Boss, I've found something,' said Greg, sticking his head out from the entrance to the kitchen.

Louise stepped through, the musty smell intensifying.

'Another locked door,' said Greg.

'Shall I?' said the uniformed officer, still holding the enforcer.

'Maybe we should try that first,' said Louise, pointing to the key taped to the chipped paintwork at the side of the door. She pulled the key down and tried the lock, which creaked open, revealing a staircase to the cellar.

'After you then,' said Robertson, handing her a torch.

Louise smiled, taking the torch, wondering if Robertson would have been so flippant had he known she was pregnant. She crept downstairs until she'd reached the cellar floor, shining the torch around the basement area which took up the whole length and width of the house.

'There,' she said, rushing to the far corner of the basement where there were two more locked doors, wondering, as she ran, if they would find Julie and Patrick Longstaff within.

Chapter Thirty-Eight

Louise sensed the hesitation in her colleagues. They'd come so far, only to be presented with two more locked doors. Silence descended as Louise stepped forward to the first, her colleagues watching – no doubt thinking and fearing what awaited them behind the pad-locked barriers. She placed her ear to the cold, wooden door. She couldn't hear anything beyond her own beating heart, but that didn't mean Patrick and Julie weren't waiting inside. With no time to waste, she wrapped her knuckles on both doors calling Julie and Patrick's names before instructing one of the team to pry open the locks.

It didn't take long for the rusty locks to be crowbarred off their hinges. Her pulse racing, Louise creaked open the first door and shone her torch within, half expecting to see another murder scene. All tension left her body as both rooms were confirmed to be empty. She was desperate to find the missing pair, but frustratingly it wasn't to be this way.

With thoughts of Aisha Hashim never far from the front of her mind, she put on protective gloves and stepped into the first room with her torch held out in front of her. She'd learned over the years that some places had a certain type of feel to them. Any locked room in a basement would feel slightly incongruous, but in this circumstance that wrongness seemed palpable. Louise sensed it in the trapped, fetid air, and in the roughness of the exposed brickwork; it didn't come as much of a surprise when she uncovered metal restraints in the walls.

She had to bend her head to enter the second room. Fighting her own burgeoning claustrophobia, she manoeuvred her body into position. Both rooms were barely big enough to hold one person. Louise struggled to imagine the mental and physical torment someone would have to endure with the door locked behind them.

Shining her torch on the side wall, Louise revealed a number of gaps in the brickwork, the holes big enough to see through. 'Tracey, go into the other room,' she called, her voice dull and lost in the confined walls.

Tracey stepped into the first room. Louise lifted her hand up. 'Can you see me?' she said, lowering her voice.

'This is creepy as hell,' said Tracey, nodding before reversing out of the room.

Louise did the same, moving slowly backwards into the basement as she fought thoughts of being stuck in the space.

'I think we need to get SOCO in there,' said Robertson, breaking the eerie silence.

'I agree,' said Louise. 'I think we also need to track down Meryl's siblings.'

Louise stood outside the Hutchinson house with Tracey and Greg as the SOCOs arrived. 'Check in the house and in particular the locked rooms in the cellar for traces of blood and DNA,' she said to the head of the team, Janice Sutton.

Both Tracey and Greg were smoking, a thing Louise hadn't seen either person do for a number of months. 'You think Meryl was kept in those rooms?' said Greg, sucking in the last of his cigarette before flicking it on to the driveway.

'It seems feasible,' said Louise. 'Although her siblings were older. Maybe they were the ones who endured it.'

'Or the ones who did it,' said Tracey.

Greg's phone rang and he turned his back on Louise and Tracey as he answered. The three of them had faced similar scenarios before, but a profound unease had descended on the group.

'That was headquarters,' said Greg. 'Some feedback on the properties registered to Neil and Jacqueline Hutchinson. Both have been rented out. As far as we can tell, unconnected families.'

'Shit,' said Tracey.

Louise craned her head back, the night sky dotted with the occasional star. It couldn't be a coincidence that all three Hutchinson family members were uncontactable. 'We need to trace the money. If they're renting their properties out, they're getting paid. That money has to go somewhere. There was a reason Meryl was using a pseudonym,' she said. 'Maybe Neil and Jacqueline are doing the same. We should look at everyone we talked to at the port and elsewhere using the name Jacqueline and Neil. Maybe we'll get lucky.'

'I'll call Coulson,' said Greg, his phone already to his ear.

◆ ◆ ◆

Most of the work needed on the investigation would only be achievable during normal working hours, and it was nearly midnight on Sunday, yet DCI Robertson had to all but drag Louise, Tracey and Greg to their cars. 'Go home. We'll start again first thing,' he said. 'No one's answering calls now.'

It felt wrong going home when Patrick and Julie were still missing, but Louise reluctantly agreed and was back in Weston within thirty minutes. Thomas was already asleep, and she crept in next to him, savouring the warmth of his body. As she'd expected, she struggled to sleep. Every passing minute felt wasted. She was sure that somewhere Julie and Patrick Longstaff were feeling the same way, only from a different perspective. Louise tried not to think about the cupboard-like prisons they'd found in the Hutchinson house, but it was impossible not to imagine Patrick and Julie in similar positions now.

She thought back to her meeting with Meryl Gatwood. She'd found her personable – charming, even. Nothing about her demeanour had suggested she'd endured an abusive childhood, or was now a predator herself. Many victims were adept at hiding their trauma, and it was what that trauma had done to Meryl and her siblings that troubled Louise the most. These things were so often cyclical. The abused becoming the abuser. If Meryl and her siblings had been kept in the dismal prisons they'd found at the Hutchinson house, then there was no knowing what they could be capable of.

Louise jolted awake. Momentarily panicking, she adjusted to the darkness that still shrouded the room. It was only 4.30 a.m. but she was surprised she'd slept that much; sleep having hit her unawares. She crept out of the bed the same way she'd crept in only hours earlier, shivering as the cold night air bristled her naked skin.

She didn't bother showering, just pulling on a fresh set of clothes and tiptoeing downstairs and out to her waiting car. As she opened the driver's door, she heard the distant sound of the sea and the squawk of the gulls. The town was asleep, and she envied the ignorance of those still in their beds – their lights switched off, sleeping in blissful ignorance of the evils the world sometimes summoned.

She drove the backstreets to the M5 and was hit by a wave of melancholy as she drove on to the motorway. She thought about the life she would be bringing into the world. It wasn't like her to succumb to such despondency. She understood she was making a number of unprovable assumptions about what had gone on in the Hutchinson household during Meryl and her siblings' childhood but for now it was something she couldn't shake.

She was in the incident room by 6 a.m., to see Simon Coulson already at one of the desks, nursing a large thermal flask as he typed away on his keyboard.

'Coffee?' he said.

Louise shook her head and sat down next to him. 'You been here all night?' she asked.

'Ever since Greg called,' said Simon.

Not for the first time, it dawned on Louise that Simon was as effective and as important as any detective on her team. 'Have you anything for me?' she asked, knowing that praise would only embarrass him.

'I've been trying to trace the money but we need to speak to the banks when they open. However,' said Simon, turning his laptop towards Louise, showing her a portrait, black and white, of a grand-looking man in suit and tie. 'Vaughan Hutchinson. Married to Dr Hilary Hutchinson,' he said, moving on to a second picture of a demure-looking woman in a long flowing dress.

'Meryl's parents?' asked Louise.

'Sort of. Meryl was adopted. The Hutchinsons were in their fifties at this point. The older children, Neil and Jacqueline, had left home. Very wealthy background. Vaughan was a name in the city,

Hilary a private consultant based out of Harley Street. They both died about five years later when Meryl was nine.'

'Who looked after Meryl?' asked Louise. 'And who inherited that wealth?'

'I've a number for you,' said Simon. 'I believe this is the Hutchinsons' solicitors, though you'll have to double-check. I have called but . . .' He glanced towards the clock.

Slowly the incident room began filling up. Robertson arrived first, soon followed by Tracey and Greg, then more of the team they'd seconded from other departments. The calls started at 8 a.m., Tracey and Greg chasing the banks, Louise the Hutchinsons' solicitor. The first bite didn't come until 9.45 a.m. – a partner from the Hutchinsons' solicitor's firm calling Louise back.

'Ben Shimton,' said the man. 'How may I help you, DI Blackwell?'

Louise briefly summarised the situation. 'We have three missing people we're trying to locate,' she said. 'Neil, Jacqueline and Meryl Hutchinson.'

'I don't understand,' said the solicitor. 'How exactly is it you want me to help?'

'We have addresses for all three of the Hutchinson siblings. The address for Meryl is in London, and we believe the addresses we have for Neil and Jacqueline's properties are rented out. We don't have another address for them.'

'I'm sure I can double-check what we have on file. I don't think I'm breaking any privileges if I do that,' said Shimton. 'Give me a second,' he said, before confirming the addresses Louise already had for the three siblings.

'When is the last time you saw any of the family?' asked Louise.

'I've never met any of them,' said the solicitor. 'Probate for the Hutchinsons was conducted over thirty years ago. There was a trust fund in each of their names. That's why we have them on file. We pay each of them a set amount every year, or every month in Meryl's case.'

'Can you give me the figures you have?' asked Louise.

'I think you know better than that, DI Blackwell. Any request for such details would need to be done in writing and there would have to be a good reason, or a court order.'

'We have one dead person, and two missing people,' said Louise. 'Is that good enough for you?'

'I'm a lawyer, DI Blackwell. I'm sure you understand that isn't enough.'

Louise sighed. 'This could be life or death, Mr Shimton.'

The solicitor paused. 'Perhaps I can help in one way,' he said after a few seconds of silence. 'I don't know if this means anything. In our correspondence we no longer address Neil and Jacqueline as Hutchinson.'

Louise felt a familiar shot of adrenaline rush her body as she asked the solicitor to elaborate.

'They both like to be addressed as Hoskin,' said Shimton, 'which I believe was their mother's maiden name.'

Louise's stomach cramped – the name Hoskin striking a chord in her mind. Adrenaline made her nauseous as she scrolled back through her reports on the investigation, and she ended the call with the solicitor.

'I think I've met him,' she said out loud, once she had confirmation. She briefly explained to the team what the solicitor had told her about the Hutchinsons using their mother's maiden name. 'There,' she said, pointing to the crime board. 'Nathan Hoskin, the warehouse manager at the shipping container firm in Chipping Sodbury. Not Neil, but close enough. Could be a coincidence, but . . .'

'They like changing their names, this lot. Not suspicious at all,' said Tracey, as Simon began typing on his laptop.

'Got him,' he said. 'Nathan Hoskin. Warehouse manager at Raymond & Sons Shipping Containers. I have a home address. He's not too far from their plant,' said Simon, giving them the address as Louise and the rest of the team headed for the car park.

Chapter Thirty-Nine

'He'll probably be at work, though they do work shifts,' said Louise, as she got into the car with Tracey.

Tracey called the depot, putting the call on speaker as Louise spun out of the car park. 'Hello, can I speak to Nathan Hoskin?' she said, as a receptionist answered.

'Let me check . . . Sorry, he's not at work today,' said the receptionist.

Louise pulled on to the Clevedon Road, heading for the address in Chipping Sodbury, a convoy of flashing blue lights, with sirens wailing, following her in the rear-view mirror.

'You're not blaming yourself, are you?' said Tracey, who was watching Louise drive.

Louise didn't take her eyes from the road. They both knew how many people had been contacted through the investigation. It would have been impossible to have gone thoroughly into each and everyone's background but it was already nagging away at Louise that she may have missed something during her discussion with Hoskin. 'Will you upload the E-Fit?' said Louise.

Tracey sighed, but did as requested. Louise snuck glances at the E-Fit they had of the man who'd been seen with Aisha in Avonmouth, though she could recall the image with perfect clarity. 'I don't think it looks like him, though I guess there could be some similarities. If he has got something to do with this, he never gave an indication to me,' said Louise, hating having to doubt herself.

'Of course not,' said Tracey. 'I've never met somebody so attuned to people as you, Louise, you know that. It seems to me that this family are doing everything in their power to stay unobserved. If *you* hadn't caught him after meeting him, then no one would.'

Louise nodded and smiled. She appreciated Tracey's reassuring words, but knew she would blame herself if her lack of detection resulted in harm coming to Patrick and Julie.

With the traffic pulling over ahead of them, they arrived at Hoskin's house in thirty-five minutes. It was another beautiful period property, an almost-replica of the double-fronted house they'd visited the night before on the Bath Road.

'Not bad for a warehouse manager,' said Tracey as they left the car, the rest of the entourage pulling into the driveway and blocking the road at the foot of the property.

Louise stepped forward. After last night's disappointment she didn't expect much but her heartbeat increased as she rang the doorbell.

Tracey peered through the front windows. 'No sign of life,' she said, as Louise pressed the doorbell once more. She was loathe to knock down another door, but if Julie and Patrick had been abducted, then the answers to how and why could be inside the house. She was about to give it one more try when she saw the outline of a figure from within. Louise reached for her utility belt, her hand on her extendable baton as the door opened to reveal the man she'd met at the warehouse: Nathan Hoskin.

Hoskin was wearing corduroy trousers and a short-sleeved shirt, the sinewy muscles of his arms coated with folded layers of papery skin. He appeared to be standing a little straighter than the last time she'd seen him, his shoulders pushed back. His eyes were red, as if he'd just woken up or had been crying. 'DI Blackwell. Good to see you again,' he said.

Louise studied Hoskin, trying and failing to see a likeness with the E-Fit image. Everything about his demeanour had changed from that first time she'd met him at the warehouse. She recalled him being respected by his work colleagues in the warehouse, but he hadn't shown this type of confidence: a look of arrogance Louise had encountered too many times before in the past. If she could confirm his real name was Neil, it would be enough to arrest him and to bring him in for questioning, but she needed answers now.

'Can I come in?' she said.

A hint of a smile formed on Hoskin's face, his eyes twinkling as he looked behind her and replied, 'All of you?'

Louise turned to the group of officers lined up next to their cars in the driveway. 'Just us three – my colleagues DI Tracey Pugh and DS Greg Farrell,' said Louise.

'Why the hell not?' said Hoskin.

Louise followed the man inside, her hand reaching once more for the baton on her utility belt, Tracey and Greg falling in behind her and leaving the door open.

'Can I get you some tea? Coffee, perhaps?' said Hoskin, as he led them through to a large sitting room – an updated version of the dust-strewn living room they'd visited yesterday evening. The décor was just that little bit more modern, the furniture and floors cleaner, though still coated with dust.

'Do you know why we're here, Mr Hoskin?' said Louise.

'Why don't you tell me?' said the man. 'Please, take a seat,' he said, sitting in a lone armchair as Louise lifted a cushion from the sofa opposite him.

'I believe your original name is Neil Hutchinson,' said Louise, sitting down as Tracey joined her, Greg walking around the room looking at the pictures and ornaments on the sideboard.

'I prefer Hoskin,' said the man.

'And Nathan?'

Hoskin shrugged.

'Hoskin. That was your mother's maiden name, wasn't it?' said Louise.

'Very good, DI Blackwell. I presume you're going to get to the point soon.'

'I've already questioned you about Aisha Hashim, haven't I?' said Louise.

Hoskin didn't respond.

'Do you know Julie and Patrick Longstaff?' said Louise.

Hoskin pursed his lips and nodded, his eyes widening slightly.

'Do you?' repeated Louise.

Hoskin gave all his focus to her. Such was the intensity of his gaze that it was difficult not to look away. 'I'm sure you're aware that I know Patrick. We work in the same industry.'

'But how do you know him?' said Louise, noting the frown on Hoskin. 'He's a senior partner in a shipping insurance firm. You work as a warehouse manager.'

'Our paths have crossed,' said Hoskin, the frown disappearing.

'I met your sister a few days ago,' said Louise, for the first time since she'd arrived noting a twinge of indecision in Hoskin.

'Sister?' he said.

'Like you, she changed her name but not to Hoskin. I wonder why that is,' said Louise.

'Ah, Meryl,' said Hoskin. 'She's not really my sister. She was adopted.'

'But you're still in contact?' asked Louise.

Hoskin didn't respond, his hand resting on his chin.

'How about your other sister?' asked Louise.

This time the indecision was evident, Hoskin's eyes darting from Louise to Tracey and Greg. Louise was about to ask the question again when there was a knock on the front door. It was PC David Jackson, the officer who'd come to her about Julie's disappearance. 'Ma'am, there's something in the garden I think you'd like to see.'

Louise turned back to Hoskin, the confidence on his face restored. 'Anything you need to tell me?' she said.

'Not at all, DI Blackwell. I'm as intrigued as you are to find out what has got your colleague so excited.'

PC Jackson's concern became obvious the second Louise walked through the back door into the overgrown garden. She glanced at Tracey and Greg, making sure Hoskin was within reaching distance.

At the end of the garden, shielded by overgrown plants, stood a metallic blue shipping container.

'That?' said Hoskin. 'I think you call them shoffices nowadays. A cross between a shed and an office. Sometimes they sell the containers off. I had that one converted. Such a good space.'

Louise wasn't sure if his smile was mock confidence, but she was coming close to arresting him just to see it vanish from his features. 'What are we going to find inside?' she said.

In an instant, all of Hoskin's bravado disappeared. Louise was stunned to see the man start to cry. 'I should have told you earlier,' he said, between sobs.

Although disconcerted by the sudden change in Hoskin's demeanour, it was enough for Louise. 'Nathan Hoskin, also known as Neil Hutchinson, I'm arresting you for the murder of Aisha Hashim and the abduction of Patrick and Julie Longstaff,' she said, as Tracey handcuffed the man.

Louise nodded to Greg who, along with PC Jackson, guided Hoskin along the thick grass to the rear of the garden.

Despite his claims that it was a home office, there were no windows in the container, which looked identical all but in colour to the one they'd found Aisha inside of at the docks.

'The door's at the rear,' said Hoskin, his tears having dried up. 'It's open, but please be careful.'

'Is that a threat?' said Louise.

'No. No, you misunderstand,' said Hoskin. 'She's inside. Please be careful with her.'

Louise opened the door, the hinges creaking. She could hear her breath echoing within the container as she tried to push back the memories of finding Aisha Hashim's body at the docks. Inside, her torch alighted on a secondary door. Louise opened that and stepped through, her eyes assaulted by a bank of lights in the distance. The room itself was little bigger than the small area where Aisha Hashim had been found. Inside was a small leather loveseat. On the seat, cramped into a foetal position, was the corpse of an unknown woman.

Louise was about to leave, not wishing to contaminate the scene, when she looked back towards the lights that had first drawn her on entering. Squinting, she realised they were a bank of television screens – each little more than fourteen inches in diameter. There were eight in total but only one contained any images. Louise stepped forward, her progress impeded by a glass divide. Peering through the obstacle she stared at the black and white television screen to see two people semi-naked lying in a confined space. The image was so blurry that Louise couldn't be sure if they were breathing, but she'd seen enough images of the two people in the last few days to know she was looking at Julie and Patrick Longstaff.

Chapter Forty

Louise crept out of the container, sucking in lungfuls of fresh air. She told Tracey and Greg what she'd discovered. 'We need SOCOs here immediately,' she said. 'No one else is to go inside until they arrive,' she added, before turning her attention to Hoskin. 'Who's the woman on the sofa, Nathan?' she demanded.

Hoskin was crying again, his fluctuating behaviour becoming more erratic with each passing second. 'That is Mother,' he said, between uncontrollable sobs. He revealed his canines as he spoke, biting down on his lower lip before he scrunched his eyes shut. 'My sister,' he corrected, before Louise could respond.

Louise glanced at his cuffed wrists, at the ring on his wedding finger. 'Your sister, Jacqueline?' she asked.

'Yes,' said Hoskin.

'How did she die?' said Louise.

'It was cancer,' said Hoskin, lifting his head to look at her in defiance.

'She died from her illness?' asked Louise.

'How else?' said Hoskin, looking confused.

Louise would have liked to have conducted the interview at the police station, but there was no time. 'How long ago did she die, Nathan?'

'Yesterday, and for God's sake call me Neil.'

'And why haven't you informed anyone?'

Hoskin shrugged.

'Is it because of what is on those television screens?' asked Louise, Hoskin's eyes returning to the ground. 'That is Julie and Patrick Longstaff isn't it, Neil?'

Hoskin shrugged, his eyes not looking up.

'Is it a live feed? It looks to me as if they're still alive, Neil. Can you tell me where they are?'

Hoskin lifted his head once more and stared at her. His facial muscles quivered as he tried to smile. 'They're in a much better place,' he said.

'David,' said Louise, calling over PC Jackson. 'You need to get Mr Hoskin here back to the station. I want an immediate psych evaluation and have him ready for questioning. Unless you have anything to tell us now, Neil?' she added.

Hoskin's face contorted into another parody of a smile, before Jackson led him away.

'Greg, stay here and supervise the SOCOs,' said Louise. 'Tracey, could you call Simon? Get him down here as soon as possible. We need to know if he can trace where the video is coming from.'

They were still alive. It was the one thing Louise clung on to as she rushed back to Portishead. She thought about what Hoskin had said, calling the dead woman *Mother* before confessing it was his sister. The dead woman in the container – who was presumably Jacqueline Hutchinson – had been wearing a wedding ring too, though neither sibling was married according to the records they had. Had they lived together in some strange alliance, watching their victims, cramped together on the miniature sofa? Had they watched Aisha in the same way until she'd given up her last breaths?

At that precise moment she feared for Hoskin's sanity, but with Patrick and Julie still missing he had to be interviewed as soon as possible.

All eyes were on her as she reached the station, news from Chipping Sodbury having filtered back to headquarters. PC Jackson was waiting for her in CID, and stood as she entered the office. 'He passed the risk assessment, ma'am,' he said. 'He's waiting in interview room five.'

'Solicitor?' asked Louise.

'He's declined legal representation,' said Jackson.

'OK, make sure everything is ready. I'll be there in five,' said Louise, walking over to DCI Robertson, who was loitering outside his office.

'I've already questioned him, Iain. Earlier in the investigation,' said Louise.

Robertson shrugged. 'So? I've read your report already, there's no way you could have known anything. He was calling himself Nathan Hoskin, no?'

'That's not the point, is it?'

'Let's not do this now,' said Robertson. 'The video feed shows the Longstaffs are still alive, is that correct?'

'Julie, definitely; her husband . . . I'm not so sure.'

'What about Hoskin? Are we calling him Hoskin for now?'

'He wants to be called Neil. Neil Hoskin. It appears he may have been living in an incestuous relationship with his sister, though that's yet to be confirmed. He accidentally called her *Mother* when we found her body. It's quite possible he is the *Father* we found on Your Eyes – the one who paid to watch Helen Norrell sleeping in a confined space.'

'We play on that,' said Robertson.

'You're joining me, are you?' said Louise.

Robertson held his arms out, breaking into a rare smile. 'I thought why not get the dream team back together,' he said, his smile vanishing as quick as it had appeared.

◆ ◆ ◆

The station and the surrounding areas were on high alert. Search teams had been sent to all the previous sites linked to the investigation, including the depot in Chipping Sodbury where Neil Hutchinson had been the warehouse manager under his alias. Each previous piece of evidence – interviews, witness statements, observations, online correspondence – was being rechecked as the SOCOs worked through the shipping container at the Hutchinsons' house.

Louise had received confirmation that Jacqueline Hutchinson had been a terminal cancer patient at the local hospital. Her last treatment had been over two weeks ago – three days before Patrick Longstaff had gone missing. Louise walked with Robertson towards the interview room, all eyes in the busy CID office focused on them. Hutchinson was sat behind the desk as they entered, his back straight, the squinting blue eyes Louise had missed on the E-Fit glancing from her to Robertson. He appeared serene, as if he thought this was all one big joke.

Louise began recording, informing Hutchinson of his rights before confirming that he didn't want a solicitor.

'I'm happy to talk, but wish to be addressed as Mr Hoskin,' said the suspect, his elbows propped on the table, his interlinked fingers showing off his gold wedding band.

'Mr Hoskin it is. But Neil, not Nathan?'

Hoskin nodded.

'Married?' said Louise, nodding towards the ring.

'In a way, yes,' said Hoskin.

'Your sister, Jacqueline, was wearing a similar ring, I noticed.'

Hoskin withdrew his elbows from the table, folding his arms. 'You're not here to question me about that are you?' he said.

'She'd been ill for some time now,' said Louise, undeterred. 'That must have been difficult for you, especially these last few days.' She was still puzzled by the extremes of Hoskin's emotional responses, and half expected him to break out crying again.

'It was harder than you could ever imagine,' he said. 'But she's gone now. She's at peace.'

Louise clicked a button – a white screen to the side of the desk showed the E-Fit image they had of the man seen with Aisha.

'Is that you?' said Louise.

'Not much of a likeness, is it?' said Hoskin.

'Did you abduct Aisha Hashim and place her in a shipping container?' asked Robertson, abruptly changing the tone of the conversation.

'I'm talking to you, now, am I?' said Hoskin, his voice full of indignation.

'Aisha Hashim?' repeated Robertson.

'I didn't abduct her, no.'

'A witness report we have suggests that Aisha wasn't willing to go into your van.'

'Aisha was willing. They all were,' said Hoskin, returning his focus to Louise.

Louise was momentarily distracted by his use of *all*. 'But it was you who abducted Aisha Hashim?' she said. 'You're the one who trapped her in the shipping container?'

'How do you sleep, DI Blackwell?' asked Hoskin.

Louise glanced sideways at Robertson, who raised his eyebrows. Sometimes it paid to humour a suspect, and she decided it best to keep Hoskin talking for now. 'How do you mean?' she asked.

'On your side? Beneath a blanket? A duvet, I presume?'

Although she wanted to keep him talking, she wasn't prepared to indulge his fantasies. Instead, she smiled and waited for him to continue.

'Foetal position, I guess?' asked Hoskin.

'How is this relevant?'

'Tell me, DI Blackwell, how do you feel wrapped up all snug in your bed? In your foetal position? I imagine you feel lovely and secure, don't you?'

Louise had a feeling where this was going. 'However I sleep, it's my choice,' she said.

'And it was Aisha's choice to be left in that container. In the darkness, in that beautiful, restricted space. Imagine, DI Blackwell . . . you're lying in bed, asleep, and someone puts up walls around your position. You wouldn't notice, would you? You'd be so comfortable, you'd remain asleep. It's like being in the womb, isn't it?'

Louise felt her hand reach for her belly but managed to stop herself in time. 'I would certainly feel different when I woke up,' she said.

'Aisha didn't.'

'You're saying Aisha wanted to die?' asked Louise.

'It was all voluntary, I promise you. Aisha had reached the end and it was the only way she wanted to go.'

'Not that it matters, but do you have any proof of that?' said Robertson.

'I don't need proof,' said Hoskin.

'And what about Meryl?' asked Louise, feeling the interview slipping away from them already.

Hoskin sat back at the mention of his younger, adopted sister. 'What about her?' he said.

'She helped you with Aisha. Did she help you with all your victims?'

'She helps those in need,' said Hoskin, 'but I don't want to talk about her now.'

'Maybe we can talk about Patrick and Julie Longstaff instead?' said Louise.

'Let's do that,' said Hoskin, with a humouring smile.

'You say your victims volunteer, but I don't believe that was the case with Patrick and Julie.'

'Once again, DI Blackwell, you've got me. You're right, the others wanted to die. Patrick, however, deserves to die.'

'And why does he deserve to die?' asked Louise.

A look of hatred crossed Hoskin's face. He snarled dismissively, not answering.

'What about his wife, Julie? You saw her on that screen. She didn't seem to be enjoying herself. Why is she there? Why is she being punished?'

'It was the last one, do you understand? I needed to do something a little special. A surprise for Mother.'

'The last one? The last people you were to kill, you and your sister?' said Louise.

Hoskin grimaced at the mention of his sister. 'I thought it was fitting.'

'To have a husband and wife go together, is that what you mean?' said Robertson, unable to hide the anger in his voice.

'If you say so,' said Hoskin.

'Tell me about Jacqueline,' said Louise, taking on the role of good cop. 'You must have loved her very much.'

Hoskin eyed her suspiciously. 'Are you married?' he asked.

'Maybe one day. You have to find the right person, I guess.'

Hoskin looked vacant, as if he was just remembering Jacqueline's death.

'Tell me about her,' said Louise, trying to play on Hoskin's insecurity while she had time.

'We're twins, did you know that?'

'No, I wasn't aware.'

'That's not why we are the way we are,' he began, nodding his head as if lost in reverie.

'We've been to your old house,' said Louise. 'We've seen the rooms in the cellar.'

Hoskin shuddered, a lost look crossing his face, as if he'd been caught out. His features slackened, and there was no one behind his eyes as he looked back at Louise.

'Would you like a drink?' asked Louise.

Hoskin grabbed the beaker of water in front of him, some type of humanity returning to his features. 'If you've seen the house, then you have an idea. I'm not sure if they meant to be cruel, but that is where they would send us. Those rooms. At first, we were sent there when we were misbehaving or so we believed. But growing older, we realised they sent us there for *different* reasons. You don't know the hours we spent alone in the darkness. Always separate, you understand? That was part of it, I'm sure. In the end, we pried open the brickwork so we could see each other.'

However grievous his current crimes, it was impossible not to have empathy for the little boy Hoskin had once been. 'And Meryl?' asked Louise.

'We were too old when Meryl came along. She was adopted, you see. They'd had their fun with us so they wanted a new victim.'

'Did they do the same with her?'

'They would have, DI Blackwell. We had no option.'

'What are you saying?' asked Louise.

'What do you think?' said Hoskin, turning from Louise to Robertson and back again. 'There's no point making a secret of it now. We killed our parents. I'd do the same again, given the same circumstances.'

'You killed your parents?' said Louise.

'Poison,' said Hoskin, as if it was the only explanation needed.

'There's no record of that,' said Louise, bluffing; she hadn't yet read any medical reports about the deceased parents.

'Just a little drop here and there makes it look like natural causes.'

Louise considered suspending the interview. 'I'd like to ask you again, Mr Hoskin, if you would like a solicitor present? You've just admitted to killing your parents.'

'No need for that,' said Hoskin.

Louise glanced at Robertson for confirmation, the DCI nodding.

'Let me get this straight, Neil. You killed your parents for the way they treated you. That I can understand. You wanted to protect Meryl, and they inflicted so much anguish on you. But why did you do what your parents did to you to others?'

Hoskin stared hard at her, but didn't answer.

'I'm presuming from the set-up I saw at your house, you and Jacqueline used to sit on that sofa, watching the video screens? To me it looked as cramped as it did in the rooms we found in your parents' cellar.'

Hoskin shook his head. 'We may have suffered, but we were together then. It's the only comfort we've known. I understand that must be hard for you to imagine, let alone accept. We like being together. As close as possible.'

'But why inflict that sort of pain on others?'

Hoskin shrugged. Louise knew then that there was no point in trying to get a rational response from him. Again, she wondered about the cyclical nature of abuse. How the Hoskins had recreated the trauma of their childhood for some kind of release. The only positive thing she could take was that it was all now close to an end. Hoskin would pay for his former crimes, but for now her main concern was finding Julie and Patrick.

'OK, if you're sure you don't need a solicitor, I'd like to ask you some more about Patrick Longstaff,' said Louise.

Hoskin squirmed in his seat, the distaste evident on his face. 'What about him?' he mumbled.

'You said earlier that he deserved it. What did you mean?'

Hoskin looked at the ceiling, lost in thought. Louise and Robertson knew better than to interrupt him, and eventually they were rewarded.

'Patrick was always a meddler. I don't suppose you've checked but we both went to the same school, St Cuthbert's – a lovely little boarding school in the countryside where buggery and abuse were still a thriving business. Probably strange for you to imagine but my time there made me long for home, made me long for my confinement with Jacqueline.'

'And Patrick was at school with you at that time?' said Louise. 'Did he ever do anything to you?'

It was there for a fraction of a second, but Louise caught it. Hoskin let his mask slip and Louise saw the indecision, and perhaps even the hint of pain in his features. For that merest of glimpses, he was no longer the self-assured killer playing games with the police. He was that lost little boy who'd been locked up in his parents' cellar.

'No, nothing like that. I think he'd forgotten about me until we met years later,' said Hoskin, but Louise knew he was lying. 'It was one of those insufferable conferences I don't normally get to attend, being a warehouse manager and all, but my boss invited me. I think he saw it as some sort of reward for my hard work. Patrick was there, his wife too, though her attention was elsewhere. Patrick was pissed out of his mind and it took him a while to recognise me, but when he did it didn't take him long to resume old times.'

'In what way?' asked Robertson.

Hoskin shook his head. 'The funny thing is, he always thought he was better off than us. He used to wear all the fancy new clothes, have all the worthless gadgets, whereas I always had the bare minimum – but the truth was our wealth could have drowned his family. He just never knew. My mother and father didn't like spending. They only sent me to a boarding school because Father couldn't risk Mother looking after me, us, on our own when Father was at work. She was something of an alcoholic, you see. Anyway, Patrick Longstaff always looked down on me and then, once, he started repeating rumours he'd heard from his family.'

'Rumours?' said Louise.

'About me and Jacqueline. I laughed them off to begin with. In fact, I laughed them off permanently, but it stung.'

'What did he say?' said Louise.

Hoskin's mouth curled, the anger forming around his eyes. 'He used to, you know, say we were together.'

Louise wondered how Hoskin viewed the relationship he'd had all these years with his sister, the woman he'd earlier called *Mother*. 'And he repeated those same slurs when he met you at the conference?' she asked.

Hoskin's face went slack, the humanity slipping once more from his eyes. 'He did. Mother – I mean, Jacqueline – was already dying at this point. Seeing Patrick gave me the impetus to create something special for her. I set up cameras. You probably didn't know that about me when you questioned me, did you, but I was in charge of the CCTV installation at the warehouse – something I'd mastered over the years. I bugged their house and waited for the right time. I knew they both couldn't go together so I took Patrick first and then his wife . . . when she was ready. Thankfully, Mother got to see them both together before she passed,' said Hoskin, no longer continuing with the pretence.

'But what about Julie? Why should she have to suffer for the things Patrick had done?' said Louise.

Hoskin slammed his fists on to the table. 'You think we deserved what happened to us? You think we wanted our lives to go this way?'

'I understand, Neil,' she said. 'Or at least I can try to understand. No one should have to go through what you did. But Julie is still alive?'

Hoskin nodded.

'And Patrick . . . has he passed over yet?'

Hoskin shrugged.

Louise's patience was fading. She glanced at Robertson, and was once again back in the allotment with him and Bryce Milner, the gun in her hand. Despite her continuing doubts about her behaviour that day, she wished she could have been in the same situation now. If it was in her power, she would beat the truth from Hoskin if it meant saving Julie and Patrick. She sensed a similar tension in Robertson as well, and wondered if that was the way it would be from now on. She sucked in a breath, composing herself. Hoskin was lying about Patrick and Julie, and she needed to find out what he was hiding. 'You strike me as an intelligent guy, Neil. I can't say I understand what you do, but I can see there is some sort of method behind it.'

'That's very kind of you,' said Hoskin.

'Because of that, I have to say I don't think you're telling us the whole truth about Patrick and Julie.'

'Is that so?'

Louise offered the man what she considered a conciliatory look. 'I can only guess at the things you and Jacqueline have been through. But I know that your hardships have toughened you.' She hated placating the man, but if it meant finding out the truth, she was prepared to do it. 'I don't think petty rumours would hurt you.

Then or now. There's a reason you've targeted Patrick and Julie that you're not sharing. Isn't that so? What did they do, Neil? Wouldn't it feel better to get this off your chest? Make everyone understand why they deserved to be punished?'

The mask slipping lasted longer this time. It was as if Louise could see Hoskin reliving his past, his eyes twitching as he considered every incident that had shaped his life. 'You're right, they did deserve to be punished,' he said eventually, the glee she'd heard in his voice earlier replaced by a sombre weariness.

Hoskin closed his eyes, and Louise knew this was a now-or-never moment. She made eye contact with Robertson, both understanding there was nothing else to say at this stage. They had to wait, and hope Hoskin was willing to give them the details.

'The truth is, not a day has gone by over the last thirty years where I haven't thought about Patrick Longstaff. Pitiful, I know. When I spoke to him at the conference, he didn't even know who I was. Can you believe that? That's when I started putting things in motion. I wanted one last thing for Mother, one special goodbye.'

'How did Patrick hurt you?' asked Louise.

Hoskin shook his head. 'Meryl told me it would end like this,' he muttered under his breath, before looking up at Louise. 'It wasn't me he hurt. It was Mother. Things could have been so different. He was her first . . . you understand? When we were teenagers, we used to have these parties by the river, and I always brought Jacqueline along for moral support. One night, I saw her talking with him. I didn't like it, but I thought . . . I don't know what I thought. That maybe there was a proper life for her out there. Away from me. Away from all this. But that was just another mistake. Patrick never knew, but he got her pregnant. We couldn't go through with it. Jacqueline barely left the house after that.'

Louise felt punch-drunk. Hoskin's warped grip on reality was like nothing she'd come across before. 'So you targeted Patrick and his wife for revenge?'

'Mother was delighted,' said Hoskin, his face lighting up. 'That bastard started dating his now wife straight after her. When Mother was having an abortion, he was fucking Julie. In what type of world is that fair? Seeing them both suffer was the greatest thing I could give to Mother before she passed.'

'But she's gone now,' said Louise, managing to keep her voice soft, when all she wanted to do was scream at the man. 'Please tell us where they are. I'm going to do everything I can to help you but I need to know where Julie and Patrick are being kept. Meryl told you it was a mistake, didn't she? Does Meryl know where they are? Is that how we will find them?'

Hoskin scratched the side of his face. The mask was still gone, as if the revelations had drained him. He didn't answer, but it was enough for Louise, who terminated the interview.

Chapter Forty-One

In the incident room, the feed from the Hoskin house was on the white screen. Louise and Robertson had suspended the interview with Neil Hoskin, and they both stood staring at the grainy images of Julie and Patrick Longstaff fused together in the tiny space of their prison cell. Now and then, Julie Longstaff's eyes would blink open, but it was impossible to tell if her husband was alive or not. Did either of them have any idea why they were being targeted? From what Hoskin had told her, it was more than likely that Patrick Longstaff had no idea he'd been the father of Jacqueline Hutchinson's child.

The whole station was now working on the investigation. The NPAS had two helicopters on standby, and officers on leave were being called back into work. Teams were trawling areas they'd gone through before and interviewing people at their houses, despite the late hour, everyone desperate to locate the missing husband and wife.

Simon Coulson called from the Hoskin house and Louise put it on speakerphone. 'As far as I can tell the feed you are seeing is live,' he said. 'It's routed via an IP address in South Africa, but that's easily masked. It's the same set-up as we found with Aisha Hashim.'

'And the other feeds?' asked Louise.

'Dormant screens not connected to anything. At least, not right now.'

Next, Louise spoke to Tracey and Greg, passing on the details of her interview with Hoskin. 'I am confident Meryl knows where Julie and Patrick are being kept. We may have to change our search to find her,' said Louise. 'I know it's late, but I think we need to find out where Hoskin purchased that shipping container office thing in his garden.'

'When do you want to speak to Hoskin again?' asked Robertson, once she'd hung up.

'I want something specific to question him about first,' said Louise. As Robertson went to fill up his coffee mug, she went back over her notes from the interview, trying to process everything Hoskin had told her. The pivotal turning points in Hoskin's life appeared to have occurred in the house he'd been brought up in, and the school he'd attended. She ran a search on St Cuthbert's School on the outskirts of Winterbourne where Hoskin had claimed to have met Patrick Longstaff.

Hoskin had alluded to the fact that abuse had been rife in the school. After a few clicks Louise discovered that the place had been shut down ten years ago after being mired in scandal, although no prosecutions had been forthcoming.

Louise searched the area on Google maps, zooming in on the aerial footage in desperation and searching for anything that resembled a shipping container. She continued her research, finding an alumni group from St Cuthbert's on Facebook. Patrick Longstaff was a member but there was no mention of either a Neil or Nathan Hoskin or Hutchinson in any of the group chats.

Tracey called as Louise began messaging people on the Facebook group. 'I have a name for the company who makes the refurbished offices. I just spoke to the MD at home. He's looking through records as we speak, and is going to call me back,' she said.

'Shit,' she added, before Louise could respond. 'Are you seeing what I see?'

Louise turned to the white screen where a new figure had emerged, blocking out most of the shot.

'Who the hell is that?' said Tracey, as the figure turned to the camera and the outline of Meryl Gatwood came into view.

'That's the sister,' said Louise, as Meryl's hand moved towards the camera, just before the screen fizzled out to black and white static.

Julie tried to wiggle her fingers. She detected some small motion on the left side of her body but couldn't be sure if she was imagining the movement. In truth, she couldn't feel any of her limbs. The pain was internal, as if her bones were in a vice and her innards were being rubbed raw. She was entwined with Patrick. Didn't know where she began and he ended. She'd grown accustomed to the smell emanating from both of them. She thought Patrick was still alive, but couldn't tell for sure if the weak heartbeat she occasionally heard was his or hers. He never responded when she spoke, though even that was not something she could confirm she'd done. She pictured herself speaking, imagined the words leaving her mouth, but it was like being in a dream.

All she could do was concentrate on surviving, and try to banish the thoughts that haunted her: that this was all her own fault, that it was some kind of retribution for her betrayal. But why would anyone want to do anything so terrible to her? To both of them?

She hadn't seen or heard from the man since that last time he'd placed her in the prison with Patrick. There'd been no food or water since. Her body felt insubstantial, her throat razor dry as every breath became something she had to endure. Even as light filtered into the prison cell, she was too confined, too wrapped in pain to lift her head to look as a rumbling noise reached her ears. She sensed the noise coming from behind, and managed to muster the last vestiges of strength to crane her neck an inch. The light was blinding as she snuck a look behind her, just in time to see the door of her cell opening.

◆ ◆ ◆

Louise stared at the screen as if she could will the picture back into view. Everyone surrounding her watched in the same dumbstruck way. 'That was Meryl,' she said to Robertson. 'I'm sure of it.'

'She must know we're on to them,' said Robertson.

'I think she might be moving them, though for the life of me I can't understand why.'

Robertson cursed under his breath. Neither of them were used to being so powerless, and once more Louise thought back to that time at the allotment where she'd held a gun to Bryce Milner's head. She could still feel its weight, the indecision when Milner had let Robertson go and she'd hesitated before lowering the gun. Whatever her misgivings about her actions then, she knew she would do exactly the same again if it meant saving Julie and Patrick's lives.

Tracey called and interrupted her from her reverie, Louise's eyes still focused on the flickering screen as she answered. 'The MD from the home office company has called me back,' said Tracey. 'He has the purchase record from Neil Hoskin from seven years ago.'

Louise glanced down to see both of her hands cupping her belly. She glanced at Robertson, who looked away. 'I'm hoping to God you've got some good news for me, Tracey,' she said, moving her hands back to her side.

'I hope so. He purchased six of the containers, nearly two hundred grand's worth. One of them was shipped to this address, the other five to a different address: a disused warehouse in some farmland in Rangeworthy. I asked the MD why Hoskin had wanted them. Hoskin had told him they were using them as temporary offices while they were rebuilding the place.'

'That's near Winterbourne, where Hoskin went to school. Do you have an address for me?' said Louise.

'Pinging it to you now,' said Tracey, hanging up.

The address was thirty minutes away. Louise wasted no time, ordering local police to the disused warehouse as Robertson rerouted the helicopters.

Chapter Forty-Two

The last time Louise had been in a car with Robertson they'd been rushing to the Grand Pier in Weston-super-Mare with Bryce Milner in the back. Neither of them had known what to expect then, and they had no real idea what was awaiting them now as Robertson took the country lanes with the enthusiasm of a rally driver.

'Maybe it would be better if we got there alive,' said Louise, holding on to the side handles on the roof for dear life, the now familiar sensation of nausea rising in her chest.

'Are you OK? You look pale,' said Robertson, glancing towards her as he hammered the car around a tight corner.

'I'm fine. Keep your eyes on the road, sir,' said Louise.

Robertson nodded. 'Is there something you need to tell me?' he asked.

Louise thought of the men in her life. Her deceased brother, who'd endured a tragic life of addiction that had contributed to his eventual demise. Her father who'd always been a rock, despite the challenges that had faced his family over the years. And Thomas, who was proving to be as special as she'd hoped. Robertson was almost as important to her. She trusted him implicitly, had gone through things with him during their time together at work that she'd never shared with anyone else. Yet, however much she wanted to, she couldn't tell him about the baby just yet. For one, he would immediately start slowing down and although, in a way, that was what she wanted, she was as keen as he was to get to the disused warehouse as soon as humanly possible.

Above them, two police helicopters cut through the night sky as if guiding them to their destination. Robertson swung a left, almost driving into a ditch, before being forced to slow as he reached a narrowing lane. His car had flashing blue lights, but despite the best intentions of the drivers coming in the other direction he sometimes had to slow right down to allow them past.

Further along the road, he was forced to come to a halt. 'Move it, you useless bastard!' said Robertson, glaring at the shocked face of a man driving a Ford Focus estate who'd wedged his car in diagonally against the side of the road and was struggling to clear the space.

'Forget this,' said Robertson, winding down his window and pulling in his side mirror as he manoeuvred past the vehicle, clipping the man's bumper as he drove away.

'Best take a note of that number plate,' he said, his voice now a low, deep growl, as he sped up to 50 mph, only to slow at the sight of a white transit van coming in the opposite direction.

Louise had already memorised the number plate of the Focus estate and gripped the dashboard as Robertson pressed heavily on the brakes. She almost didn't look up as the white van manoeuvred around them. If she hadn't, she wouldn't have caught sight of the driver, who had her head turned down, trying to avoid detection. 'Shit! Iain, that was Meryl!' she said.

Robertson brought the car to a dead halt before reversing into a bush and turning the car in two fell swoops until he was in pursuit of the transit van that was already a hundred and fifty yards away and accelerating, as if the driver knew she was being followed.

◆ ◆ ◆

Julie had no idea who the woman was, but she was either very strong or Julie had become insubstantial over the last few days. At first, Julie had thought she was being rescued. The frail-looking woman appeared confused as she opened the door to Julie and Patrick's prison. But that had changed as soon as the woman had handcuffed her and dragged her outside, before putting her in a fireman's lift and dumping her unceremoniously into the back of the van where she'd chained Julie to a makeshift rig.

Julie had begged the woman to take Patrick too but wasn't sure if her words had left her mouth. Her throat was still razor dry and nothing that was happening made sense any more as she bounced around in her new mobile prison. Julie didn't recognise her limbs. She was caked in her own filth, and in constant pain, which intensified every time her captor rushed a corner or drove recklessly through potholes and over speed bumps.

Julie couldn't remember the last time she'd had so much space to herself, but she could barely move. Her joints were locked in place, every nerve ending in her muscles alive with pain. Had Patrick been breathing when they'd left? She couldn't tell. She thought she'd whispered encouragement to him during their hours together. But for all she knew she was back home in bed, experiencing this never-ending nightmare from the safety of her own home. At least that was what she hoped for as the van crashed to a stop, Julie's head smacking against the metal insides before the driver spun the wheels of the van and accelerated away, faster than before.

◆ ◆ ◆

Louise rerouted the police helicopters as Robertson followed Meryl back through the narrow country lanes. The DCI was an experienced driver and kept a safe distance. He had to be mindful of the general public, unlike Meryl who was now taking blind corners at speed. The helicopters were back in view within minutes, and however fast Meryl was driving it was only a matter of time before she was caught, though it soon became clear that the woman was either not aware of the fact, or for now was wilfully ignoring it.

Louise winced as Meryl rushed past an oncoming car, causing the driver to turn hard to his left, the car catching in a ditch. Robertson slowed down as he passed the vehicle, checking on the driver who appeared unhurt, before continuing in his pursuit.

'There's a main road up ahead,' said Louise.

'I know,' said Robertson, who was going 55 mph and not making any headway on the white van. 'She's not slowing,' he said, easing on the brakes as the main road came into view.

Louise could barely watch when Meryl increased her speed and drove through the crossway without slowing. Seconds later, an articulated lorry drove past from the left and Robertson skidded to a halt as he reached the give-way sign.

'I can still see her,' said Louise, watching Meryl's van disappearing around a corner into a small village.

Robertson drove across the main road with caution, but by the time he'd rounded the corner, Meryl's van was parked up, the front door hanging open. Robertson pulled the car over and Louise was out in seconds, catching sight of Meryl careering through the back garden of a small, thatched cottage towards a woodland area. 'I'll go,' she said, setting off at a run, her heart hammering in her chest as, for the briefest of seconds, she forgot about the baby growing within her.

'Meryl,' she screamed, and ran after the woman, the two helicopters thundering above them drowning out her cry.

Meryl was quick and agile, meandering her way through to the entrance of the woodland. Louise didn't know the place very well but the trees looked dense and stretched as far as she could see. She glanced up at the helicopters that were already hovering above the trees. Each would be packed with thermal cameras, so there was no way Meryl could escape. Even so, Louise couldn't take that risk of letting her go. It was possible Julie and Patrick were not at the warehouse and she needed to hear directly from Meryl as to where they were.

'Meryl!' shouted Louise, as she entered the darkness of the wood, the dank smells making her stomach turn, the sound of a twig breaking on the woodland floor alerting her just in time to the sight of a large, fallen branch hurtling towards her.

◆ ◆ ◆

Julie hit her head as the van careered to a stop once more. She strained to listen while noises came to her from outside. It sounded as if the driver's door had opened and another vehicle was close by. She heard muffled voices before the whirling blades of helicopters obliterated all other sounds.

She tried to scream when she heard the back door of the van opening. She cowered away in the corner, acknowledging the irony of trying to make herself as small as possible when she'd been confined for so long. The door creaked open, torchlight blinding her. Whatever fight she'd had within her had long since disappeared and she was ready to succumb to whatever they wanted. Even as they said her name, she just wanted it to be over.

'Julie Longstaff?' came the sound again. The man who was shining the torch moved it away from her eyes, the light falling on her semi-naked body.

Julie pulled her knees into her chest, the movement causing her to scream in pain.

'Julie, my name is DCI Robertson. I'm not going to hurt you. It's all over now. We've got you.'

A split second later and the branch would have hit Louise square in the face. As she ducked, the force of the branch hit the tree behind her. Meryl came into view, freezing for a split second before drawing the branch back once more, ready to finish the job. It was time enough for Louise to respond. She sprang forward, forcing all her energy into her right leg, which she jabbed hard at Meryl's right knee. It was a move she'd used before – a former colleague of hers now serving a long stretch in prison could testify to that. Tim Finch would forever walk with a limp, and if the sound of cracking bone was anything to go by, so would Meryl Hoskin.

'Meryl Hoskin, aka Meryl Gatwood, I'm arresting you for the murder of Aisha Hashim, and the abduction of Patrick and Julie Longstaff,' said Louise, cuffing the woman who was rolling on the woodland floor in agony.

'I need an ambulance,' said Meryl, through sobs of anguish.

'Where are Julie and Patrick Longstaff?' said Louise.

Meryl was struggling for breath. 'In the van,' she muttered.

Louise radioed Robertson. 'I have Meryl Hoskin in custody,' she said. 'We need an ambulance. Do you have Julie and Patrick?'

'Just Julie,' said Robertson. 'She's pretty incoherent . . . but from what I can gather, I think her husband might still be at the warehouse.'

Chapter Forty-Three

Access to the disused warehouse was down a single-track road that wasn't big enough to take any of the emergency vehicles. Louise and Robertson were forced to abandon their car on the verge and make their way on foot to the area, having left the paramedics and uniformed police to take Meryl and Julie to hospital.

As Louise walked into the metallic hull of the warehouse, she caught sight of Tracey at the other end of the building, accompanied by a team of firefighters who'd also made the journey by foot. The whole area was how Louise imagined a film set would look. Lighting rigs were set up to illuminate the interior and cameras hung from rafters around the building, the majority pointing towards the five shipping containers.

'We've only just managed to get through,' said Tracey, as Louise ran over. 'Cameras are pointed at each unit,' she added, as the firefighters worked on the locks.

A sense of déjà vu hit Louise as the rusting doors were pulled back and torches were shone on the inside of the first container. Two cameras were perched at either inside corner of the container but the interior was empty.

'There,' said Louise, shining her torch on two metal chains that came from the side walls of the container. 'We'd better let SOCO look at this,' she added, noting signs of blood on the floor, the unmistakable smell of human waste in the trapped air.

It was a numbers game now and it felt churlish going from one container to the next though as the fire officer opened container two, it became apparent that the search was now over. Inside the container was a sliding glass panel, behind which the container was divided in half by a second glass wall. On the left-hand side, semi-naked and lying in his own waste, was the dormant figure of Patrick Longstaff.

'Paramedics – now!' said Louise, summoning the team as she retreated from the container and gratefully sucked in fresh air.

'He's still alive,' called one of the paramedics who had followed them to the warehouse. 'A weak pulse but we've got him.'

Relief surged through Louise's body but the moment ended as quickly as it had arrived. Patrick and Julie had been rescued but there were still three other containers. 'Open the next three,' she said to the fire officer.

The sound of chains snapping echoed within the warehouse and, as the paramedics busily worked away on Patrick Longstaff, Louise opened the next container, gagging at the smell that reached her as the door was prised apart. She didn't need the paramedics to check this time, the decay on the body chained to the container wall enough for her to determine she was looking at a corpse.

She left the container, shaking her head at Tracey and Greg, who both poked their heads inside.

'What the hell is going on?' said Greg, his face ghost-white. Louise didn't know how to answer. She feared what they would find upon opening the last two containers, but it had to be done. Container four was empty and Louise hoped that was the end of it, but that relief was also short-lived as container five was opened.

The smell was reminiscent of the other containers and, as Louise had feared, a second corpse was found within. Curled into a foetal position, the body was entombed in a corner. Two cameras pointed directly at the victim, the lights of which were red. Louise needed to be sure, and as she walked over to the victim to check for a pulse, which was non-existent, she turned her head back to the red lights and realised she was probably being filmed.

Chapter Forty-Four

Louise shut the door to the cubicle, dropping to her knees just in time to be sick in the toilet bowl. It was the day after the discoveries they'd made at the disused warehouse in Rangeworthy. Patrick Longstaff was currently in intensive care and the two corpses had been identified as Lesley Maddron and Claire Entwistle, two young women who'd been reported missing in the last year, neither from the local area.

Both Neil Hoskin and his stepsister Meryl were waiting to be questioned. Meryl's leg injuries were not as bad as Louise had first thought. As was sometimes the way with police work, Louise had stumbled on something significant due to nothing more than hard work, diligence, and a dose of good luck. The truth was, if she hadn't been so dogged about finding Aisha Hashim's killer, then these further atrocities may never have been uncovered. And although his sister was dead, it was conceivable that Neil and Meryl could have continued with their work for an indeterminate amount of time.

Louise wiped her mouth, her stomach empty. Her sleep last night had been plagued with nightmares of confinement, and she couldn't wait until the questioning was over.

Tracey was waiting for her in CID, her colleague looking her up and down as she returned from the bathroom. 'Meryl's waiting for us. She has a brief,' she said.

'Well, that's going to do her a lot of good,' said Louise. 'Let's go.'

Meryl was a different prospect to the woman Louise had first seen in London the other week. Her faux charm had disappeared, the coldness in her eyes now evident. Louise was sure that if the branch the woman had swung at her last night had made contact with her head, she would probably never have lived to face this moment.

Meryl smiled, as if reading her thoughts. Louise went through the preliminaries before getting to the first of her many points. 'We have records showing that you befriended Aisha Hashim before she moved in with you in London. Why was that, Meryl?'

Louise kept her eyes focused on Meryl as she answered, wondering how she hadn't noticed the darkness in the woman the first time around.

'No comment,' said Meryl, not even exchanging looks with her solicitor.

As far as Louise was concerned, Meryl could say no comment all day long. She'd been caught driving Julie Longstaff away from the warehouse, and that alone would be enough to put her away for a number of years. 'I spoke to your brother yesterday. Interesting dynamic, your family. He explained to me what happened to him and to your sister when they were children. That must have been truly horrible for them. I don't condone what they've done for a second, but I can understand how it happened. But with you, Meryl, I'm not so sure,' said Louise.

Meryl didn't answer, her only response a subtle shake of her head.

'You didn't go through what they did, did you, Meryl? In fact, they stopped that happening to you. So why, then, have you got such a big part in their activities?'

'There are lots of things you don't know, DI Blackwell,' said Meryl. 'In fact, there's so much you can't even guess at. I can tell you everything. But I want to strike a deal.'

'We're not in America, Meryl, so I'm afraid you're not going to plea bargain your way out of this. We've already got enough evidence to put you away for a long time. I'm sure your solicitor can testify to that.'

Meryl glanced at her brief, who didn't respond.

'What we can do, if you fully cooperate, is put a good word in with the judge for you. We can tell them how you helped us and they'll take that into consideration when it comes to sentencing. But I won't be messed around on this, Meryl. I need to know everything from the beginning to the end.'

Meryl's earlier confidence diminished as she sat back on her chair. 'You're wrong in what you said. I did experience it. The cellar you found at my parents' house. They locked me up there for six months on and off – every time I'd been *bad*,' said Meryl, making air quotes. 'That's why they did it, Neil and Jacqueline.'

'Why they did what?' asked Louise.

'Why they killed my parents. They saved me, and because of that I owed them everything. They raised me as their own, you know that?'

Louise dwelt on the enormity of what she was being told. Neil Hoskin had already confessed to killing his parents, but it seemed he'd also raised Meryl with his twin sister. Now didn't feel like the time to get into family dynamics. She already knew for a fact that three lives had been lost, and Patrick and Julie Longstaff had come close to losing theirs. No doubt there were many more victims, and it seemed such a high debt to pay. But Louise couldn't say so, not just yet. She needed Meryl to keep talking. 'So how exactly did you repay them?' she asked.

'I'd like a minute to speak alone with my client,' said Meryl's solicitor.

'Be my guest,' said Louise.

Meryl held her hand up. 'It's fine, I'm ready to talk,' she said.

'I must insist, Miss Hoskin.'

'It's fine,' said Meryl, raising her voice, the coldness reappearing in her eyes. 'Due to the circumstances of our parents' death, the probate was held up for a very long time. Daddy was very wealthy, as you may well know. But none of us were seeing that money any time soon so Neil came up with an idea. Back then it was video cameras and VHS tapes. I don't know how he found the market, but he did.'

'What are you saying?' said Louise, a shiver running through her body.

'It started when I was young. We would find these runaways and film them in confinement. Neil and Jacqueline would sell the tapes. Things have progressed from there. Now it's online, streamed to select clientele. We make hundreds of thousands of pounds.'

Louise felt the walls closing in on her, and forced herself to take a deep breath. If what Meryl was saying was true, the list of victims could be significant. 'Why did you live in that tiny flat in Sydenham then?' asked Louise.

'Money doesn't mean that much to me . . . and I needed a convincing cover story anyway. And I like small spaces . . .' said Meryl, with an unholy grin.

'Why did you take Julie Longstaff from her captivity?'

'I didn't want her to talk,' said Meryl. 'She was the only one alive.'

Louise didn't correct the woman on her mistake. 'Was that the only reason? Or did you have something else planned for her?'

'What does it matter now?'

Louise lowered her eyes. Meryl's genuine lack of remorse made her skin crawl. 'And your brother and sister? We've seen their house. They enjoyed watching their victims, didn't they, Meryl?'

Meryl shrugged. 'You'll have to speak to Neil about that. All I know is what I experienced for six months, they experienced for over a decade. You can't imagine what it's like. Confined in an area where you can't literally move – and their parents did it to them.'

'So why would you do it to other people?' said Louise, heat rising in her cheeks.

'It wasn't for me,' said Meryl, as if she thought she was innocent. 'I didn't watch the people we had in captivity.'

'And you think that excuses you?'

'No. I guess it doesn't, but the truth is I don't really care either way.'

◆ ◆ ◆

Louise saw the same coldness in Neil Hoskin's eyes as she'd seen in his sister's. 'Meryl's told us everything,' she said. 'Do you have anything to add?'

'What difference would it make?' said Hoskin. 'Jacqueline's dead, and Meryl and I will be going to prison for a long time. I understand it. In fact, I look forward to it. What better way to spend the rest of my life than in the same way it started – cooped up in a tiny cell?'

'Meryl explained about the videos and the online streaming business. She's begun providing us with a list of names of clients. Would you be able to verify them for us?'

'Meryl doesn't know everything. I know how this works. I might be going to prison, but there are privileges for good behaviour, aren't there?'

'That will be for another time. For now, tell me about Aisha Hashim. Your other victims you kept in secret, but you placed Aisha in a shipping container that was due to go abroad.'

Hoskin smiled. 'As I said, there are some things Meryl didn't know about. Aisha wasn't the first person we shipped.'

Louise closed her eyes. Her stomach was fluttering, her baby active in her womb. It felt wrong being in the presence of such a monster while pregnant, but she continued. 'And Patrick and Julie Longstaff? You told me why . . . but what was the long-term goal? Were you going to ship them as well?'

Hoskin's face contorted, his features morphing into something resembling a smile. 'Life couldn't continue without Jacqueline. Not in the way it had. I told you before I wanted to do something special for her.'

'Something special?' said Louise, trying again not to lose her temper.

'It's how we spent our final hours,' said Hoskin. 'You saw the sofa. We sat together, bodies entwined, and we watched Patrick and his wife. I only wish Jacqueline had lived long enough to see their end.'

'It sounds to me like you wanted to get caught, Neil. Maybe you wanted to atone for your sins?'

Hoskin laughed, the noise grim and humourless. 'You're right in one way. This was personal for us. I wanted them to pay the ultimate price.'

'But they both survived,' said Louise.

'You might think that,' said Hoskin, his eyes narrow and cruel. 'But I know for a fact, they'll never be the same again. You're just like them, like all the others. We've been ignored all our lives, but now not a day will go by that Patrick and his wife don't recall us. Patrick will know the life he destroyed, and his wife will understand what she married. People will know what happened to us. They'll understand.'

Louise saw it then. The helpless little boy, locked in the cellar, desperate for the world to come to his rescue. She felt the baby shift inside her, and ended the interview before she said or did something she regretted.

Epilogue

Louise's thoughts occasionally turned back to Hoskin's words from that day: *I know for a fact, they'll never be the same again.* He'd been talking about himself as much as Julie and Patrick Longstaff, but that didn't excuse him in any way. Usually, she was able to compartmentalise her previous investigations, but the case lingered.

Even now, sitting in the reception area, waiting to see the midwife for her twenty-week scan, she was plagued by images of Aisha Hashim in her shipping container prison, and Julie and Patrick Longstaff's imprisonment. Louise was desperate to banish those images to the recesses of her mind, where she kept so much unwanted information, but for now they were stubbornly forefront and she had to shake them loose as the midwife called her and Thomas over.

With the legacy of the Hoskins' crimes still not yet fully explored, Neil and Meryl were in remand, awaiting a full trial. Now that he'd been arrested, and his sister was dead, Neil Hoskin was willing to discuss his crimes in full but, like so many in his position, he was drawing the process out. Already, he'd led them to two unmarked graves and was drip-feeding them details of the other unfortunate souls who'd crossed their path over the years.

'You OK?' asked Thomas, grabbing her hand.

Louise smiled, nodding, though she was more nervous now than she'd been on the first scan. She cupped her hand around the small bump and hoped the news was going to be positive. She'd declared her pregnancy to Robertson a few days after the Hoskins' arrest. She'd never seen the man smile so much, and she'd been overwhelmed by everyone's response ever since. What would happen now if things were wrong with the baby? It didn't bear thinking about, but she'd been thinking about little else as this day approached. It was as if all her future was going to be determined by the midwife, by the results of the test, and now the moment was minutes away she felt terrified to face the truth.

'Louise Blackwell.' The world stopped turning as the midwife called out her name, the other expectant mothers watching Louise as she got to her feet and walked hand in hand with Thomas to the midwife's office.

'Hello, Louise, come on in. How is everything?'

Everything is a complete mess, and how are we being so calm? thought Louise. 'Everything is fine.'

'Excellent. Let's take a look, then, shall we?'

Maybe this would be the story she told her child one day, when they were grown up. Maybe it was a tale she would forever keep to herself. Louise unbuttoned her trousers and lay back on the bed, the midwife smearing her swollen belly with the cold jelly.

As the midwife busied away with the scan, murmuring to herself as she took measurements, Louise had to fight off images of Aisha Hashim, Julie and Patrick in their captivity. She tried to focus on what was happening, but the temperature in the room felt cloying.

'Everything OK, Mum?' said the midwife.

Louise grabbed Thomas's hand, trying not to think about how close the walls and ceiling were to her. She focused on the positives from the investigation.

Patrick Longstaff had survived, and – for now – was back with his estranged wife. Records showed that Jacqueline Hoskin did have an abortion as a teenager, and, despite there being no proof, Louise had informed the Longstaffs of Hoskin's suggestion that Patrick had been the father in advance of it becoming public knowledge during the trial. The potential impact of that had been hard for them to hear, especially considering their failed attempts with IVF, but both Patrick and Julie would be the bedrock of the prosecution case, and despite Hoskin's threat that they would never be the same again, Louise held out some hope for the couple.

The midwife jabbed the scanner across Louise's abdomen. She was smiling, and Louise hoped it wasn't through pity. 'I have some very good news for you,' she said, after a prolonged silence. 'See here,' she added, pointing to the blur on the screen. 'Baby has finally shifted, and we can finally see the bowel. No obstructions. We'll get you back in for another scan in a few weeks, but you have a very healthy baby . . . Do you want to know the sex?' said the midwife, handing Louise a roll of paper towels.

Louise was breathless. She glanced at Thomas in time to see him wipe his reddening eyes. 'Shall we?' she said.

Thomas smiled, nodding as he clasped her hand tighter. 'Yes, please,' said Louise.

'Wonderful,' said the midwife. 'I'm pleased to tell you that you're expecting a healthy baby boy.'

Louise turned to Thomas, who had been adamant they were having a girl. But if she'd been searching for any sign of disappointment she'd come to the wrong place. His face was one gigantic smile.

'I'm going to be a mummy,' said Louise.

Thomas grabbed her hand. 'The best mummy ever.'

◆ ◆ ◆

The sun was trying its hardest to poke through the low-lying clouds hovering over Sand Bay as Louise walked hand in hand with Emily towards the rockpools. Thomas was following behind, his attention on Molly, who kept making a beeline for the murky seawater.

'So, the baby will be my cousin?' said Emily, her face a mask of concentration as they stepped over the jagged rocks.

'That's right,' said Louise. 'Don't you think it will be nice to have a baby cousin?'

Emily pursed her lips, giving the question a full consideration. 'I think it will, yes,' she said, as Thomas and Molly caught up with them.

Molly's face was covered in wet sand, and she swotted at it with her right paw before shoving her snout into one of the rockpools. 'There was one more thing I wanted to ask you,' said Louise, as Molly emerged, shaking herself before heading off to another rockpool for some more exploration. 'That we'd both like to ask you,' she added, smiling at Thomas.

Emily looked at her aunt, her puzzled face a treasure to see. 'You know Thomas and I are having this baby together, and we will be living in the big house?'

'Yes,' said Emily.

'Well, we were hoping you would stay with us. I've spoken to Grandma and Granddad, and they don't mind as long as you're happy to do so. What do you think?' said Louise.

The conversation with her parents had gone easier than she'd imagined. Her mother had admitted that they'd been waiting for Louise to bring up the idea. The plan now was for Louise and Thomas to move into the shared house so Emily's life wouldn't be too disrupted, and for her parents to find something smaller nearby. They'd already made an offer on a bungalow half a mile away, and promised to offer as much childcare as they felt able to give.

Emily was wide-eyed. 'Are you sure they won't mind?'

'They will miss you, of course, but you'll still get to see them all the time,' said Louise, overcome by her niece's consideration. 'So what do you say?'

Emily glanced at Thomas, smiling, before rushing towards Louise with such force she almost knocked her over, wrapping her arms around her in a vice-like grip.

'I'll take that as a yes,' said Louise, a strange sensation in her belly making her pull away from her niece. 'Here,' she said, unbuttoning her coat, taking Emily's hand and placing it on her belly. 'Can you feel that? I think your cousin wants to speak to you.'

ABOUT THE AUTHOR

Photo © 2019 Lisa Visser

Following his law degree, where he developed an interest in criminal law, Matt Brolly completed his Masters in Creative Writing at Glasgow University. He is the *Wall Street Journal* and Amazon bestselling author of the DI Blackwell novels, the DCI Lambert crime novels, the Lynch and Rose thriller *The Controller*, and the standalone thriller *The Running Girls*. Matt lives in London with his wife and their two children. You can find out more about him at www.mattbrolly.com or by following him on Twitter: @MattBrollyUK.

Follow the Author on Amazon

If you enjoyed this book, follow Matt Brolly on Amazon to be notified when the author releases a new book!

To do this, please follow these instructions:

Desktop:

1) Search for the author's name on Amazon or in the Amazon App.
2) Click on the author's name to arrive on their Amazon page.
3) Click the 'Follow' button.

Mobile and Tablet:

1) Search for the author's name on Amazon or in the Amazon App.
2) Click on one of the author's books.
3) Click on the author's name to arrive on their Amazon page.
4) Click the 'Follow' button.

Kindle eReader and Kindle App:

If you enjoyed this book on a Kindle eReader or in the Kindle App, you will find the author 'Follow' button after the last page.